ASCEN
Rebelutions
Martyr

Hugh Phœnix-Hulme

Copyright © Hugh Phœnix-Hulme 2021

This novel is entirely a work of fiction. The names, characters and incidents portrayed within are the work of the author's imagination. Any resemblance to actual persons, living or dead, is purely coincidental.

All rights reserved. No part of this publication may be reproduced, distributed, or transmitted in any form or by any means, including photocopying, recording, or other electronic or mechanical methods without the prior written permission of the publisher, except in the case of brief quotations embodied in critical reviews and certain other non-commercial uses permitted by copyright law. For permission requests, please contact the publisher.

Concept by Hugh Phœnix-Hulme with input from Aven Kelly & Aleta Lovelace

Written by Hugh Phœnix-Hulme with assistance from Aven Kelly & Bandi Crawford

Edited by Andrea Leeth & Aleta Lovelace

Page Art by WASP ZOLA (Sophie Pake)

Cover art by DKMRGN Design

Calendas typography has been designed by Atipo. www.atipo.es

Prologue

EverDawn, for all their ethical questions, were considered to be one of the top employers of the day. Aside from the hugely competitive benefits and wage package, Alice could never quite figure it out. Sure, a job was a job, and she was good at what she did, but that didn't make the corporation trustworthy, or its mission necessarily moral. Long gone were the days when people would work themselves to death – almost literally – for their employer, showing loyalty to a company that had a replacement lined up the minute they kicked the bucket or called in sick one time too many. EverDawn claimed to not share the ethos of past corporations. It was an attractive claim, relatively speaking. After all, it was mainly blind trust in corporations that had led to the issues of the past, a past that no one wanted to repeat.

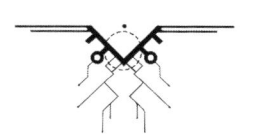

The past had seen corporations backing governments with colossal sums of money finding their way into the coffers of politicians representing individual corporate backers. In totality it amounted to a huge advertising game, or so it seemed from the outside. People would be offended if someone supported one corporation or politician over another, and eventually everything boiled over. The world of politics had fused into one colossal mega-system. Unity had finally happened. It had only taken many centuries for people to come together and to start working for everyone, not just themselves. Truly, the world was together under one nation. Perhaps it was the sense of hope the people of the world clung to; the desire for peace after so much chaos, but things had changed, and for the better. And this change curiosity occurred in the midst of chaos; when the people stood up and said "enough". Enough hate, enough killing, enough. We are people and we stand united.

There had been corporate blocs and cold wars between governments, and that was when everything got convoluted and dangerous. CEOs and Presidents lived and died in devotion to some ever-escalating rivalry or other. All they wanted to do was to fill their pockets, line them as heavily as the gluttonous capitalist machine did its stomach; eating itself from the inside out and belching a noxious gas that sickened all around it. Those that held back the antidote for a price soon learned that there were side effects to their expensive drug. Money couldn't save them, at least, not when there was someone better off. And until President Mason, there was always someone better off.

That was forty years ago, though. A lot had changed. In many ways the dream of unity came to fruition, although its seeds were sprung from the manure of the past. Still, things grow where they can, and sometimes a thing grown in shit has the same nutrition as one started in a hydroponic garden, or the toxins. Who knows until they take a bite?

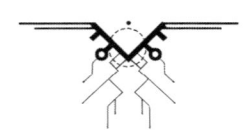

A new vision of Earth had materialised. One in which people worked together to create a better life. Over-farming and climate change had been issues in the past, bringing with them widespread famine, but the ingenuity of the people to solve their own issues meant that many began to grow food for themselves, keeping the cost of feeding their families at an all-time low. Low in cost, but often high in wealth as they pulled together. Many people had chosen vegetarianism or veganism due to the challenges of farming meats and animal products, but not everyone. People collected their own rainwater and generated their own power through solar and wind, and essentially began to become more self-sufficient, having to rely less and less on the market. It was something President Mason – an ardent capitalist – wasn't a fan of.

He seemed decent enough to start with. Decent enough to be voted in. He pulled every string and exercised every power to make radical changes that echoed around the world. Tax money was quickly and quietly diverted into the pockets of his associates, a good proportion without a doubt finding its way back to his own. Life would have been bordering on great for most people had it not been for President Mason. His greed truly was a dark shadow on our species and all it had accomplished in building a near utopia.

EverDawn itself was one of the key ways in which the world was different. Their highly sought-after service had been developed and given to the people as a gift, of sorts, for all who wanted it. The opportunity to become almost immortal – or what passed for it anyway – was an offer many people couldn't pass up, but at the same time it was a one-way ticket, a permanent decision. Many more people chose not to take the gift of Ascension, but to remain in the natural world to care for family and carry out responsibilities they had to others as well as themselves. For some, the objections were moral or religious. But the technology of Ascension, as it was known, was designed to usher a new era of human existence. Taking human consciousness and elevating it to the realm of pure energy meant that a person could live forever.

Alice was one of those with doubts about Ascension. Wasn't it playing God? Maybe. Were people ever meant to live inside computers? She often reminded herself that if they weren't, mankind would never have found a way to do it, so maybe it was meant to be. One thing she did know was that the money she made doing even basic administration for EverDawn meant she had a significantly more comfortable life than many.

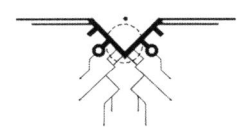

People who were less fortunate might brand her as one of the elites, but she was far from it. Sure, she had money. She had a decent job. But those things alone didn't put her among the elite. Not at all. The people in charge were the elite. And their friends. It brought to her mind the stories of hard-line communism in the 1900s, when members and associates of the Party were treated to fine dining, exquisite wine, finery that was denied to the masses who'd worked so hard to provide for the many.

She didn't have to worry about the ethics of Ascension technology for much longer. She'd be retiring in a few years and she could forget all about it. Advertisements everywhere promised an "escape from human misery" and the opportunity to live somewhere better than the here and now. She would consider herself lucky if she never heard about Ascension again in any form. But she knew it was here to stay.

Of course, she never shared her misgivings about the project and the technology. Or about the people who ran it. She kept such opinions close to her chest, under lock and key. The last thing she needed was to rock the boat and risk her job and all the comforts it afforded her in a very uncomfortable world. No, she needed the job, even if it meant doing things she didn't necessarily agree with in order to make sure her family were cared for now, and after she'd gone. She was old fashioned that way, perhaps a bit too much, but she had been raised to put family first and foremost and had tried to instil that sense of responsibility into her own children and grandchildren.

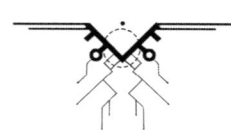

It wasn't the technology she necessarily had the issue with. It was how it was being used. Or, rather, how it came to be used by the directors and their elite friends. The Ascension technology had been free in the past, allowing anyone to Ascend who wanted to, but recently the government had been rolling out a pay scheme for everything attached to it. Regular people would now need to purchase credits in order to access the interface where their friends or family had been ascended, and likewise within the program itself there would be payments needed for features such as chat rooms where you could meet with your loved ones. It was all part of President Mason's grand vision. He and his elite group of friends and colleagues realised they could strong arm the little guy out of using services intended to be free, to make the system serve only those they deemed worthy.

Paid-for access to EverDawn was a relatively new development and hadn't yet been rolled out globally. Alice thought it was unwise to enforce such a system, forcing people to pay to speak to their Ascended loved ones. It could cause problems. Big problems. Especially since the masses were not typically as blessed as she was when it came to money, good health and fulfilment. She could see it causing an uproar, but she was just an administrator and no one special, so who would listen to her thoughts on the issue.

She looked at the clock on the wall. It was going for four. Luckily the workday ended at about 4:30 and she could be off home to her cute house in the suburbs with a small kitchen, two bedrooms and a comfortable air. She'd bought it around forty years before and it had been her home ever since. She'd raised her kids in it, and those old walls had seen some great times as well as some darker times. The darkest was the time around her husband's passing. The next darkest, perhaps, was when Mason was elected President. She'd had reservations about him from the start, and they were beginning to be justified.

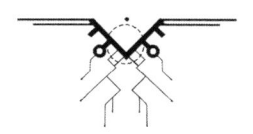

President Mason wasn't announcing the rollout of paid access to the program and the interface. He was springing it on people and that was liable to cause anger and resentment towards his administration. People were not going to be pleased, especially that they were asking something like fifty thousand dollars to ascend now. Fifty thousand up from free. Alice wasn't sure how President Mason could not see how this was a bad idea. Especially with no prior warning nor time frame for the expected full roll out of having to pay. It was a ticking time bomb. She sighed.

There were two files left she had to process. They were people who were lucky and got in while Ascension was still free. She recognised one of the names, of a guy she'd gone to school with, back just before the war had started. They'd been friendly with each other and had known each other outside of school too. He'd lived just up the block, a fellow named Jack. She remembered him well. Their fathers had worked together at one of the companies in town, back at the height of corporate power, just before the downfall.

She punched the details into the computer system and created their Ascension profiles. It was easy enough work, and she actually liked making new profiles for people. It was one of those tasks that somehow left you with a feeling of accomplishment, and data entry was definitely her preferred task when it came to her role. Nice and mindless, not stressful. Easy. Just the way she liked her life. Of course, there were other aspects of the job that required a lot of finesse and training, and it was for this reason the company had already hired an intern to replace her when she retired. The intern's name was Jade. She was a nice girl, around the same age as Alice's granddaughter, Lex. Alice often wondered if they knew each other outside of work. With fewer people in the world, it was more and more likely people would know each other. Especially people in the same age groups.

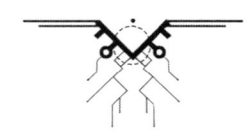

It probably didn't matter though. She looked at the clock again. Jade had already left for the day, needing to do something at home with her ailing father. Alice felt bad for her. She knew what it was like to have sick parents. Both of her own had passed away from illness, something that she wouldn't wish on anyone. It was ironic: for all the general strides they'd made in the world at large, people still got sick and it killed as indiscriminately as before. Fortunately, since her parents passed from different illnesses, mankind had made huge strides toward developing cures, vaccines and other treatments. Illness was still prevalent, but it was far less intense than in her parents' time.

She glanced at the clock in the corner of her computer screen. 16:15. Just fifteen minutes. She took her time with the last file, trying to draw it out as long as possible to kill the rest of her workday. It was Friday, the final day of the work week. For all the various developments and changes from the old way of the world that had worked into the new, she thought, it was funny that one thing mankind seemed intent on keeping around was the sometimes slave driving work week. If anything, the hours had become longer, and there was little if any wiggle room in terms of overtime pay in most job sectors, but it had pushed many people to do their own thing in terms of growing their own vegetables and providing freelance services where they could. It allowed them to make their own hours and focus on doing other things with the time they'd otherwise have to devote to being in the office or commuting.

16:20. She took her handbag out of her desk drawer and put it on the back of her chair. It was a brightly coloured brand name thing, large enough to carry almost all of her everyday items, plus a sweater or jacket in the event that she got hot or cold. She put her wallet inside, small and hand-embroidered, a Mother's Day gift from Lex years ago. It had been sitting on her desk since she paid for her lunch from the food cart that usually made the rounds around noon. Her colleague Sarah would be along momentarily to get her on her way out of the office. They always went for a drink at their local bar on Fridays. They lived just up the street from one another, walking distance from the office. The bar, "SpeakEasy", was on their way home, placed precariously and somewhat strangely under an old railway bridge, almost built into the supports. It was hard to tell whether the bar had been there before the bridge or vice versa. It was a dark old thing, often frequented by the older generation, which was somewhat comforting in a world that had grown and changed so much since the old days. Topics of conversation were frequently rooted in the past, and the barman often played what was now considered to be extremely old, classic music from nearly a century prior.

16:25. She could hear a jingle of keys and Sarah's tell-tale steps as her long heels clacked against the pristine white floor of the EverDawn hallway. She shut down her computer and stood from her desk, stretching her ageing back as she did. She was going for sixty-five, but some days she felt over a hundred. She wondered if maybe she had some health issues herself, but never bothered seeing a doctor. Partly due to the inability to get time off from work while training Jade, but also partly due to fear as to what doctors may find if she did.

Sarah poked her head around the corner then.

"You ready?" she asked.

"Yes. I'll just grab my coat," Alice replied.

She walked to the coat rack on the far wall and took her trademark bright red pea coat off the hook.

"I have three more files for you. But just do them Monday, obviously. Or get Jade to do them. That's what interns are for, after all." Sarah said, handing the files to

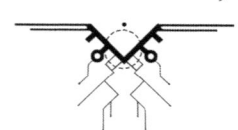

Alice, grinning as she did. They both knew that interns were ideal for grunt work and the often boring data entry.

Alice glanced at the names on the tabs and took a sharp intake of breath. She recognised the names, not just from school or work or any past affiliation. They were family. Her daughter, son-in-law and grandson. Only three files. A fourth file would be Lex's, but it was clear that Lex hadn't decided to take Ascension. At least not yet.

"What is it?" Sarah asked, shifting her handbag from one arm to the other.

Alice thought about telling her but decided not to. "Nothing. Come on. I think I really need a stiff one to forget this week."

They left the office together and walked out into the dreary afternoon that was common at that time of year. Alice's mind flooded with thoughts and worries about her family going through with the Ascension process, knowing that she'd voiced her displeasure about it, but her protest had obviously fallen on deaf ears. She took out her phone and tapped a message to her daughter Lin quickly. She hoped she could change their minds before they went through with it. She had the weekend to try, anyway.

Chapter One

As Lex wandered through her district the air was filled with the heavy smell of barbecuing pork, combined with the high humidity, a hazard of living right next to the ocean where storms would begin to roll in mid-afternoon. The mix made breathing laborious, even though the pork smelled succulent. The clouds hung dark in the sky overhead, a tell-tale sign that yet another storm was brewing. Lex looked up into the inky mass and felt a pang of irritation. Another fucking wet and dark day. Just what anyone needed.

She'd thought that living by the ocean was going to be enjoyable, and it was for a while until the continued dampness just got into everything, especially in the winter. The climate wasn't great and both the over-farming of the last two centuries combined with heavy uses of fossil fuels; continued pillaging of the Earth's resources and huge consumption using single-use plastics and other materials had meant people had needed to change fast. There were new and fantastic ways to live, something the people of the past intent on their individual greed would never have likely agreed to. People had become innovative and cooperative. Gone was the personal way of thinking, and now it was more about community. Sure, there were a few things that Lex, as well as other people, would change if given half the chance, but there wasn't anything unbearable about life. It could be pretty good when you got down to it. People grew fruits and vegetables in hydroponic setups in their own homes or gardens, often selling or trading with neighbours. Some raised chickens and traded eggs for carrots, cucumbers or other fruits and vegetables. It was a great way to live.

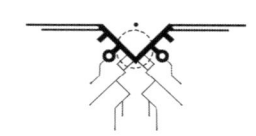

Rebellion's Martyr

The churning clouds overhead foretold of a potential deluge soon to come. It was the tail end of September, the time of storms. The storms could change everything very quickly, causing havoc as floods ravaged the streets and knocked out power, an issue especially for hydroponics systems which often relied on still sediments or liquids to let their plants thrive on the nutrition below. Blackouts took a while to resolve. Being by the sea meant that rains were frequently heavy in the autumn, but everyone knew what to expect. It was welcomed by those who collected their own rainwater, that was for sure. After one or two storms you had enough water to last you at least a week, or longer.

With the winter coming soon and storms sometimes lasting for long periods, people began to stockpile various means to keep warm. Batteries, what fuel they could manage to get their hands on and wood were the most popular options, with wood being the cheapest. Anyone could walk into any forest and start chopping trees – something that was causing issues as more and more people began to take this drastic, desperate step. Still, though, it was either that or freeze, so fuck trees. Fuels and batteries for heating systems were expensive ever since President Mason signed some kind of treaty into place restricting access to certain types of power sources, so most people went with wood, when and if they could.

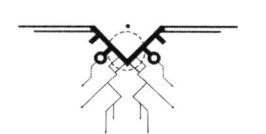

A couple of raindrops fell on her face as she looked up at the sky, dark clouds twisting and contorting. The breeze was picking up, forcing the smell of barbecues and other street side vendor food stalls into her nose mixed with the early scent of petrichor. It smelled divine, but she didn't have time to stop now. She needed to get to the LAI, more commonly known as a "Spot". LAI – 'Location for Ascension Interface' – just didn't roll off the tongue as well. LAIs were complexes of rooms where real humans could connect with and speak to the ascended people in the EverDawn computer network through Augmented Reality. In the past they had often been full to capacity. More recently, fewer and fewer people were able to afford "interfacing" to connect with loved ones – something that was a growing frustration. The prices were going up, and it was all thanks to one person: President Mason.

Mason was not a well-loved leader, amongst the rationally thinking at least. He had bought his way in to power, coercing officials and even procured help from other major world powers like Russia and China. It was nothing new. Politics had always been dirty, practically since the Boston Tea Party on the shores of America in 1773. This situation had been brewing for a long time, and with more modern means of distributing disinformation and propaganda, it had been possible to fool enough people to a great enough extent to narrowly scrape an election victory. That's all he had needed – the legitimacy of an official electoral success, no matter how dirtily it had been achieved.

Lex glanced at her watch as she rushed past various street food vendors. It was a little after three but she still needed to buy credits to pay for her time at the Spot. That involved stopping at Mr. Meshi's small hole-in-the-wall shop where he sold all manner of things from the everyday essentials to the weird and wonderful. He was the only person she went to for credits, amongst other things. She had been going to him for years and the price he asked for credits never increased – at least, not yet, even in an environment where everyone else was jacking the prices up by forty or even fifty percent. Meshi was a good man. His wife, like Lex's parents and brother, had ascended and so he understood the importance of being able to reach them in cyberspace.

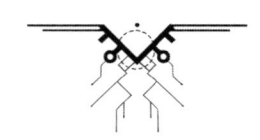

She turned onto the bustling street where Meshi's shop was nestled between a busy cafeteria with a long line, and a shoe shop that sold all manner of strange and new cyberpunk style boots. That was all the shop sold, and Lex had been a patron in the past. The window reflected a rogue ray of sun that managed to break the heavy cloud cover, briefly dazzling Lex as she walked through the beam. Meshi's shop looked out of place between these two – it bore more than a passing resemblance to the fanciful stereotypical Chinese shops in movies like Forbidden Kingdom, or Gremlins, run by eccentric elderly men intent on selling all manner of strange artefacts. Meshi almost played to the same stereotype. To have a shop full of esoteric knick-knacks and objects of unknown origin was a concept that juxtaposed well against the modern world of electronics. He always had a solution to every problem and tried to up-sell at every opportunity, but he knew Lex. She wasn't going to buy anything more than she had to. Not usually anyway.

Meshi's old, wooden door looked less like it should be the entry to a shop and more like it belonged in some dark, dank house that hadn't been inhabited for a hundred years. The paint was chipped, and the wood was rotting in some places. Meshi would have it patched up as much as was required for it to function while maintaining the image. That sat well with his financial ethos too. He was frugal when money was involved, but for good reason – with fewer and fewer options to make a living, people had to save what they could. Hell, it was considered a luxury to be able to eat out at a proper restaurant. If the costs of interfacing continued to mount, it too would soon become a luxury.

Lex pushed the door open, the bell ringing out. Meshi's previous customer, clad in a long jacket and a Fedora or similar, pushed past, without saying a word, and walked briskly away, holding their jacket closed around them.

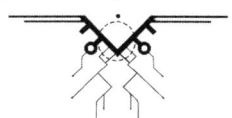

"You're welcome, asshole," Lex said under her breath. Her grandmother had always taught her good manners, and she found it frustrating that most people didn't seem to share the value. She closed the door, the darkness of the shop enveloping her. The windows hadn't been cleaned in years – maybe decades. The coagulation of grime and dust on the outside was so thick you could probably write a marketing slogan in it, and it made what was already a dark shop even darker, obscuring what little daylight was able to penetrate the glass.

Lex looked around, trying to see if Meshi was in. She heard something scuttling about in the backroom and figured it was him. He'd be out in a minute. In the meantime, she perused his other offerings: dusty shelves of random bits and bobs, many things he'd collected on excursions around the world before travelling became almost impossible, pointless for the most part, considering the world was all one nation now. Back in her school days Lex had learned that the world used to be divided by continents and countries. That was ridiculous though, people drawing up invisible lines and then fighting over them. Imagine, being born just a few metres across from a line you can't see and therefore being unable to walk across the street without paperwork. Ridiculous! That was around twenty-five years ago, around the time she was born, maybe slightly before. Lex's mother had travelled in her youth, and she'd met Lex's father in a foreign land. She couldn't remember which, somewhere in Europe.

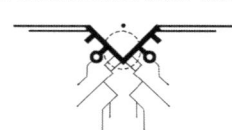

But now, everything was different. Her father had told her about other cities, or at least what they used to be like. He told her that there was once a Cathedral in Italy called the Sistine Chapel whose ceilings were a wash of wonderful colours and religious scenes. In Poland, there had been churches with roofs of gold and entire cities that had been rebuilt after a world war. He even once told her of China and its firework festivals. That was a hard one to get her head around, there being a China. As far as Lex knew there was a Chinatown in every district. She had asked him whether China had exploded and scattered little parts of itself across town. Gosh, how silly! That's a child's mind though. And it wasn't exactly her fault, she hadn't a clue what the words he threw around had meant at that age; post-capitalism, communism, progression. Still, those had been some of her favourite bedtime stories, but she was all grown up now, and travelled enough to know that the world looked the same. Not that she had travelled particularly far herself, but it was enough. Now all of those places would be slums, dark and dangerous unless you had the cash to buy a little comfort, like everywhere else. The Chapel probably houses the homeless, the gold would be stripped back to the rafters and as for fireworks? Yeah right. How the hell were they able to see such things through the smog when you could barely see your hand in front of your face? Fireworks seemed like a pretty big trade off when the whole area was choking on plastic fumes and the industries were built on the burned-out bodies of workers. President Mason didn't see it that way. Then again, Lex was pretty sure his eyes were blinded by the reflection of all those coins. Hopefully, the glare would burn out his retinas like ants under a microscope one day. That way he might actually be able to truly see.

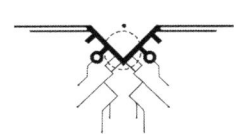

Lex walked carefully between the precarious shelving that housed almost anything and everything a person could imagine. Dusty books from some of the last century's most famous authors, a stack of ancient newspapers that had seen better days – presumably great for historical research for those kids who could afford to be in school – teapots and cups that appeared to be from Asia somewhere. A basket of numerous boxes of incense sat on the floor against one shelf, some with Arabic writing on them suggesting they'd come from the Middle East somewhere. Lights of all shapes, sizes and varieties hung from the ceiling, but none were turned on. She crouched down to get a closer look at a tea set with what looked like traditional Chinese writing on it. She wasn't sure what it said, but she wagered that her grandmother would love it.

Meshi walked into the front of the shop from the back room, the kitschy beaded curtain rattling as he pushed it out of the way.

"Lex? That you?" he asked in the general darkness. If anything, she was timely and usually visited him at the same time of day every couple of days for her credits for the Spot.

"Yeah, it's me," she replied from the darkness. Meshi walked over to her, a small, lanky man in his late 40s or early 50s from Yunnan in China, dressed in grey trousers and a short-sleeved white button-up shirt. Not very fashionable compared to the style of most people of the time, including Lex, with their cyberpunk clothing, shoes and hair. He was like something that burst through time from the past, and it strangely comforted Lex for some reason.

"You like that tea set!" he exclaimed excitedly. "For you, special offer."

"No. Not today, Meshi," she said, standing up and brushing her dark hair from her face. "Just the credits."

"Always only credits. When you buy something more?" he asked, jokingly.

"When I get more money," she smiled. "Maybe my grandmother will give me some for my birthday next month. Then I promise, I'll buy something more."

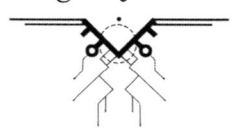

They walked through the small, dimly lit shop to the till by the door. Outside the grimy window Lex could see the rain beginning to come down more heavily. It was a good thing the Spot was only about a five-minute walk from Meshi's place, especially as she wasn't wearing anything waterproof.

Meshi reached under the glass counter-top and produced a baby formula container. "Today I have enough for thirty minutes."

"That's it?" Lex asked, disappointment clear in her voice.

"These days credits hard to come by," he replied.

"Yeah but thirty minutes?"

"Take or leave."

She stood at the counter for a minute about to mull it over, but she knew she was going to relent. It had been two years since her brother and parents Ascended and she was finding it difficult without them. It felt like going to the Spot was almost the only thing keeping her sane some days.

"Fine. How much?"

"For you, still special price this week. Twenty-five dollars."

"That's not a special price, Meshi. That's nearly a dollar a minute."

"I say again, take or leave."

"Can't you do any better?"

Meshi grumbled and counted on his fingers for a minute before nodding once. "Okay. Twenty. But you bring me some of Alice's special sweet and sour." He passed over the card that contained the Ascension credits.

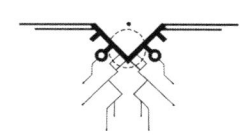

"Okay, deal," she agreed.

She left Meshi's just as he turned on the lights, finally relenting to the darkness. His 'Open' sign buzzed on in bright pink lettering, flickering with strain as water undoubtedly got into the electrics from the now more substantial rain. With half of the electrical devices he had rigged up in his shop, it was a wonder the place hadn't burned to the ground yet. A relief for Lex, of course, but a mystery nonetheless. One thing was certain: after the collapse of the old Libertarian government, no one much cared for health and safety – not that they had before, but somehow it grew worse. The state of buildings, electrical wiring, cars (for who could afford them) and anything else that might have benefited from some regulation at least fell into danger and decay.

She rushed through the rain to the Spot trying to protect her velvet jacket from getting watermarked. She cursed her stupidity for wearing velvet at this time of year. She knew well that September brought ferocious storms. She had only lived there for most of her life, after all.

The street got slicker with the rain, a rain that was heavy and cold. It bounced off Lex's skin, beating down and drenching her in moments. She hopped a puddle that had an ominously sparking wire near it. Nobody moved it, nobody cared. They just did what Lex did, stepped by it and continued about their day without getting zapped. At least in the city she could duck in and out of cafes, Spots, and shops for respite from the seemingly never-ending drizzle. Even overhanging ledges that were precarious at best made for decent coverage, so long as they didn't fall on those sheltering.

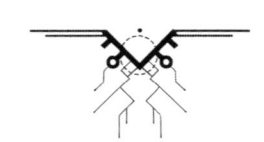

Chapter Two

Lex managed to get to the Spot a little before four and right before the rain really let loose. She sighed with relief that her velvet coat would live another day, as she walked through the glass doors and into the Spot's pristine reception lounge. A long, tall, white desk was toward the back of the room and several white sofas were set in one corner with magazines, books and the like on a glass coffee table, ready for people to peruse them while they waited for their turn with the technology. There were several rooms to use and, until recently, they'd almost always been packed.

Lex walked up to the counter, and the very put-together receptionist barely glanced up from her tablet, supposedly carrying out administrative tasks, although her prods and swipes told a different story. Tapping her keys on the glass, Lex looked up at the clock, wanting desperately to get online as soon as possible. The receptionist sighed and begrudgingly looked up, her black hair shining under the track lighting as she did.

"Yeah?"

"I have credits for half an hour," Lex said, passing over the credits she'd bought from Meshi and putting her hands on the desk expectantly.

The receptionist took the credits and looked at Lex for a moment, then down at something on her desk. "Room seven. I assume you know the drill," she said as she handed Lex a key card and cast her eyes back to her tablet again as though she didn't really care. Lex nodded, not that it mattered.

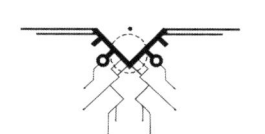

Lex rushed down the hall to the room. She'd been in that room before, right at the end, the last door on the left tucked in a corner. She wondered why the receptionist had sent her all the way down when there was clearly no one else in any of the other rooms. Lex dismissed the thought as she opened the door and flicked on the light, illuminating the space where the interface would take place.

The off-white neon light flickered for a moment as it surged with power and brought the room alive. There was a coat stand near the door to her right, just past the light switch, and a small couch next to that. In the centre of the room was a glass pedestal with a headset on top of it, connected to nothing physical in the room – it was all done wirelessly. The room itself had small sensors all along the tops and bottoms of the walls to create the visage of a virtual space right in the room, when the user put on the headset. It was then that they could access the Ascension interface and meet with friends and family who had chosen that particular path.

She hung her jacket on the hook and put her bag on the couch before rushing over to the headset, inserting the card in the back and pulling it on over her straight, dark hair. In the reflection of the visor she could see her own eyes, almond-shaped, dark brown, a subtle touch of makeup. She touched the left side of the headset to turn it on and was greeted by the usual digitised woman explaining Ascension and the process of both ascending yourself and interfacing with those who already had.

"Welcome to the Location for Ascension Interface," the woman began in a crisp, light and almost slightly robotic voice. "I'm your assistant, Tina."

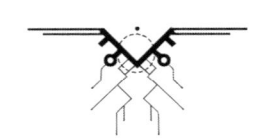

The digitised woman paused for a moment before continuing. "The Ascension process is a ground-breaking technology that allows human consciousness to exist as pure energy in a computerised system. There are a number of benefits to Ascension, including – but not limited to – eternal life, eternal youth and instant travel. The Ascended consciousnesses that are already in the program can be accessed in this store file."

Tina brought up a file onto a virtual desk that sprawled out in front of Lex. Without needing to think, Lex tapped her finger on it quickly and typed her family last name – Atov – into the database. In seconds her family's photos appeared as Tina continued explaining the process.

"Select the individual or individuals with whom you wish to interface. You may select up to five individuals at any one time. Once selected, tap 'next'."

Lex hurriedly clicked 'next' after selecting the photos of her family. The program began to load but seemed to take much longer than usual. She glanced at the clock on the wall. It was ten past four already.

Suddenly, the room came alive all around her in brightly coloured lights. She was inside the program, at least virtually. This was one of the best ways to exist in her opinion: being able to visit when she wanted, without having to completely divorce herself from biological existence. Visitors were able to see parts of the Ascended world but being a part of it was another thing entirely. She looked around the room, cleverly digitised with the virtual world overlapping the real one. She could still see the physical aspects of the real room – the coat rack, the couch and clock – but they were overlapped with the digital Ascended world.

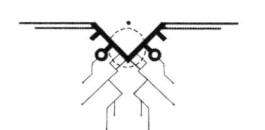

The interface to EverDawn was like a lounge or reception area. It was where the interface always started and you could wander the halls and pop in and out of various rooms, some with themes, waiting for your family or friends to join you. Lex was about to head down the hall to the room they always used – a standard lounge type room where you could sit on virtual plush sofas and drink virtual drinks. She always ordered the same: a virtual TI – Tonic Infusion. She wasn't exactly sure what was meant to be in it, or how they got the sensation and taste of something not real into a person's tastebuds, but it was refreshing and delicious all the same. Usage of the lounge and drinks had always been included in the credits purchased to access the interface, but in recent months they had started charging separately. She always made sure to have a few more credits on her to at least pay to access the lounge.

Lex opened the door to the lounge and looked around. It was almost entirely dead. There were two people interfacing in the corner, but that was it, aside from the room staff such as the bartender and the doorman. Each room had a doorman now to ensure payment was provided upon entry, and sure enough before she had enough time to take in the room, he was already tapping her on the shoulder telling her to pay up. She dug around in her physical pockets and inserted five more credits into a slot in the wall, three to get in and two for a drink, on top of what she'd already paid for room 7. It was highway robbery, but there was no other way. She was all too aware that it would be more than a week before she could afford to do this again.

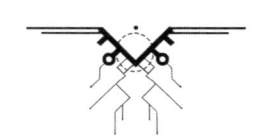

The clink of the coins in the machine was loud in the general silence of the room. A low mumble from the couple in the corner filled the deafening quiet, a welcome respite from what was getting to be far too quiet for her liking. They weren't even playing music anymore, or so it seemed. When the coins settled in the machine and the sound of the clinking and clanking of metal on metal ceased, the doorman let her enter the room properly, allowing her to access the bar for her drink.

She walked up to the bar and looked at the bartender – the usual guy, named Jori. He was tall and lanky with dark hair that seemed meticulously styled. She always wondered if the Ascended AIs had to get up in the morning and do "people" things like styling their hair, or whether their digital consciousness was just downloaded into a pre-built avatar. She thought about asking Jori, but she'd noted a tendency for AIs to natter on about how great Ascension was with an air of self-importance and arrogance. She wasn't sure Jori would be like that, but she also didn't want to get him started on some long-winded sales patois of the ins and outs of EverDawn before her family turned up. Instead, she asked about the music – a small bone of contention for her.

"Jori. Where's the music?" she asked as he passed over her drink. It was also missing the usual fanciness, a paper umbrella and straw. It didn't even have ice.

"We had to cut back on the music," he started. "Especially when we're dead like today. We can only play music if we have at least ten patrons in here."

"Ten?!" she exclaimed. "Jori, with the price of interfacing now you'll be lucky to get five. No-one can afford it anymore."

"Not my area of expertise," Jori began. "I prefer soups and stews to crackers and tofu."

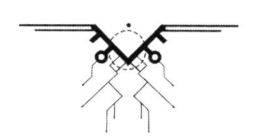

"What?" Lex replied, somewhat baffled by the strange and seemingly useless commentary that had just burst forth from his mouth. Jori didn't respond, instead busying himself with wiping down the bar and arranging virtual glasses on a shelf – tasks that were obviously unnecessary, but were designed to make EverDawn feel more comfortable and familiar.

Lex chose to ignore it, aside from her initial query as to what he was on about. Instead she continued, "What is with this cheapo drink?" she asked again, tipping it toward him. "I know times are tough but not even any ice? Come on, Jori."

He shrugged. "Another cut-back."

She looked at the drink and then glanced at the doorman about twenty feet behind her. "Cutbacks on ice but not on doormen and they charge for rooms now?"

Jori just shrugged again. "Not my department. Hey, have you thought about Ascending?"

Lex could see she wasn't getting anywhere with him and decided to leave it before he started. Besides, her family could be there at any moment and since she only had limited time, she wanted to maximise it.

She sat in the corner, at their usual table – designed to look like some iridescent glassy substance as an advertisement for EverDawn's ultra-futuristic image – and looked up at the clock. Quarter past four. She had twenty-five minutes now.

As the clock ticked down closer to twenty minutes left she began to wonder where exactly they were. She'd done all the preparations and the downloading of profiles correctly, so where could they be? It wasn't at all like them to be late. Just as she was about to get up from the table to go ask Jori if it was another cutback, the door opened, and her parents Michael and Lin along with her brother James all came into the room.

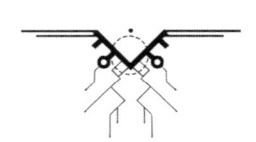

"Lex!" her mother called, rushing over to her, followed closely by her father and brother.

"There you guys are," she replied, rising from her seat at a table and hugging her mother. "I was beginning to think you wouldn't show up."

"Sorry we're late, honey," Lin began. "We had trouble getting into the interface."

Lex looked at the three of them. "What? What kind of trouble?"

"Oh, you know. Just not loading, not completing. Error messages." Michael said, going in for a hug from Lex himself. "It happens."

"Hey sis!" James said gleefully, reaching out for the huge bear hug they were both accustomed to from each other. "Nice to see ya!"

"Nice to see you too. It's been a while."

"Hopefully not as long next time," Michael said, raising his eyebrows.

"Well, it seems like they're making it harder and harder to get in here," Lex said. "As it is I've had to pay extra just to get in the room here and for drinks."

"We heard they were going to start charging extra," James chimed in without thinking. "President Mason seems to be getting greedy about Ascension."

The mention of President Mason elicited a few raised eyebrows from Jori, the doorman and the couple on the other side of the room. Everyone suddenly seemed to be interested in their conversation. Her parents looked a bit skittish at the reactions from the other people in the room.

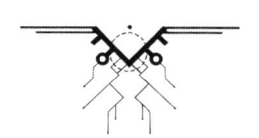

"Maybe... now isn't the best time to talk about that." Lin said tentatively, looking around with slight anxiety rising. "We can discuss that another time."

Michael nodded as he sat down at the table. "There will be plenty of time."

Her parents and James all sat down at the circular table with Lex, who looked over her shoulder at the other four people in the room, making sure they'd gone back to minding their own business.

"How have you been Lex?" her mother asked. "How's Damian?"

"He's good. Last I heard," Lex replied. "He's travelling right now. France I think. For work. But he will be back tomorrow."

"He should just do Ascension. He wouldn't need to travel so much," James piped up. "Go anywhere in an instant. Makes life so much easier."

"Only he never would," Lex said, rolling her eyes. She'd heard this insistence a thousand times from people who were Ascended. "He doesn't believe in it."

"Who doesn't believe in Ascension?" Michael asked. "It's been an idea for decades and been possible for almost as long."

"You know Damian," Lex sighed. "He's not into that kind of thing."

"Have you thought any more about it?" Lin asked

"No. Not really."

"Why not?"

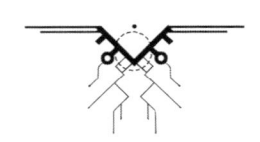

"I just haven't. I've been busy. Grandma Alice is getting really old now, so I don't want to do anything until she's gone or decides to Ascend for herself."

"That makes sense," James said. "At least we have you to count on for taking care of Grandma Alice."

"Are you seeing her today?" Lin asked.

"I see her nearly all the time. Most days."

"Tell her we say hi and that we love her and wish she'd consider joining us."

"I will."

"I miss her sweet and sour pork." James sighed. "I miss food in general."

"What? Ascension isn't as perfect as you thought?" Lex playfully asked, teasing him on purpose. There was a bit of serious questioning on her end. They'd been pressuring her to Ascend for months and kept going on about how amazing it was. She wasn't sold on the idea though, at least not yet.

"Oh be quiet," James said looking down, slightly irritated.

"Hey kids, don't argue," Michael began. "Lex didn't pay to come here to fight."

"No I didn't," she admitted. "I miss you guys. I feel like this might be the last time for a while."

"Why's that?" Lin asked. "Have they cut your hours at work again? How are you getting on? Do you have enough money? We can send some through the wire transfer from our account since we don't need it here."

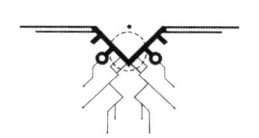

"No. No. That's okay," Lex began, before lowering her voice so Jori, the doorman and the couple in the corner couldn't hear. "The credits are ridiculously expensive now. It's getting out of hand. The only way I can afford any is because I keep going to Meshi. He still sells them at the old price. To me anyway."

Her parents and James looked around at each other then, as though they knew something she didn't.

"What?" Lex asked.

"No one interfaces anymore." James said. "For the same reason: the cost."

"We suspect that Mason is trying to make it so only the rich people can enjoy Ascension. We've heard rumours from people on the inside that suggest that's the case," Michael said, almost half jokingly. "But it's all speculation."

An alarm rang inside her headset, warning her that only five minutes of her interface time remained. Her heart flipped. It always went far too quickly, especially for the cost.

"Five minutes left," she told her family. "Way too fast."

"There will always be next time," Lin said. "It's not like we're going anywhere. We'll be here whenever you want to come back to see us. Don't feel like you need to rush and put yourself in financial trouble just to see us."

"I'll send you some money from the account," Michael said. Lex didn't argue the idea this time. She knew that she could use the money − if not for credits to interface, then for things like food, medicine and basic necessities. The cost of everything seemed to be going up exponentially.

"Thanks," she said sheepishly.

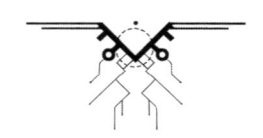

"Don't worry about it, Lex. We know times are hard on the outside. That's why we so want you to come join us in Ascension," Michael told her, reaching across the table and taking her hand. They all held hands briefly for a moment together in a circle before Lex couldn't hold it in any longer.

"I want to know what you guys heard about President Mason."

Lin, Michael and James looked over at Jori, polishing glasses behind the bar and the doorman who seemed taken with fixing something on the wall. The other couple in the corner had ended their session and so it was slightly more awkward in the room, especially if they were about to talk about the president – something it seemed was frowned upon if you were going to discredit, disagree with or otherwise try to make him look bad.

James started, and didn't need much coaxing. "Well, we heard from at least twelve different people that their families can't interface anymore – this is people all over the world we're talking about here. In some cases their families are outright being refused access to Spots, even if they have dozens and dozens of credits to use."

"I heard it's quite bad in other places," Lin said. "A lot of places don't even sell credits anymore unless you provide ID."

"ID?" Lex asked. "You don't need ID to buy credits."

"You shouldn't, but apparently in some places you do," Michael said. "Just be aware it could come down like that here…"

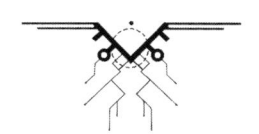

Lex opened her mouth to press them for more details, but the interface cut off without warning. She took off the headset and put it back on the table it was usually on. She looked at the clock and realised that it had cut off about three minutes early. It was either the tech being shitty like it had been today or it was something more sinister. The administration believed even the smallest words of dissent could potentially prove damaging to President Mason. It was possible and quite potentially probable that someone had been eavesdropping, and had cut her session short. She didn't want to think about it, though. She supposed she had no real way of finding out which it was, but that she might soon find out.

Turning around and picking up her bag from the couch and coat from the coat rack, she got herself together and opened the door to leave, hoping only that the rain had stopped and her velvet coat would live to see another day.

Chapter Three

The rain had slowed to a trickle, but the thick cloud cover and nightfall had made the darkness almost oppressive. If it hadn't been for the bright, neon glow of various shops, cafes, theatres and restaurants, the streets would be a never-ending maze of dark alleyways and confusing intersections with no real discerning appearance to help night wanderers find their way. It was lucky for Lex that she'd grown up in the city and could find her way easily, even taking the dark backstreets, but she was in a rush this time and dallying about taking new and curious ways home in the dark would only lengthen the trip.

Her grandmother lived almost clear across town from where she was and walking wouldn't get her there on time. She needed to take public transport or a taxi if she wanted to get there anytime that night and in relative safety. She rummaged around in her pocket as she walked, producing what little money she had left. She had enough to take the seriously, shitty metro or a bus. The metro hadn't been updated in years and it was like something out of a history book – it was slow, cumbersome and uncomfortable. To make matters worse, the city's gangs had made their headquarters in the stations. It was common knowledge that in most stations you got off the train and made a beeline for the exit to avoid a confrontation. It had been that way for some time. Some people just had a preference for that way of life, it seemed, and there was nothing anyone could do to stop them.

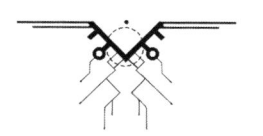

There had been times that joining one of these gangs had seemed appealing, especially after her family had ascended and she'd been more-or-less on her own with the exception of her grandmother. Her best friend, Damian, was often travelling and so had it not been for Grandma Alice, she'd have been entirely alone. She had some reservations about Ascension and doing it herself, but she couldn't quite work out what they were. Something just didn't sit right with her. Memories of the arguments that had transpired when her parents and brother had broken the news about ascending flooded her mind. It was something that had caused a couple of issues, but nothing major. At least she knew they were safe and seemingly enjoying life 'on the inside'.

She looked at the money in her hand and thought about dodging the gangs in the underground between the closest station and her grandmother's house. It wasn't something she really wanted to do, but she also wanted to save the money her dad would be sending her – possibly for more credits to use the Spot – but she wasn't sure yet. Maybe she'd treat Damian to a night out when he got back since it'd been ages since they'd seen each other. They could go to their favourite restaurant: a strange sushi place near Meshi's shop but tucked in a back alley so unassuming that if you didn't know it was there, you'd pass it by every time. It was perfect in that sense – only the people who really gave a damn went there and none of the tough guys who liked to play up every now and again. It was just ordinary people eating ordinary sushi. Or what passed for ordinary sushi anyway.

She turned the corner onto the main strip that led into the heart of Chinatown, the closest, and strangely the roughest, metro station. The bright, neon lights of the neighbourhood shops and restaurants broke the monotony of darkness both on the street and overhead, shimmering and reflecting off the puddles of water that had pooled on the streets and pavements, making the whole area come alive in colours of pinks, purples and blues. It was nice, in a way. She definitely loved how the darkness seemed to make the colours brighter and stand out more.

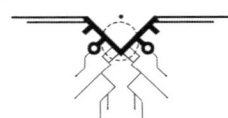

The metro station was just ahead, its trademark M glowing a muted incandescent yellow against the cacophony of colourful neon. Rushing past street vendors putting their smoked joints of meat out on display and yelling at passers-by to buy their wares, she avoided eye contact and tried to dodge harassment by the desperate shopkeepers looking to make a sale. The food, no doubt, smelled absolutely divine, but there was a home cooked meal waiting for her at her grandmother's house. It would only take about an hour to get there, maybe less this time of day, after rush hour. It depended on whether or not the gangs were behaving themselves tonight; taking the Metro was a fairly high risk just to save some money. The gangs could do any manner of thing: throwing garbage on the tracks, throwing glass bottles at the trains. It wasn't unheard of for them to push people onto the tracks either. There'd been a few fatalities that way. Some poor soul in the wrong place at the wrong time and ending up fodder for the trains. The police never really did anything. They couldn't. Down in the metro, the rule of law was lawless, and anything was fair game. Enter at your own risk.

She took a deep breath at the top of the stairs and started the descent. The metro line was quite deep in, and she had to traverse around seventy-five worn and broken steps to reach the terminal and then would need to go down another fifty or so to reach the platforms. Layers of graffiti covered the walls, some of it completely nonsensical and some of it just your typical gangland symbolism. She was entering Hong gang territory, a gang of primarily Asian descent like she was, so she was hoping she could walk through without much interruption as on occasion any hassle you did get was based on race, which should have been wrong, but it'd been that way for some time, or so her Grandma Alice had told her. It almost brought segregation to the fore again, making people only see others based on where in the world they'd come from, and many only hung out with those from their specific regions of the world. It made the environment a bit rougher when it should have been better. But it was seemingly the way people had wanted to go, and the way the media and perhaps politicians had orchestrated it. Divide and conquer. With the masses suspecting each other in many cases it made it easier to be a slimy sleaze at the top. No one could do or say anything when they didn't have the numbers to back it up.

Stepping off the last of the steps she turned the corner into what was a surprisingly quiet realm. A few people were hanging around smoking or presumably taking drugs as was common for the Hong gang to do – amongst others. Spray painted murals on the wall depicted President Mason in various poses. In one, he was being beaten up. Another had him burned at the stake, and one particularly graphic image of him in a sexual position while members of the gang had their way with him. She tried to hide a smile at that. It was kind of poetic justice in a way: the person doing the fucking gets fucked by the people he fucked. Brilliant, in a weird and twisted way. Clearly there was no love lost between the Hong gang and Mason.

She walked through the terminal and tried not to make eye contact with anyone who was around. It was almost too quiet, leading her to wonder where the other members of the gang were, or if they were lying in wait, just biding their time until some unsuspecting person came along to rob or rough up. Her guard was up as she approached the self-payment kiosk and took her money out. If they were going to strike, it'd be now.

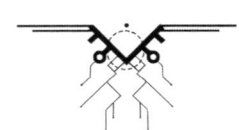

As suspected, she felt someone behind her and she turned slowly, trying not to show signs of being spooked or startled. They fed off that. As she turned, she realised she was face to face with Akoni, the leader of the Hong gang. He was tall and lanky, dressed in an overcoat that had seen better days and was ripped to hell in places across the front, casually and haphazardly mended in some spots but not others. He was wearing a few small, silver chains that dangled from various pockets, and had shaggy black hair that sat over one curious eye and fell over his face slightly, a look that strangely worked well.

He had four of his minions with him, all dressed similarly with chains, spikes and a whole lot of leather on display. Some carried bats or swords but Akoni was carrying a large kitchen knife. He didn't need something flashy to get what he wanted, he was a pro at taking whatever he desired and had been raised on the mean streets of Chinatown where he learned the hard way how to be tough. A scar over his left eye told that tale – an eye that he'd lost in a fight years back and had been replaced with some strange cyborg hardware he'd stolen from a black market trader. If they hadn't been living in the times they were living in, Akoni would have looked like something out of the future with that eye. It glowed an iridescent blue and was made of titanium plates that rested around the socket on the outside of the skin, presumably nailed into his skull, but she wasn't sure how it worked. All she knew was that those cyborg eyes gave the owner a lot of perks and worked far, far better than average human eyes. They could also access information systems if used correctly, as well as provide casual information such as bus times, recipes and more in augmented reality, right from your own eye socket.

"Give me your money," he said levelly. He'd done this same old song and dance countless times before.

"What? My whole thirty cents?" Lex replied just as levelly. Questioning Akoni was probably not the cleverest of moves, but she wasn't in a mood to be pushed around. Especially by some Metro punk.

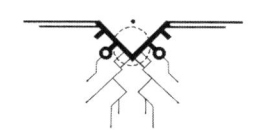

"Everything you have," Akoni said.

"Well that would be thirty cents then."

"Fuck off, is it." He turned then to his minions. "Grab her bag."

Akoni watched as two of his friends pushed Lex against the Metro self-pay kiosk and grabbed her cloth bag off her shoulder. She had her hands up and let them rummage in her things. There was no point fighting back, especially since she had next to nothing they'd be interested in.

One of the street toughs brought her bag to Akoni who looked inside it briefly before taking out a book, '*The Art of War*' by Sun Tzu.

"What the fuck is this?" Akoni asked, waving the book around. "You wanna learn how to fight or something?"

Lex didn't answer him right away. She didn't know how to explain that she just liked reading old classical books and some of the things in '*The Art of War*' were wildly fascinating. She gathered that someone like Akoni wouldn't read just for fun.

"You wanna fight?" he asked.

She stammered. "N… no."

"Why not?"

"I'm not the fighting type."

Akoni didn't know what to make of this so he put the book back in the bag and rummaged around in it some more. There really wasn't anything he wanted or could use. A packet of gum, a pen, the book and some sunglasses – not that they ever got used since Lex tended to be a lover of the night.

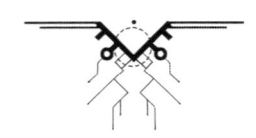

"This bag is shit." he said, tossing it back aggressively to Lex who caught it then held it close. She didn't know what was going to happen next or how to get out of this rather unpleasant situation, especially since she got the feeling Akoni was losing patience and the whole thing could turn nasty in seconds.

"I like your murals," she said, remembering how her parents and James had alluded to issues with Ascension interface stemming from President Mason's elitist and greedy self-serving views.

Akoni seemed taken aback by this sudden comment. He looked over his shoulder at the murals on the wall depicting President Mason essentially getting everything that was coming to him.

"That?" he asked, almost incredulously. "You like it?"

"Yes," she replied, trying not to sound hesitant.

"No one's ever said they like that."

"Well I'm saying it now."

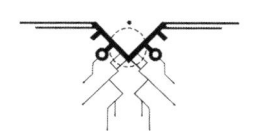

Akoni looked back at her, tilting his head and squinting his one normal eye as though he were trying to figure her out. He raised an eyebrow and seemed to give up on the quest for extracting money and began to ramble off the story of how the mural came to be. A lot of issues with the welfare system and childcare issues meant that a lot of kids ended up having to do things on the streets they normally wouldn't in order to get money to either help at home or buy their own meals. It was the rise of the Hong gang really, a bunch of kids who banded together to help one another out but along the lines somewhere they'd lost their way and began to take their misfortune out on innocent and unsuspecting individuals. That's when they decided to go underground to the metro station, so they could have shelter and funnel victims into areas where it was easier to target them. They'd by this point grown to a group of at least thirty individuals, ranging in ages from ten to twenty-five or so.

Akoni himself was in his mid-twenties, around the same age as Lex. In fact, the two had gone to school together for a year or two before Akoni disappeared, presumably because of various social welfare problems that caused his family to no longer afford education, prompting him into his life as a no-good street punk. Lex felt bad for him and she vaguely remembered him as a really sweet kid, very obedient and trustworthy. She wondered if it was worth mentioning it to him, just to ease the situation.

"I remember you, in fact," she said to Akoni.

His normal eye narrowed. "From where?"

"School."

"Ha! I never went to school!"

"Yes you did – we were in the same class for two years. You always brought a lunch box that had some galaxies or something on it."

There was a glint of acknowledgement in his eye. "Maybe you did know me."

"You were a nice guy," she said. "I'm sure you still are. After all, anyone who supports a mural like that is a great person in my books."

"So you hate President Mason?" Akoni asked.

"Doesn't practically everyone?"

Akoni smiled. "You're in good company here then."

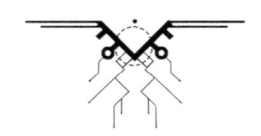

Chapter Four

It was a little after nine that Lex finally got to her grandmother's house after being held up for nearly an hour by Akoni and his gang of miscreants. For all the bad things they did to many, many people, she felt some compassion toward them having been merely products of a horrendously failed system that was meant to help people who were less fortunate but didn't. It wasn't their fault they ended up how they were, but it was entirely up to them how they used their past experiences to shape the future.

The door opened as Lex walked up the path, her grandmother standing at the door in a worn old dress and an apron that had seen better days. Overhead, the sky flashed with lightning and a rumble of thunder rolled in the distance, bringing news of a coming storm. Grandma Alice started shouting at her before she'd even reached the house.

"Where have you been? It's hours past dinner! I had to put it in the fridge and now it will be disgusting!"

"Sorry. I had to take the metro. I got held up. You know how it is."

"The metro! Are you a crazy girl? You know people get killed down there!"

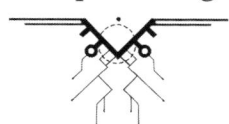

She thought about telling her grandmother about what happened at the Chinatown metro with Akoni and his gang and how she had somehow become friendly with them purely by complimenting their grotesque yet enjoyable mural of President Mason being given what he deserved. She erred on the side of caution though – she didn't want to worry or upset her grandmother nor give her imagery of Lex running with gangs, shoving people in front of trains purely as some misguided way to get back at the establishment for years of mistreatment, mismanagement and misleading promises that never materialised.

Her grandmother held the door open for her and she walked through into the porch area and began to take off her jacket and calf-high, thick soled punk boots. The familiar aroma of home cooking, mothballs and Grandma Alice herself filled the air, reminiscent of old times when her family were still fully human and not in the Ascension interface and she could physically touch them instead of having to use a computer to access a conversation. The smell in the house, combined with just being in her grandmother's presence reminded her of those seemingly easier days of childhood when she didn't have to worry about much aside from getting decent grades in school, maybe the occasional wondering where the next dinner would come from with food scarcity, a relative thing of the past given Grandma Alice's extensive hydroponic set up in her basement.

Grandma Alice followed her into the porch area, closing and locking the door behind her. It was past her bedtime, but she had to get Lex's dinner sorted out for her. Grandma Alice still wanted to dote on Lex, despite Lex being in her mid-twenties and more than capable of caring for herself, but it was, after all, what grandmothers do best.

"Did you speak to your parents today?" Grandma Alice asked as she climbed the six stairs into the proper part of the house, wiping her hands on her apron.

"Yeah." Lex replied. "Only for like twenty minutes though."

"Why so short?"

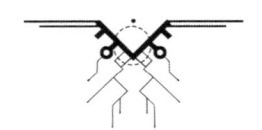

"The price. It's getting so expensive now." Lex stopped in the kitchen, noticing that the dishes from her grandmother's dinner were just sitting in the sink. She started washing them.

Grandma Alice scowled at her. "Don't go doing that. I'm capable of cleaning the mess on my own. I've been waiting all day for you."

"Sorry Grandma Alice."

Grandma Alice made to pull dinner out of the fridge.

Lex, her hands wet with soap suds, said, "I ate already, actually."

"Must have friends in good places then." Slowly, she put the carefully wrapped plate back in the fridge. "We'll sit on the couch, then. Tell me about how your family is doing in that computer."

"It's not a computer exactly."

"Well, it sounds like one."

Lex followed her grandmother into the living room, but she didn't sit down. Just stood beside the couch, which was under-stuffed, old, and lumpy. This was the living room where she had spent almost all of her youth. The room where she had slept on the couch. Where she had been swaddled in blankets while running a fever. Where her grandfather had picked her up and swept her around the room in a dance just meant for the two of them.

It was a small room, like the rest of the house. Her grandmother bustled in and sat down on the couch, sitting a tin of biscuits on the table. "Just in case."

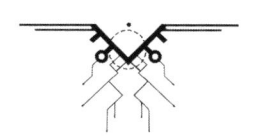

"I really-" Lex shook her head. There was no point in it. She didn't have to eat, but she could let her grandmother attempt to fuss if nothing else.

The table was piled up and cluttered, barely any room for the biscuits. There were newspapers spread out over it. Bills that were sitting unopened. Letters from people her grandmother knew. A lighter, despite the fact that neither of them smoked, and every odd bit, bob, and titbit that Alice found over the course of the last week.

The tile floor hadn't been replaced in easily seventy years – long since before Lex was born. Even before her parents were born. The former owner of the house had a thing for Middle Eastern design and had the tiles flown in from Iran, Iraq, Egypt or some such. She wasn't sure where, but she knew the man had done a lot of extensive travelling from back before the world closed up a bit. The tiles were worn, cracked and occasionally missing a chunk from a corner or two. Those tiles where the patterning was still visible had a brown almost mandala shape and style to them, edged in black and highlighted in white.

She caught herself staring down at the lesser worn tiles that ran alongside the edge of the wall, where feet rarely, if ever touched – at least not enough to wear the tiles. Her mind wandered and wondered what the world must have been like back then, in the time of her father's stories. She had to wonder if he had walked on tiles like this. The sights, smells, sounds and experiences that could have been had, and what the culture was like. She wondered what it was like now. Was it much different to where she found herself? If all of the world was one, wasn't it all going to be the same? How long would the blending take? Not long, she wagered. She wasn't sure. She wasn't sure she wanted to know. A world with so many divides didn't seem worth thinking about.

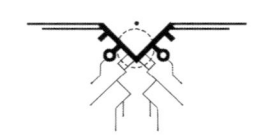

"You didn't answer my question," Grandma Alice said as she kicked off her shoes, and patted the couch.

"Sorry, what question?" Lex asked. She didn't sit, instead propping her hip against the arm of the couch. The fabric had worn smooth over the years.

"About your parents. And James. How they are."

"Oh. Yeah, good I guess. As good as you can be when you Ascend, which I guess is better than here sometimes."

"Hmpf." Grandma Alice sneered.

"They were asking how you are. If you'd thought about it anymore."

"Hell no. They can keep asking and I'll keep telling them. It isn't for me. I don't trust that nonsense not to lose me in some program."

"It's not like that, Grandma Alice."

"How can you be sure? Have you done it?"

Lex paused at that. She definitely hadn't done it, although she'd thought about it. She wasn't sure why she hadn't done it by this point. There was little on the outside world left for her, especially after James ascended, the only real people she had left were Damian – who travelled extensively – and Grandma Alice, who was getting on and would probably pass away within the next five to seven years. Maybe she would later, after Grandma Alice passed away.

They sat in relative silence for a few moments, her grandmother picking up a piece of paper and jotting something down. It looked like a thought about the hydroponic system. An upgrade, maybe.

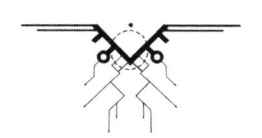

Lex suddenly remembered her agreement with Meshi about the sweet and sour pork though.

"Can I get some of your sweet and sour pork to go? Maybe some rice too?" Lex asked casually.

"You're not feeding street kids, are you?" Grandma Alice asked.

"No." She frowned, mouth cutting into a severe look. "It's for Meshi. He said he'd keep giving me a good price on credits for Ascension Interface if I brought him some of your sweet and sour."

Grandma Alice looked at her over the paper, pen paused. It pressed down so hard it made an ink blot spread. "How much does it cost for that these days?"

"Too much." Lex replied, sighing. "It's ridiculous. It was dead when I went there today. No one was there. One other couple aside from Mom, Dad, James and I."

"When do you go see him again?"

"Probably Thursday. So, day after tomorrow."

"Okay. I'll make you a big plate of it so he gives you a better deal."

Lex smiled. "Thanks Grandma Alice. That's a good idea, by the way."

Alice looked at the paper. Then she crumpled it up. "Too much work. I would never get it finished."

"Oh. Well… the garden is doing well anyway?"

"I'll get the food for you," said her grandmother, putting the pen back onto the mess that was her table. Then she stood up and announced, "it's later than I thought."

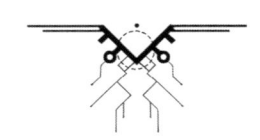

Grandma Alice more or less went to bed at the same time every night. She might read or watch the news, but then she'd be out like a light and early to rise the next day, often tending to her indoor garden in the basement or out playing cards with friends at someone's house.

Lex watched her go, waiting until she was gone from sight to go and double check that the door was locked and then flicked out the lights before walking down the hall toward her own bedroom, grabbing her bag as she went. Her room was adjacent to Grandma Alice's, and she could see Grandma Alice's light still on and the door slightly ajar, the thick smell of incense wafting out into the hall. Grandma Alice was praying at her shrine again, or at least had lit incense. She was a firm believer in ancient religion, especially Taoism and Buddhism with a sprinkling of ancestor worship in there. She'd kind of made her own mix of things, something that seemed to work for her amid the chaos of life and occasional uncertainty of the world. It brought her peace and comfort and at the end of the day, that was all Lex could ask for.

She opened her bedroom door and stepped into the darkness of it. The cool air from her having left the window open made her shudder a bit – the temperatures were dropping off quickly at night now. It wouldn't be long before she'd be unable to have the window open at all, but she loved having an icy room. It made it so much more comfortable for sleeping, especially under her heavy duvet that her other grandmother had made for her before she'd died.

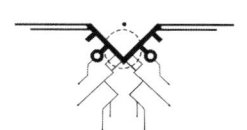

She flicked on the light and the whole room came into view. Her single bed with the bright blue duvet cover, crisp and clean was the highlight of the space, drawing attention to it immediately due to the colour. She had an old ratty stuffed animal on the pillow, one she'd had since she could remember, a stuffed dog that had seen better days especially with its patched ear and tail – both jobs Grandma Alice had done back when Lex was only six or so and James had tried to tear the dog apart to upset her. He'd got in some serious hell for that, no question about it.

The carpet was a flat, dull and beige thing, rough to the touch which was why Lex had found a huge pinkish purple shag rug from somewhere and put that down to make up for the lacklustre carpeting of the room. It was soft and bouncy when you walked on it, and often she'd lay on it and read a book or play on her phone at night, just because of the feel of it. On one wall, parallel to the bed was her computer desk, her laptop stowed away on the part underneath that slid out for keyboards – or so they did in times past when people still used those archaic old desktop computers, things that hadn't been used in decades at least. Grandma Alice kept this old desk from way back in her childhood – it had been her own – mainly due to the workmanship on it. It was in amazing shape considering the age, which was estimated to be at least fifty or sixty. Grandma Alice was about seventy-seven, and so Lex could just see her sitting at this very desk doing her homework when she was young.

She went to the window and pulled it shut. It really was getting cold outside. She might have to stop leaving the window open, especially if the storms kept coming as they were now. She could figure they'd be almost constant so there was probably no point in leaving the window open unless you really didn't mind damp chills. The smell of rain was worth it, sometimes. Other times the chill could be biting and closing the house up against those seaside winds that could whip up was the preferable choice.

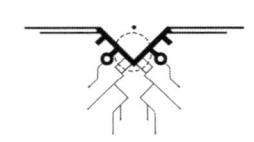

Her pyjamas were laid out on the bed, right where she'd left them. Not exactly laid out, but tossed casually to one side since she'd been in a rush that morning. She put them on – a comfortable t-shirt depicting some local band and plaid pyjama pants with a hole in the thigh where she'd accidentally walked past a loose nail in the wall one night. She couldn't remember where she'd got them from , but they were her go to for some time.

A pinging sound emanated from her handbag, the built-in screen depicting a message from someone on her phone. She pulled her phone out, and the tell-tale purple fluorescent light flashing indicated a text message. There was literally one person in the world that had the tendency to text her that it could be.

Damian.

She tapped her security code into the phone and it came alive with flight, illuminating her face bright green from her background – some pretty bright sap green leaves – a fantastical enhanced image of a forest, bringing to mind images far from the straight lines and grey concrete of the city.

Navigating to her text messaging application she saw she did indeed, have one new message. She tapped it to open it up and sure enough, it was from Damian.

To: Lex
From: Big D
About: I'm on my way home!

Yo L, I'm on my way home.

You, me and a bottle of Chianti on my return. You pick the spot.

I get in at 11.30am. Meet you for dinner – 5?

See you tomorrow!

She shut her phone and put it on her bedside table. Five would suit her fine.

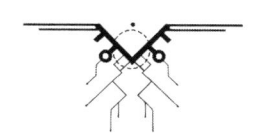

Chapter Five

The restaurant was dimly lit but candles graced the tops of each table. It wasn't meant to be something romantic. In truth romance had somewhat died out long ago and the only thing that candles were used for was necessity as a person never could tell when the power would go out. There was the added benefit of the candles providing a bit more light than the grimy wall sconces did, and so the whole thing worked well together and did give the place a bit of an ambience that could have been almost quoted as 'nice', if the threat of rolling blackouts hadn't been real. It wasn't that the blackouts themselves were the issue, it was more the rather obscure confirmation as to when light would be restored, often being quoted as 'anytime from now'. It was that very inconvenience that had led many to produce their own power through small scale solar and wind farming. At least then you knew you were covered. Lex wondered why restaurants and places didn't do the same, but perhaps they needed so much they weren't able to produce it. It was one thing to power a single-family home. Quite another to power a full restaurant.

Lex looked at her phone in her lap. It was five past five, but not unusual for Damian to be at least a few minutes late. She was habitually punctual, something people often got on her case about – after all, who bothered with punctuality in the world they lived in? Most people had a rather relaxed view of timekeeping, something that was definitely not in her comfort zone. She had been raised to be on time in any and every situation whenever possible. It shouldn't even be a difficult concept to be on time. It wasn't to Lex anyway.

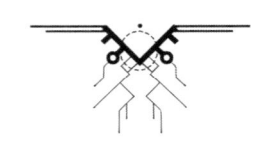

The door opened and Damian's familiar figure walked into the restaurant. He saw her immediately and flashed his huge, white-toothed grin. His hair, mostly silver-grey, hung over one eye, and she saw he'd clearly had a change in hairdo whilst in France. She liked it. It definitely jived with the whole new Earth, new dawn kind of age they lived in.

"Lex!" he called, opening his arms for a hug. She stood and they embraced, patting each other on the back like old friends. She'd forgotten just how nice it was to be in Damian's upbeat and positive presence, a presence she was slightly envious of, especially since having a less than enjoyable interface with her family the day before. How he was able to maintain such a cheery demeanour among all the shit he put up with between work and his own family was something she never could quite get a handle on, and yet was a little jealous of at the same time, but not in a malicious way, not at all. At least when she was with him, some of his cheeriness rubbed off on her.

"Damian!" she exclaimed, stepping back out of the hug. "How was France?"

"Oh, jeez. You know." he said, waving his hand to the waiter to bring him a menu. "Tiresome. Boring. Almost as bad as here. Except worse!" he laughed.

She took a sip of her wine. "Worse than here?" she asked, not getting the joke.

"I'm kidding. When did you get to be such a Serious Susie?"

"Oh. Ha-ha." she tried to laugh. She still wasn't sure if he was joking or not, so she just played along as best she could. The waiter arrived with the menu and handed it to Damian.

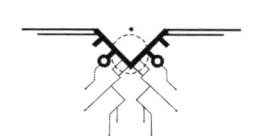

He looked over the wine list first. "Château Margaux, a bottle please. And the chicken breast with green salad." He looked over the menu at Lex. "What are you having?"

She stuttered for a minute. Chicken was expensive. "Uh. The tomato soup."

Damian raised an eyebrow at her. "Be serious. Come on. I'm buying. Don't worry about the price."

"Are you sure?" she asked. "A lot of this is really expensive."

"Yes, besides – I recently got a promotion." Damian replied nonchalantly like it didn't much matter, handing her the menu. "Have what you want."

She took the menu and quickly skimmed it, being conscious of picking something more appropriate for a dinner with Damian, while also being careful to not fully take advantage and order something like lobster. Lobster was almost entirely extinct and had to be farmed. Even then it was difficult; overfishing and acidification of the oceans in decades past had left many species in an endangered state, and so to get uncontaminated, decent lobster that one could legally serve as food, the price was often into the hundreds.

"I'll have the mushroom risotto and garlic bread then," she said. "And another glass of wine."

"Good choice." Damian remarked. The waiter noted down the orders and took the menu away.

"So, a promotion…" Lex started, smiling. She was happy for Damian. He worked hard and deserved it.

Damian held his hand up. "It's nothing. Really."

"What will you be doing now?" she asked.

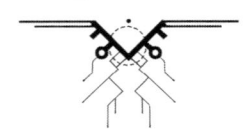

"Pretty much what I did before, just with more responsibility."

She took another sip of wine. "What exactly did you do before?"

He smiled and looked down at the table. "Sales. Selling things people need to the people that need them."

"That doesn't answer my question very well."

"I know. I sell a lot of different things."

They sat in silence for a minute before both laughing.

"I'm glad you're back," she said.

"I'm glad to be back. I'm honestly exhausted." He leaned back in the chair and stretched. "I can't wait to get home and sleep in my own bed."

"You haven't been home yet?"

"No, I had to go drop off some paperwork. Then the boss wanted to chat for a bit, so I ended up having to come straight from work."

"We could have rescheduled."

"What? And miss dinner with my bestest buddy? Never," he said. "Besides, I'm an energetic powerhouse."

Lex smiled. It really was good to have Damian back. He provided comfort to her and had become like a brother ever since her family had ascended. He was, without a doubt, her best friend in the world.

"What's wrong with you today?" he asked. He did always have a way of knowing things.

"Oh. You know. Nothing really."

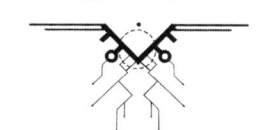

"Come on. I know something's up."

She thought about holding it in and insisting nothing was wrong but she couldn't. It had been bothering her since she used the Spot the day before: the cost, the issues, the growing unease when she interfaced. And it wasn't just from her side. Her family experienced issues too.

"I spoke to my parents and James yesterday," she started.

"Oh yeah? How are they?"

"They're alright, yeah," she continued. "Just that there's a lot of problems using the Spots now. They're getting so expensive, and when I did get in I had to wait forever for them to get into the room. Oh, speaking of which, they're charging for rooms now."

"Charging for rooms?" Damian raised an eyebrow again. "That's new."

"Tell me about it. You go fuckin' broke just trying to say 'Hi' to the people you love." Lex said, exasperated. "At least my Dad sent me some money. I'm going to put it towards my next interface and try to get longer. You know, there were only two other people there yesterday?"

"What time did you go?"

"Four. Four-ish. I was done by twenty to five."

"Really? That's usually the busy time. Right after work kind of thing."

"Exactly. No one can afford it anymore. It's ridiculous."

The waiter arrived then with the bottle of wine Damian had ordered along with the glass for Lex. He put it on the table and Damian reached for it right away.

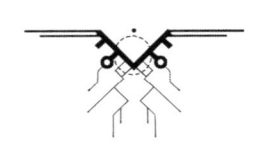

"Finally. I've been dying for this all day." he said.

"I don't blame you. I'm still surprised you were up for coming out."

"Don't worry. I didn't want to cook tonight anyway."

She looked around the restaurant. It was surprisingly full, with people just like them, casually having a meal or drinks after work – if they worked for corporations. People who worked for EverDawn were easily spotted. They were always very clean looking, tidy and wore nice clothes. They just had an air of wealth about them. She remembered when her grandmother worked there and how well she'd dressed and looked. Grandma Alice had only retired three years prior and received a hefty pension from working there so many years. Lex didn't know just how much, but it was enough that she knew she didn't need to worry about Grandma Alice starving or ever needing money.

Lex looked nervously over at a group of women who clearly worked for EverDawn and then down at her glass of wine.

"What?" Damian asked.

Lex glanced over at the women again and sighed. "There's rumours going around that President Mason is behind the issues with the Spot interface," she whispered. "My family heard it on the other side too."

"Wouldn't surprise me," Damian replied, picking up the wine bottle and inspecting the label.

"Why not?" Lex asked, surprised.

"He's a dick. Plain and simple."

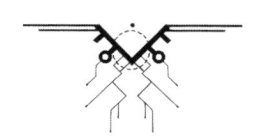

"They said they heard he's trying to make it so everyday people can't access the Spots. Only he and his cronies."

Damian put the wine bottle down. "Again, it wouldn't surprise me."

"Really?"

"Nope."

"And you think it's okay?"

"I didn't say that."

"Then what are you saying?"

Damian looked over at the group of women who suddenly seemed to be glaring at the two of them. "Well, nothing changes unless action's taken," he said in a low voice. "So, unless you have a clever plan to stop Mason from banning everyone from Ascension based on wealth and financial background, then I guess you just have to accept it. Or make more money. Or both."

It hadn't occurred to Lex to take some form of action. After all, she was just one person. But perhaps if she could get Damian on board, along with several other people who were sick of being shorthanded by President Mason's stranglehold on the Ascension technology, then maybe they could organise a protest or something and make their voices known.

"What about you?" she asked Damian as their dinner arrived.

"What about me?"

"Aren't you pissed off about Ascension being potentially phased out to the masses?"

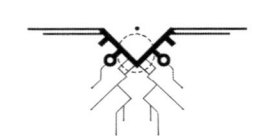

"Well, yeah. But I don't need to use it as much as most people."

"Still. When you do need to. What will you do?"

"Pay."

"Well it's easy for you to say, Captain Promotion." Lex said. She felt bad about getting annoyed with Damian and his ability to just pay his way for the things he wanted or needed while the rest of the masses suffered and were left out in the cold in terms of Ascension interfacing with family.

"Hey, hey! I know it's easy to do things around here if you have money, but don't let that get to you. The real problem here is President Mason." Damian replied.

Of course, he was right. Lex knew it, and knew that he had to be stopped, or they had to make their displeasure known. Something had to happen. Sitting around dining on risotto and wine certainly wasn't going to help. Neither was complaining about it.

"Okay. I'm going to ask around." Lex said, determined to do something. It was hard for those who were still existing in the everyday world to just live in it, never mind having access cut to those closest to them who had ascended. She was sure to get at least a few people organised to do something about it. Even if they started a petition or something. She knew she couldn't just sit idly by and let her contact with her family dwindle away to nothing.

"Well. Good luck in any case." Damian said, sipping his wine. "I have to say I'm definitely glad I don't need to use the interface much. I'd probably be just as mad as you are."

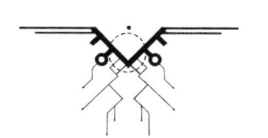

Rebellion's Martyr

The EverDawn women still seemed to eye up the pair from across the restaurant for a moment or two longer before gathering their things and leaving, being sure to walk right past the table Damian and Lex were at, almost as though to prove some kind of a point. Lex watched them go, wondering how it was that people could work for a faceless corporation hell-bent on separating families.

Chapter Six

Dinner went on much longer than either of them expected. It seemed they had a lot to catch up on, and not all to do with the shadiness of Ascension technology and how difficult it was to access these days. Damian had been having some family troubles of his own – none of them had ascended like Lex's family, which sometimes made things far more difficult than if they had. After all, if you ascended you weren't around to cause troubles. If you ascended, you lived inside the technology and couldn't cause issues on the outside with friends and family.

His brother had always been a bit of a character. He had been heavily into drugs for a long while about two years back and after three stints in rehab had sworn off it for good. Or so he claimed. It seemed he was back on the pills, something that didn't sit with Damian well at all. It caused a lot of family issues, his parents were a wreck with worry and it was believed his brother had started running with one of the gangs, presumably to help fund as well as source his habit.

Lex felt bad for Damian. He was so hard-working and had a fairly stressful job. He didn't need more issues on top of what he had to deal with on a daily basis. He definitely had enough on his plate, and with their parents getting older it was only a matter of time before their brother no longer had the security net of their parents and Damian would be on his own having to deal with a brother that seemed to not give a damn.

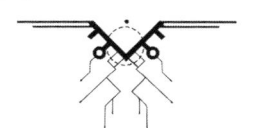

Lex walked home through the park, a place she used to come all the time as a child with her parents and James. It was your standard park – leafy, green trees were plentiful, there had been a play park with a slide and swings at one point, but it had been long since torn down. Today there were mainly just benches to sit and relax on, a decently sized lake filled with different waterfowl and water plants. Watching the ripples of the water could be an enjoyable and relaxing way to spend some time, and many people could be found doing so, especially at weekends. Children didn't come to the park much these days, it had seemed to evolve into something primarily for adults, but that wasn't an issue. It was more enjoyable that way. You could actually hear yourself think.

She rounded the pond and watched the ripples in the night reflect the few streetlights that dotted the area. The sky was again obscured by thick clouds and the stars hid behind this thick, wispy curtain, awaiting such a time that they'd be able to shine through on a clear night again. The chill in the evening air was crisp and damp – autumn had truly arrived, even if the trees were still primarily green and not the tell-tale shades of oranges, reds and yellows that autumn usually brought.

The path out of the park and to the taxi stand was lined with high pine trees. Someone had been harvesting pinecones, judging by how many had fallen and crunched under her boots as she went. Pinecones made a particularly delicious and healthy syrup-come-jam which many used as a remedy for chest problems and colds. It tasted of rich pine scent, something that reminded her explicitly of cold Christmas days when she was a child and she'd struggle to sleep overnight on Christmas Eve due to excitement. Those had been good times with her whole family coming together to celebrate the holidays. They'd often exchange home-made items such as jam and handicrafts with cousins and their house would often be filled with family – sometimes numbering well into the thirties.

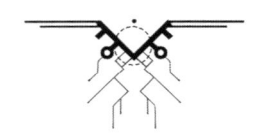

That was all over now. Most of the family had either passed away, moved abroad or ascended and it was just Lex and Grandma Alice left in town. There were one or two cousins in neighbouring towns, an hour or two away from where they lived but it seemed that as life ticked by and everyone got older, the less and less contact you had with cousins. Lex thought it was sad, but it was also a two way street: her cousins didn't go out of their way to contact her, and vice versa. It was just how it was and she supposed that she could make more of an effort, but wasn't sure why she'd overly bother.

Her cousins did keep in touch with Grandma Alice occasionally. Probably not as often as Grandma Alice would like, but life could get in the way sometimes. It was strange how the modern world could seem to make families be too busy for each other, what with work and other responsibilities, but that was just how it went. It had been getting progressively worse and worse over time. Perhaps mankind was changing in ways they didn't expect, becoming more self-sufficient in living day to day as well as whether they needed family around or not.

She pulled her coat closed and did two of the buttons on it to protect from the chill. The wind was bitingly cold and she still had a way to walk before she'd be home. The list of things she needed to do that evening sprung up in her mind and she quickened her pace, wanting to get home before too late so she could get her chores done and possibly still have a bit of time to play a game she'd got into. Help Grandma Alice with the garden in the basement, clean the bathroom, do some laundry and clean up after dinner. It wasn't a huge amount to do, but it was enough to take about an hour or two, and it was already going for nine.

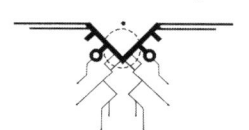

Her handbag buzzed and vibrated – it was a text message for sure, with its long tell-tale vibration, different to phone calls and other notifications. She pulled her phone out and tapped in her security code, a number based off her old high school locker combination: 73456. It was simple to remember, which was a benefit for her since she had a terrible memory at the best of times. The screen came to life with bright lights illuminating the darkness around her, save for the occasional streetlight. She saw the text messaging application was again, showing one message, and she opened it up. It was from Grandma Alice.

To: Lex
From: Grandma Alice

Dinner's on the stove. I've gone out for the evening with Emily. See you later. X

She closed her phone as she stepped out onto the main street. There was a bank machine just across the street where she planned to take money out before getting a taxi home. She was due to go to Meshi's shop the next day and she needed cash. He preferred to deal in cash, why, she wasn't sure, but she didn't want to press the point home either.

As she crossed the street to the bank machine she heard a rumble of thunder overhead. The wind picked up and the chill already present in the air became more prominent. It was a good thing the taxi rank was so close by – she didn't want to have to walk the seventeen blocks in what was soon to be pouring rain, gusting wind and potential lightning hazard. She took out her bank card, a black thing with raised numbering and a holographic picture of what looked like a phoenix in one corner.

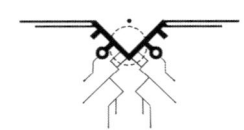

The machine had a glowing green slot where the card was to be entered into the terminal. A mechanical, yet chirpy voice, very similar to that of Tina, the computer assistant in the Ascension interface, welcomed Lex to the bank machine and asked for her PIN number. She entered it – the same as her phone to save her having to remember multiple numbers – and the next screen loaded asking how much money she wanted to withdraw from her balance which, to her surprise, was now a whopping $536.71. Her father had sent her the better part of four hundred dollars.

She took two hundred of it out, grinning about how many credits for the interface she'd be able to purchase at Meshi's, assuming he had them in. The thought of Meshi reminded her that she had to take him some of Grandma Alice's sweet and sour pork to keep up her end of the bargain. She hoped he'd have more credits than he'd had the last time she'd been in the shop, but she tried not to get too hopeful on that. It seemed they were becoming hard to come by, just more proof of President Mason's supposed plans to turn interfacing and the whole Ascension process into some elitist thing for only him and his friends.

Putting the money in her wallet and the wallet in her handbag, she began to walk away from the cash machine, the robotic voice thanking her for using their services. The street was lit well toward the taxi rank and she saw several cars waiting for patrons, dashboards lighting their faces in the darkness of the cabs, music playing on the radio, news stations giving out various stories of goings on in the city. She walked toward the nearest cab, the rain a steady drizzle working its way up to a good downpour. Out of the corner of her eye she spied a poster, encouraging the viewer to re-elect President Mason. His bony face prominent on the literature, a phony tagline of 'Helping families help each other' below the line to re-elect him to office. Lex stopped and looked at it, anger rising in her chest. She ripped the poster off the wall and folded it neatly before putting it in her handbag. She didn't quite know what the plan was with President Mason, but it was a start. Besides, crunching lines into his face was highly satisfying.

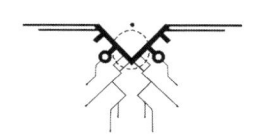

She stopped at the driver side door of the cab and knocked on the window. The cabbie rolled it down halfway to protect himself from the rain.

"Yeah?" he asked in a gruff, monotone voice.

"How much to Morrow Avenue?"

"Thirty bucks." he replied.

"Okay," she said, slightly annoyed at the high price, but not wanting to walk in the cold and wet of the imminent storm.

She got into the taxi and sat in the back behind the driver so he couldn't see her very well. She wasn't keen on taking taxis at the best of times, but this was a special circumstance given the weather and how long dinner with Damian had run. Not that she was annoyed, it had been great to catch up with him after so long. It had been nearly a month since he'd left and she realised only after they'd had dinner that she had been missing him and his humorous anecdotes terribly. She hadn't many friends as they'd moved away or ascended, and so the last month had primarily been a combination of Grandma Alice, Meshi, her family, when she could see them, and a select number of gamers she played online with.

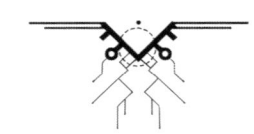

The taxi pulled away from the rank and moved down the street to a set of traffic lights. She looked out the window at the passing shops – mainly clothing boutiques that had the same thing over and over on display in their windows, all gallantly lit with soft lighting to try and entice buyers in. A message "Buy this jacket / skirt / pant suit and be as classy as this mannequin is!" was what seemed to be portrayed by the display. It was a message that fell on deaf ears for the most part as the style of the day – particularly with the under thirty crowd – consisted of dark clothes, chains, velvet. It had become a kind of gothic-come-cyberpunk look that went well with the development of not just technology but also the new buildings which had a somewhat grim facade yet were highlighted well in the darkness by neon lights that brought the nights alive.

The radio crackled and the tell-tale music for the news channel started. Lex never really paid much attention to the news, but something about the news tonight made her listen in. Especially when the music was interrupted with the words 'Breaking News'.

'President Mason has today signed a new order making the collection of rainwater for personal use, including renewable energy, illegal. Critics say that he's trying to drive citizens into using EnerGlobe Energy – a company that Mason himself has invested billions in. This comes following rumours of his slow and gradual changes to Ascension technology and the use of the Spots where humans can interface with loved ones in the Ascension platform. Many have reported issues accessing the Spots, and nothing but continual problems with the technology once inside. An EverDawn spokesperson told us that there's nothing wrong with the technology.'

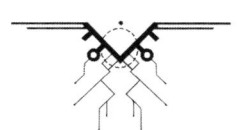

Lex craned her neck to look at the driver in the rear-view mirror of the taxi. He seemed unfazed by the reports of corruption and greed that were being reported. Perhaps he was like her – having been suspecting it for some time. She didn't know though and she didn't mention anything. She was beginning to suspect that people stood on two sides of the fence when it came to President Mason – you loved him or you hated him. It was hard to tell who was on which side and how far they'd go to defend their position. It was a risk that was too great to take one on one, and so she remained silent. A plan was building in her head though. She only hoped she could pull it off and get at least some people on board with it. It would be easier now that the media were reporting that President Mason was trying to mess with Ascension and limit who could use it and who couldn't, it would hopefully incite many people to stand against him and join her in her quest to stop him.

The taxi pulled onto her street and stopped in front of Grandma Alice's house. The rain had picked up but at least she didn't have far to go at all, just up the path past the old garden that was now mainly shrubbery and the occasional small tree, and then into the house. Grandma Alice had stopped working in an outdoor garden some time ago, mainly due to the difficulty with getting up and down off her knees to do things like plant and weed. The hydroponic garden in the basement was much easier for her – everything was table height and so there was no need to crouch, kneel or sit down when tending to it. There weren't any weeds either, something that delighted Lex as it had been primarily her job to weed the garden when she was around, a job she absolutely loathed.

She entered the house and flicked the porch light on before locking the door behind her. The house was dark except for a small lamp that Grandma Alice always left on in the living room. The house took on an eerie quality when it was only her, alone, and Grandma Alice was out. She could hear the hydroponics in the basement, the lights buzzing away and the steady bubbling sound as the filters worked to keep the water of each pod clean. The clock ticking in the kitchen reminded her that she had some things to do for Grandma Alice before she went to bed, but first she wanted to get her new project started.

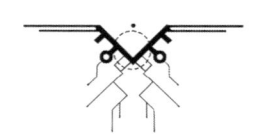

Lex pulled her boots off and rushed upstairs to her bedroom, turning on the kitchen light as she went. She took her phone out as she walked down the hall, opening her bedroom door and turning on her desk lamp. She had read something about some leader in the past who had been loathed more than anything, someone who had caused a lot of issues and had been complicit in what was considered to be genocide of entire populations. But what was his name? She tried to research it on her phone quickly but came up empty. Instead, she took the poster of President Mason out of her bag and unfolded it, folding it back over the initial folds so it laid flat on her desk. Staring at that creepy, gaunt and ghoul-like face made her shudder. Something had to be done indeed.

Chapter Seven

Her legs burned as she walked quickly down the main strip of Chinatown, desperate to get to Meshi's shop before three thirty. It was important that she got her credits for Ascension interface before four so she could beat the rush – if there was one. Otherwise, she'd be left waiting for ages. That's how it had always been in the past, anyway. Except the last time she went, that level of quietness was unprecedented. She expected a rush today though, what with the news breaking that President Mason was suspected of trying to tamper with access to Ascension and the interface technology – something she anticipated would bring the people out in droves to try to access the system before they got potentially cut off for an undetermined amount of time.

She shifted her arm to make carrying the container of sweet and sour pork for Meshi more comfortable. It was surprisingly heavy. She had no idea how much Grandma Alice had made for him, but it felt enough to feed a family. She hoped he'd knock the price of credits down significantly with a pork haul like this. Surely, he had to.

Turning the corner onto the small side street with Meshi's shop, she breathed a sigh of relief. Soon she'd be all sorted out with her credits and be off to the Spot and she could relax. She wasn't sure why she was getting so worked up over it, especially since there was just as good a chance that there'd be no one ahead of her in the queue at the Spot as there was that there'd be people there. It was fifty-fifty given the latest news about President Mason and the allegations of him trying to make it so only certain people could access it, but she wasn't going to take the chance of being stuck in a line a mile long if she could avoid it.

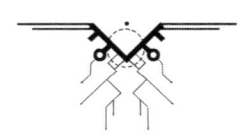

She got up to Meshi's small shop and began to climb the stairs to the door but stopped halfway as she looked up and saw a handmade sign with big, bold lettering with the word 'CLOSED' emblazoned across the door. Her chest tightened and her stomach did a flip. In tiny lettering below the word, she saw a phone number and decided to call it to see what was going on.

As she tapped the numbers into her phone she looked around for any sign of Meshi. It was entirely possible he had just popped out briefly for lunch or something and would be back momentarily. She heard the line connecting and the phone began to ring on the other end. She was about to hang up after seven unanswered rings when suddenly Meshi's familiar voice came over the other end.

"Hello?"

"Meshi, it's Lex. Where are you?"

"Closed. Shop is closed."

"When will you be open again?" Lex asked, becoming irritated that he was suddenly closed when she wanted to get online to interface with her parents and James.

"Not opening again." Meshi said sternly.

"What?" she asked incredulously.

"You heard me."

"But-"

"No but. I had problems with the government and I got shut down."

Lex wondered what problems he could possibly have had but didn't push the issue.

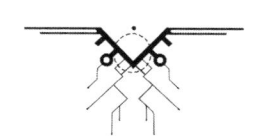

"Well," she started, "I have your sweet and sour from my Grandma Alice. Where can I leave it?"

There was a pause on the other end of the phone before she heard Meshi reply, "Bring it to me. I only live around the corner."

She did as Meshi asked and took the parcel of food to him at his apartment around the corner. It was an old thing – very run down looking from the outside with chipped paint on wooden window frames, the occasional broken pane of glass and cracking pavement steps leading up to a door that had certainly seen better days. There was a panel with buzzers and associated names on one side of the door and Lex looked on the panel until she found Meshi's name. It was a curiosity to her that she couldn't find it, especially as there were only seven names, but none sounded remotely close to Meshi.

She pulled out her phone and clicked the redial button. Meshi's voice answered again.

"You here?"

"Yeah – where's your buzzer on the door?"

"It's under my real name. Phil Kwong."

Lex looked on the list again and sure enough there was a buzzer with P. Kwong listed. She hung up on Meshi without saying anything as she pushed the button. There was a loud, metallic buzzing noise and the door clicked as it unlocked. She moved quickly so as to get inside before the door locked again and once inside climbed a small set of stairs to a door that led to a lobby. It was here that Meshi came out of his apartment and waved her over to come inside.

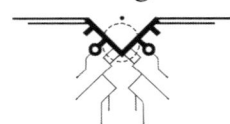

The apartment was almost identical to his shop. She had a moment where she thought that he had moved everything from the shop into the apartment, but how could he arrange it in such a way in only a few days? Or maybe he could, with some help. She decided to ask him outright.

"Is all of this from the shop?"

He closed the door behind her and locked it, looking out the peephole without saying anything at first. When he seemed satisfied that no one else was outside, he turned slowly and replied, "Yes."

"Well? What happened to the shop?" she pressed.

Meshi walked over to a dark wooden shelf laden with decanters of all shapes, sizes and colours. "Drink?" he asked.

Lex was confused but agreed. "Sure."

He poured two drinks from a decanter so blue it rivalled oceans and the sky – a deep almost incandescent ultramarine. The glasses matched and he turned back to face her, walking to where she was standing awkwardly in the middle of the room, holding one out to her. She took it and thought of how for some reason the colour reminded her of childhood. A strange thought indeed as she couldn't place where in her life she may have encountered the shade. Perhaps it was a decanter of her mother's, a plate, or something else that was kicking around their house. Her mother had, before she Ascended, been a fan of various china.

Meshi sat down and waved at Lex to do the same. He took a sip of his drink – whisky, neat and strong, just how he liked it – and sighed. Lex sat opposite to him and took a sip of the drink herself. The oak-aged flavour went down a treat, something she'd not had in what seemed to be years but was in all likelihood only a couple of months –

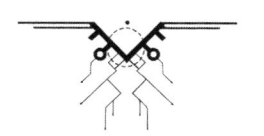

probably the last time Damian came back from some unique foreign land.

"So?" Lex asked, pressing Meshi for details. "What happened?"

Meshi swirled the whisky in the glass, watching it slide up and down the sides. Lex began to feel a bit of irritation at his unwillingness to share what was going on, but she kept it to herself for fear of upsetting him. He definitely seemed to have enough going on without her getting on his case about it, and her credits and if she'd be able to buy them still.

"Well," he finally started, taking a break to down the rest of the whisky, "the government guys came and closed my shop down."

"What?! Why?" Lex demanded.

"Oh, you know why." Meshi replied.

Lex wracked her brain for a moment, trying to figure how she'd know. She never knew where Meshi had got the credits from, the very same that she bought in order to interface with her family. She never asked and she'd never been suspicious about the low cost when everywhere else was rising in price. She'd just assumed Meshi was maintaining the price for her as some kind of customer loyalty. In exchange for sweet and sour pork, of course.

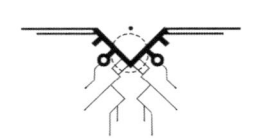

As it turned out though, he had been in bed with some unscrupulous characters through the black market and that's where he managed to get cheaper credits from. Part of Lex was disappointed – had he given her lower prices because he'd bought them at cost price and could afford to, or was he doing it because they were something that bordered on friends and not just shop-keeper and customer? She didn't ask though. She was partially fearful of what the true answer was but tried to convince herself that it was due to friendship.

"So that's why I got shut down," Meshi started after telling Lex about the black market credits amongst other things. "President Mason obviously got wind of that and didn't want someone like me to be providing people like you easier access."

"It makes sense." Lex said. "Last time I went there was literally *no one* there. Clearly fewer and fewer people can afford it."

"Not even I can." Meshi said. "I haven't spoken to my wife in weeks. I could only get so many credits and I sold them to you."

"Even when you hadn't spoken to her in forever?" Lex asked, feeling increasingly bad.

"No, no. I always kept some back for myself, but I had to save them up to make it worth it.

Lex sat back in her seat for a moment and thought hard. She wasn't sure what to do or where to go from here. With Meshi out of business and presumably cut off from his black-market supply, the chances of her getting back online to interface with her family were slim.

Meshi got up and poured himself another drink. He tipped the decanter at Lex, asking if she wanted to join him in another round. She shrugged in reply and held out the glass.

"Why the hell not. I guess I'm not getting online today anyway," she said.

"No. You probably won't," Meshi replied, reaching over and filling her glass a bit too full.

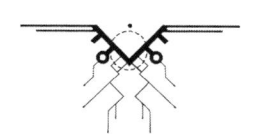

She sat there, looking into the deep, dark whisky, wondering whether to mention to Meshi the ideas she had in her head about forming an organisation to try to stand up to all these new and ridiculous rules. It was going too far too fast and someone needed to say or do something before it was too late and they lived under some insane dictatorship with a bony-faced president calling the shots. A president so far removed from the plight and issues of the everyday person that they'd stop at nothing and not worry about stomping over the smallest of people to ensure his full control over the populace. It was a terrifying thought really, someone so power mad, but it seemed to be the way that the world was going. Ascension interfacing had been targeted, rainwater collection outlawed, solar and wind power too. What was next? What could be next?

"I always thought I knew what I was doing," Meshi said sullenly. "In terms of trusting the government. But now…" he trailed off.

"And I've never really trusted the government," Lex replied. "Especially ever since President Mason got voted in. Something doesn't sit right with me about him at all. But one person can't change things," she shrugged. "Not really, anyway."

Meshi swirled his whisky in the glass again and downed it. Lex began to wonder if he was on some kind of mission to get drunk with the way he was putting it away. She figured though that he'd had a rough day or two and he was trying to let loose a bit.

"Well," he began, "what if you had other people behind you? What would you do?"

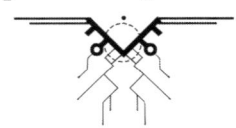

The conversation mirrored the conversation she'd had with Damian the night before so strangely that it sent chills down her spine. Maybe it was more than coincidence that she was being posed similar questions by two different people – two people who'd never, to her knowledge, ever crossed paths with each other.

"I'd organise something," she said confidently, having already thought about it since Damian asked her the same thing. "A demonstration, protest, something to show the government that we aren't happy and we mean business."

"Do you think they'd listen?" Meshi asked.

"Maybe. Maybe not." Lex replied. "But we can't just sit idly by and do nothing while we are being cut off from family and friends. I mean, I'm lucky that I've been able to get cheaper credits from you so that I could afford it. Most people can't."

"And those days are over." Meshi said sullenly. "It's the same story for other black-market suppliers. Many of my contacts say 'enough is enough' and 'something must be done', but they lack organisation. Everybody wants to talk about it, but nobody seems to feel empowered to act."

They sat there in silence for a minute, Lex holding the deep blue glass up to the light so it would catch and cast an eerie blue glow over her face. She forgot just how calming a blue light could be, something she rather needed since finding out she wouldn't be getting online today. She wasn't sure why she was so stressed about it – perhaps the uncertainty surrounding the whole situation, what with not knowing *when* exactly she'd be able to. When or *if*.

"What if we organised a few people?" she asked, not particularly to Meshi himself, but rather just thinking out loud. "Empower people by starting something ourselves?"

Meshi's eyes lit up. "That sounds like a plan."

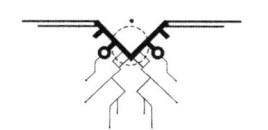

He suddenly got up from his place on the old, worn sofa across from Lex, putting his nearly empty glass on the coffee table. It was an antique looking table, low, wooden, with a lot of the varnish missing where it appeared that someone at some point in the history of the table had tried to remove the top layer but given up halfway through the job. Perhaps the person had died. Or perhaps, likeliest of all, the table had just enjoyed a number of years hidden away under various things in someone's dank old basement and that's how it'd come to look worn, weathered and worse for wear.

Meshi walked over to an old cabinet, presumably once used to house liquor in some home owned by people who were far above his station. It was very rich looking indeed – varnished oak wood, with doors made of glass featuring floral etching were above a hutch style door which opened and laid flat like a table, presumably for serving. He opened the hutch part of the cabinet and rummaged around a bit for a moment before pulling out an old, dusty mobile phone.

"Ah, here," he said, turning to Lex.

"What's that for?" she asked. "It looks ancient."

"It is ancient. Mobile phone from 2010." He walked over and handed it to her. "I think it has battery life. I will need a minute to find the charger."

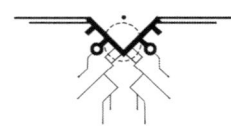

Lex looked at the phone in her hand. It was an old model smartphone, the kind that took off in popularity at the beginning of the century, capable of downloading music and applications for things like social media, games, lifestyle and so forth. She searched for the 'on' button and found it along the side, halfway down. It took a few moments, but the screen came to life in bright light and swirling colours. The name of the manufacturer appeared on the screen and she was asked if she wanted to continue as a guest or not. She figured being a guest would be the best option, considering she was planning to use the phone for somewhat illegal purposes.

Meshi reappeared with a tangle of cords, trying to sort through them. He sat back down in his seat, the ball of various chargers and cords on his lap and reached for his drink.

"I need more brain medicine to tackle this, I think."

Lex smiled and looked down at the phone. The home screen was bare except for a phone symbol, text messaging and some kind of internet service. It really was an old, archaic thing, but it would do for her purposes.

"It definitely needs a charge," she said. "There's only about twenty percent left."

"I'm working on it," Meshi replied. "I'll also get you some phone numbers. You don't need to know who they are to send them a message about a meet up, so I won't share names. I'm not sure these folks would want their names spread around anyway."

"That's fine." Lex said. "I don't need names. I have several numbers of my own of people I can invite. And I'll tell them to spread the word – discreetly, of course."

"You better hope it's discreet." Meshi said, a worried look moving over his face. "If the government catches on we'll lose a lot more than the ability to get online and one small random shop." He pulled out a cable from the mess on his lap and looked up at Lex, tipping his empty glass at her again. "One for the road?"

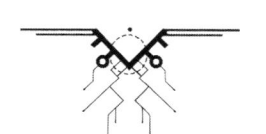

Chapter Eight

Back at home and slightly buzzed from the three rather large whiskies she had enjoyed with Meshi, Lex was laying on her bed thinking hard about everything that had happened. Everything seemed to be happening so quickly in terms of government sanctioned control over the masses – or maybe it was that she was only now paying attention to things that were becoming problematic because she was being directly affected. She hadn't been before and it was therefore easy to turn a blind eye. Things were definitely different now.

The plan she'd suggested to Meshi though could work. Since he also knew people aside from her who had been screwed over by the increased price of interfacing and who had also run into issues with Ascending itself, chances were, they could incite several at least to join their cause. Word on the street was that the actual process had increased in price – from free to something obscene like fifty thousand dollars. That would probably be the turning point for many other people, something that would indicate to them the glaringly obvious fact that President Mason didn't have anyone's best interests in mind, and in fact he was solely out for himself, his cronies and his administration.

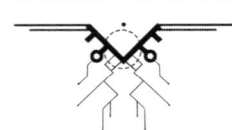

The poster on her desk that she'd taken off the wall by the bank machine would come in handy for that. She already had looked up some of history's most malicious leaders and the one that sprang to mind – Adolf Hitler – would be perfect to really rile people up. She hoped that it would be the start of something truly unique and helpful, something that would lead to an even better situation than they were all in now where humans were being forced away from ascended families and the government didn't care. Sure, maybe it was premature to compare President Mason to one of the most prolific monsters in history, but it was also rather apt. With the new changes he was putting into place it wouldn't be long before things went the same way as they had in the past.

She got off her bed and went over to her desk where she'd left the poster. It had dried out and the paper was crinkled and slightly water stained, but that didn't matter. If anything, it would make the poster have more character, and that was what she was going for. After all, she needed it to be as attractive and thought provoking as possible if she was going to get more people interested in their cause. She looked around the desk and found a black marker to deface the poster with, drawing a Hitler moustache on President Mason's bony face and the words "Is this the leader you really want?" below it. She ripped off the part that was encouraging people to vote for him again, and then took a photo with the old burner phone Meshi had given her before laying back down on the bed for the laborious task of typing out twenty-something phone numbers in text messages. It was a small relief that she could just save the message itself as a template. At least that saved some time.

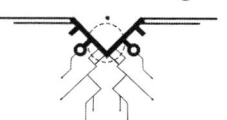

The whole process only took ten minutes or so and then the photo was out and distributed to her friends, both people she knew and the random contacts that Meshi had given her. He knew someone who was going to use their personal black-market connections to print at least a thousand of the amended posters. That was going to be exactly what they needed, and hopefully as many people as posters would be there. She sent the photo with a date, time and location: Meshi's shop's backroom – he had the store's rent paid up for another three weeks at least despite his business being shut down – 2pm, tomorrow. It would be best to get it done as soon as possible to limit the possibility of government cronies getting wind of it and coming to shut it down. Come one come all, especially if you've had enough of Mason's utterly greedy bullshit. She hoped that there would be at least a couple of people that showed up – or it would be solely her and Meshi, and she wasn't confident in their ability to bring down the government if it was just the two of them.

The point of the whole thing was to drum up interest to begin the development of some kind of resistance movement. It was in its infancy of course – just presently an idea – but she couldn't sit by and watch all of mankind's scientific and engineering accomplishments over the years be controlled one hundred percent by some greedy bastard who had no idea what the masses desired or needed. Lex only hoped that her passion could incite others to follow suit with various ideas designed to try to show the establishment that their stranglehold over the masses would no longer sit idly by and let Mason and his minions do what they liked while leaving ordinary citizens out in the cold.

Within minutes of the message going out the phone was pinging away, one every fifteen to twenty seconds, with messages from people, some she didn't even send messages to, all positive about coming to the meeting. Inside twenty minutes, she had at least ten definite attendees and four maybes – maybes that made it clear they were only 'maybes' due to other commitments on their time. It was turning out to be a fairly large gathering, she only hoped that no one from the police or government would catch wind of it and shut it down. Otherwise, she was quite excited by the prospect of so many people being fed up with President Mason's continual and gradual overtaking of their lives.

After what seemed like the hundredth ping of notifications on the phone, Grandma Alice poked her head around the corner of the door, a slight scowl on her face.

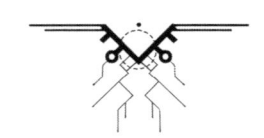

"What's all that noise?" she asked.

Lex jumped up, startled. "Nothing." she lied.

"Doesn't sound like nothing." Grandma Alice replied. "Who's messaging you so much?"

Lex looked at her phone, trying to come up with an excuse. "Oh, it's from the phone company – doing some maintenance. You know how it is sometimes. They send out one message but you end up getting it fifty thousand times."

Grandma Alice smiled at that. "Dinner will be in an hour." she said. "Kim-chi with beef."

"Awesome." Lex replied, hoping she didn't sound like she was trying to cover anything up. "I'll go for a shower now then."

As the water ran over her back she couldn't help but think about those who would be stopped from their rainwater harvesting if President Mason got his way. She grinned. It might not be a great deal yet, but the mightiest oaks were always sewn from single acorns – and that acorn was set. Not only set but germinating quickly. Hopefully, the roots would spread out enough to anchor them while they grew. One thing was for sure, it had begun.

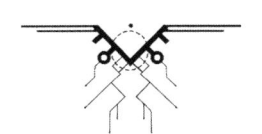

They were playing cards in relative silence, save for the shuffle of cards, the occasional creak of a chair as someone shifts. Dinner is over and done with, and they've shifted to this, a game gathered around the dining room table, plates cleared out and put up for the moment. Knowing her grandmother as well as she did, Lex knew the look in the wry old lady's eyes. Alice knew that Lex was up to something but didn't press her for details – in fact, she knew that she'd find out in time. It was always that way: Lex was the type of person who couldn't keep a secret too well and would eventually cave and let the cat out of the bag, so Alice just had to be patient. She had her suspicions, especially as Lex had never made her distaste for things like injustice at the hands of the government a secret and it was likely that's what all the secrecy was about now.

Alice just watched Lex over the top of her cards. Her mannerisms had changed slightly. She was more nervous. She seemed to be trying to avoid eye contact – something which was unusual, especially for her. Normally she wasn't shy and could hold a conversation with anyone, perhaps too well. Alice had seen the poster though and knew Lex was up to something. But then again, Alice knew all about the issues with Ascension technology, the costs, the pricing and the general bullshit that was coming down the pipeline from President Mason. The card games she attended weekly weren't just for retired EverDawn employees. They often invited current employees, such as Jade, the girl that had trained under Alice prior to her retirement.

They chatted about the company at these gatherings – the good, the bad and the ugly. Jade was a bit of a gossip as it was and she had no problem dishing the dirt. Alice had heard all manner of stories about how various employees themselves had begun to have issues with the rules, regulations and new pricing structure of both the process of ascending as well as the interfacing at the Spots. Many of the employees had joined EverDawn to help serve humanity in some way as well as to help provide a new way of living for humanity. It had always been meant to be something beautiful, but President Mason was turning it into something it was never meant to be.

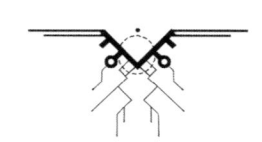

Of course, though, Lex had no idea that Alice knew about all this already. To her Alice was just Grandma Alice, matriarch of the family and a keen player of Gin Rummy. Lex had no inkling of what Grandma Alice ever got up to outside the home, except for the card game, and she wasn't sure she wanted to know. Not for any deep, dark reason, but she had her own stuff going on and what Grandma Alice got up to when she wasn't around wasn't really any of her business anyway.

"Market tomorrow." Alice said, as though it didn't much matter.

"I can't tomorrow." Lex replied. "I'm seeing Damian for lunch." It was a lie, but Grandma Alice didn't need to know that.

"Do you need anything?"

"Not that I can think of offhand."

Alice looked at her cards again, thinking about her final year at EverDawn when she'd had to process Lin, Michael and James' profiles to go through with the Ascension process themselves. It had been a bit of an emotional time, knowing they were going to go through with it, but there was little if anything she could do to change their minds. It was something they'd thought about for a while and weighed the pros and cons carefully. They were adults and they knew what they were doing, although she had been unimpressed that they'd been so willing to leave their family behind, but she figured that it was just as much her responsibility to keep communication open as it was theirs, although the one relative design flaw in Ascension was the inability to communicate unless you physically went to a Spot to do so. The onus was definitely on those on the outside.

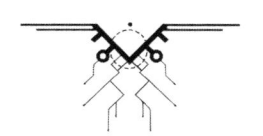

81

These thoughts made Alice realise that she'd perhaps harboured some resentment in a way towards those who were ascended and wanted to ascend. She was a fan of the old-fashioned family life – daily chatting, unconditional love, Christmas dinners together and the like. She didn't want to have to learn how to work some machine to make it work between her and those she held closest. It was for that reason she was grateful Lex hadn't ascended. She could help Alice with various things around the house as well as knowing how to access the interface. One thing was for certain: she wasn't very good at all with technology despite having been around it most of her life.

The card game continued in relative silence. It was one that they both knew well. Alice won, and when they were finished, Lex stood up.

Lex asked, "need a hand with anything tonight, Grandma Alice?"

"No. That's fine dear." Alice replied, knowing that Lex should get to bed and get some decent rest if she was going to be taking on the government. "I'll finish up here. You just head to bed."

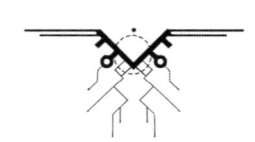

Chapter Nine

Lex was dreading taking the metro to Meshi's shop again but in the interests of saving money, it was the best option. She wasn't sure why she was keen on saving money. It wasn't like she'd be able to lay her hands on any credits anytime soon now that Meshi was out of the credits game, but something inside her was hopeful, even if she had to pay a hugely absurd price. Regardless, it would be worth the cost considering the next time she managed to get online – if she could get online – it could be the last time for a very long time if things continued to go the way they were.

Her shoes crunched along the pavement as she made her way to the metro station nearest to where she lived with Grandma Alice. It was one of the safer ones, being in suburbia. There wasn't much in the way of ability to make money shaking down patrons or bothering people in the suburbs, so many of the gangs kept it to the inner city, close to Chinatown, Downtown, Eastside and the like. She wasn't worried about encountering anyone untoward until she reached Eastside Station. That was when it began to get hairy to say the least.

The stairs down to the main platform and station area were slippery with rain. The weather hadn't budged much, if at all, and a steady stream of drizzle was the norm for the last four days, and possibly even longer. It was a dull kind of time of year. Normally, it'd have been awash with all manner of autumnal colour but this year had just been grey and dirty – probably not helped by Mason enabling dirty factories in and around the city to ramp up production by issuing waivers against Clean Air mandates.

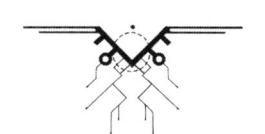

There were no beggars in the station today though, something Lex was relieved of. It wasn't that she felt malice towards them – in most cases it wasn't their fault they'd fallen on hard times. She just hated being approached and feeling like she couldn't really do anything meaningful. The train was running two minutes early, which was good for her as she had turned up a bit early so she wouldn't have to wait long. Three minutes, four at the most. She punched her ticket in the validator and stepped onto the escalator which took patrons from the main station down into the depths of the metro where the tracks were.

The station was quiet, empty and almost had an eerie feel to it. A few stragglers here and there but nothing serious. It was just after noon, so many people would be at work, but with more and more people working for themselves, she was sure she'd see more activity the closer to the city centre she got. It wasn't unusual for her home station to be quiet this time of day, but today it seemed unusually so.

The train came along, the tell-tale dinging of a bell to alert its arrival to weary passengers who may have dozed off sitting on the benches. It pulled to a stop and the doors opened. Lex stepped onto the train. This particular train was something of an enigma – modern and new from the outside, set against a wildly dated interior. The upholstery on the seats looked like it was thirty years old, and the floor wasn't much better. Brown cushions with inlaid yellowish-orange stitching and a floor so grey and worn that it may as well have not existed. It was the strangest of trains, a version of modern meets ancient that seemed to go well overall with a number of other public aspects throughout the rest of the city.

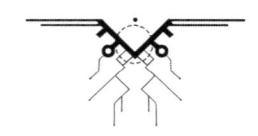

As the train pulled away from the station, destined for its next stop on the line, Lex realised she'd have to get off at Chinatown. That meant the possibility of running into Akoni again, something she wasn't sure she wanted to do. It wasn't that he was a bad person, per-se, and she'd seemingly made an impression on him the last time they'd crossed paths, so perhaps it'd be alright this time around, if he was even in the station.

Something about Akoni didn't sit right with her, even if he had been kind and relatively alright with her. Maybe it was their somewhat non-existent past and the strange familiarity that seemed to exist and yet didn't. She had barely known him when they were at school, but he was the type people seemed to know all about, even if they didn't know him personally. Something about his face and eyes told all his stories, but she wasn't sure if she was imagining things or if it was real. The thought of his eyes made her remember his strange bionic eye, screwed into his skull with a strange titanium plate, all shaded blue with yellow trimming resulting in a very robotic look indeed. Something about that eye was off putting, and maybe that's what she found so uneasy about Akoni. Was that all? He was a gang leader after all. Whatever it was, it sent a cold shiver down her that was as void of warmth as his robotic technology itself.

Her thoughts flitted from one thing to another, no one thought staying for too long before another popped into her head, but she didn't pay them any real attention. She just watched each station pass by as the train drew closer and closer to Chinatown station, the anxiety growing in her stomach as she got nearer to the meeting in Meshi's shop. She wasn't sure what she was setting everyone up to be getting into, especially since it could go one way or another. There was no real way of knowing how it'd go, but if there was one thing for certain it was that something had to be done, and at least they were taking steps toward making something happen.

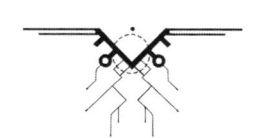

The train pulled into the last stop before Chinatown, the anxiety in her stomach becoming palpable. She started to wonder if she could really go through with it, but the thought of her family seemingly trapped in the Ascension interface, perhaps wondering why she'd not returned at her usual time, strengthened her resolve to go through with, well, whatever they were going through with. She'd have to wait and see how it developed.

The train moved away from the station and into the familiar tunnels that denoted the Chinatown area. Adrenaline pumped through her as she watched the lights of the tunnel pass by in a period of time that seemed to be too quickly. With only what felt like moments in time passing before she felt the train shift gear and slow down, the familiar ping and recorded mechanical sounding voice stating 'Chinatown' filling the nearly empty train, she'd managed to talk herself up enough to at least manage to get out of her seat and get to the door.

As she expected, she saw Akoni and his gang of miscreants lurking around near the escalator and stairs, right where she needed to pass through. It was an annoyance to her, at least in the first instance. She really couldn't be bothered to deal with them today, but on the other hand, maybe she'd be able to convince a handful of them to come to Meshi's shop with her to the meeting. A group of wayward souls like this gang would fit in nicely with other rebels looking to set the record straight and get even with an aggressive and demanding government hell-bent on creating difficulty for the masses in exchange for making their own elitist ends more enjoyable, profitable and secure.

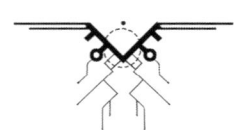

She stepped off the train after it'd come to a full stop, clutching her bag closer instinctively, remembering how they'd gone through her things in their previous encounter. She had significantly more sensitive material with her this time such as the burner phone and a copy of the poster she'd made up depicting President Mason as Adolf Hitler – all only slightly incriminating. She wasn't sure how she'd explain either if they chose to go through her stuff again, but she figured the only way to get through that was to cross that bridge when she got to it.

Akoni and his cronies were tossing a ball of some kind around, presumably stolen from some poor kid who happened to pass through their territory. Despite it being an assumption though, Lex couldn't shake the feeling that she was right in the conclusion she'd jumped to when it came to Akoni and his gang. They were just the type to steal from children – or from anyone for that matter – just for the fun of it and to see how far they could push their luck. It was a wonder they bothered with all the various other things they got up to. Surely stealing from children was far too easy and not satisfying in the least, but she figured perhaps they were doing it purely to be cruel and satisfaction had little, if anything, to do with it.

As she approached them, she noticed, much to her dismay, a slow in their game of catch. She knew she'd garnered some unwanted attention from them, and sure enough, three of the younger punks stepped forward, blocking her path.

"Give us your bag," one of them said. "Or you'll regret it."

Lex clutched her bag closer. "N...no," she replied, trying to sound brave.

"The fuck you say?" said the other street tough. "Give it to us or you won't like what happens next."

"So?" Lex said, hoping she sounded stronger than she felt as she pulled her bag away from their outstretched hands.

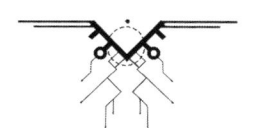

The shorter of the pair flicked his head to the side to sweep part of his bright green Mohawk out of his eyes. "Oh you're really asking for it now." he said, reaching into his jacket pocket and producing a switchblade. She wondered where a kid of this age could have laid his hands on a knife of that calibre, but figured it didn't much matter. There were ways for people like him to get anything from guns to knives to drugs and more with absolute ease.

Just as things were starting to get a bit hairy, Akoni stepped in, putting two fingers in his mouth and whistling sharply.

"Knock it off," he said levelly. "Lex is a friend."

A wave of relief washed over her. Perhaps she'd get away with all of her possessions intact after all. The two punks backed off after Akoni's stern comment about Lex being a friend, and she moved to get up the stairs to street-level as quickly as possible. She only made it three steps though before she found Akoni himself in front of her, blocking her way up the stairs. He crossed his arms slowly and looked down at her, surrounded from behind by his friends and gang members as she looked up at him through her eyelashes, hoping he wouldn't cause her too many issues.

"Thanks…." she began, trying to just press on with her mission to get to street level, stepping up one more step in an attempt to move past him. He pushed on her shoulder though, making her take a step back down.

"Hang on a minute," he said. "It's been a while."

"I have to go," she said, trying not to sound rude. "I'm already running late."

"Where to?"

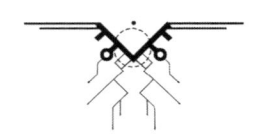

She paused for a moment, weighing up the pros and cons of telling Akoni the truth. One the one hand, it was very possible he'd want to get involved. On the other though, it was just as possible if he declined or showed no interest it was possible that he'd go wagging his tongue all over town and let it slip that there was a resistance of sorts in its infancy. Maybe. Maybe he wouldn't say a word and instead just show solidarity toward the whole operation. The more she thought about it, the more the pros outweighed the cons and so she decided to take her chances.

"If you must know, I'm going to a meeting."

Akoni's eyes narrowed. "What kind of meeting."

"A couple of people sick of how President Mason is controlling the Ascension program and making it so that only he and his cronies can use or have access to it. Amongst other things."

"Sounds like my kinda place," Akoni replied. "Given I'm not exactly a Mason fan."

"Wanna come then?" Lex asked. "You might find it useful. Maybe you even know of some ways we can make our voices heard more loudly."

"I have a few ideas. And consider me there. But it's probably best we're not seen together – either before or after. What's the address?"

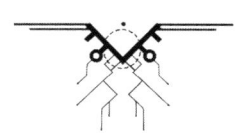

Lex looked around at the rest of the gang milling around, having moved off and lost interest in hassling her the minute Akoni got involved. Some were having a game of toss with their presumably stolen ball while others were play-fighting, or so it first appeared, before it soon got out of control and one of the punks – a guy with a bronze-coloured jacket and yellow hair – ended up with a fat lip and a bloody nose. The others hooted and hollered, laughing away and making jokes about the scuffle while Akoni turned back to face Lex.

"So. The address." he said, crossing his arms.

"Right." Lex replied, pulling a poster out of her bag. "It's on here."

"Amateur."

"What?"

"You don't write the fucking address of a meeting of this nature on the promotional invitation of sorts!" Akoni replied, waving the paper around comically, half laughing. "That's just asking for trouble."

Lex's chest tightened. She hadn't thought of that. But then again, she hadn't exactly stated that it was going to be a resistance meeting, the fact that they'd be discussing essentially the downfall of President Mason – or what they generally hoped to gain from it – or what their overall, generic plan was. All it had was a picture of President Mason depicted a bit as Hitler, some generic slander about him and the address and time.

"Calm down, would you?" she whispered. "The address is only on this copy."

"Still. That's one too many copies if you ask me." He handed it back.

"Nobody is asking you. Don't you want it?"

He pointed to his bionic eye. "Good for more than just seeing."

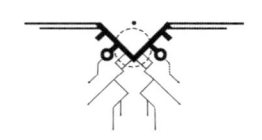

His eye made Lex apprehensive, but she also figured it must be an incredibly useful invention to have at his disposal anytime of the night or day. If it could record information, she wondered what else it could do. Could he bring up maps, get the weather forecast? She wanted to ask, but she knew she had to get going, otherwise she'd definitely be late for her date with Meshi and all the others.

"You'll have to tell me about it sometime," she said casually, trying to get the conversation to end before the other ruffians of the Chinatown crew got bored of fighting each other and decided to turn on her. "See you there then, I guess."

She turned then and half-waved to Akoni and began to race up the stairs as fast as she could go without drawing attention to herself. She hoped inviting him, and whichever members of his crew, wouldn't incite some riotous issue at the meeting.

Chapter Ten

The backroom was always small to begin with, but when it was crowded with thirty or so people, it was even like being squashed into a tin at a packing factory. Meshi hadn't got enough chairs in the whole place to accommodate everyone, but numerous people insisted that it was of no major bother and they were just excited and happy to be 'on the team' so to speak. There were several people Lex knew from previous encounters – both in the shop and from generally being active in the neighbourhood surrounding the area, but there were more people there she'd never met before than there were people she recognised. Perhaps for the best, but she remembered what Akoni had said about her being amateurish in her approach and she worried that word might reach the wrong people and she'd get done in for organising the whole thing. Meshi too. Time would tell.

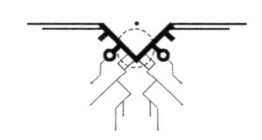

She made her way over to a small table where an old coffee machine bubbled away making a fresh pot. The smell was intoxicating and she felt her mouth begin to water. She hadn't yet managed to have her daily cup, so this first succulent cup would be well received indeed. There was a stack of mugs and various cups of different styles, colours, textures and sizes on one side of the machine, making Lex smile at Meshi's clear concern for the environment. Since things had got out of hand with some environmental issues decades earlier, more and more people had switched to reusable cups in an effort to offset some of the pollution that single use plastic had caused worldwide. For the most part it was helpful and millions had caught onto the trend, but there were still the occasional people who would almost go out of their way to use plastics, almost as though to prove a point of some kind. But Meshi had never been like that. Not at all.

She frowned at the options in terms of coffee whitener. None were too appealing – a powdered whitener she'd heard bad things about, a thick cream and 2% milk. She only ever had coffee with skim milk as it allowed the flavour to come through without being overpowered by the milk. Sugar was never considered either, something Grandma Alice had encouraged her to do for health's sake. Sugar was the devil according to Grandma Alice, despite occasionally having desserts after dinner, but she never let herself get carried away and she didn't want Lex to either. Even though Lex was a grown woman herself and could make her own food choices, Grandma Alice still looked out for her, sometimes to a point that bordered on annoying, although Lex had matured enough to know that a nag from a relative often registered their interest in your well-being and health.

The cup she'd picked had a bit of a chip in the handle, something she had to navigate mindfully to ensure she didn't cut herself when drinking. It wasn't a bad chip, but enough to be felt when you ran your hand over it, and presumably so, enough to warrant a cut. She thought about putting it back and taking another but simply couldn't be bothered. After all, if a small cut on her hand was all that happened today, she'd be lucky. Akoni's warning kept popping up in her head, but she wasn't sure if she should consider it a warning as such or if he was just having it on with her in a way. He seemed the type to joke about.

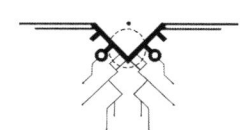

She opted for the 2% milk – after all, if you only put a splash it was enough to lighten the coffee without giving it that overpowering milky flavour. The coffee pot clicked at almost the perfect time to indicate it had finished brewing and she let the remaining few drops drip into the pot before removing it from the hotplate part of the machine and pouring it into the cup. It mixed with the coffee itself enough that she didn't need to use a spoon to combine the two liquids, the sheer movement of the coffee entering the cup was sufficient.

She turned away from the machine and looked at the crowd of people gathering in the small back room. There were several others who'd come in since she'd arrived, more people she didn't know, more strangers who were coming together in a show of solidarity, a collection of people who were encouraged by her bold step forward to join the cause and try to show President Mason and his elitist buddies that they meant business. It was refreshing to see so many new faces. Perhaps the issues they were all facing as a direct result of Mason's rule were beginning to crack the fine porcelain of a society everyone thought was sufficient and loved by the masses. That was the thing though. No one had ever voiced their opinion in a slightly negative stance against this particular establishment before, and so even if a single person in the community had been feeling annoyed with things, the fact that no one voiced the same meant they kept their mouth shut for the most part. Especially these days when it was becoming more and more clear that the government couldn't be trusted. As it happened anyway, the interface program at the Spots seemed to now have doormen employed explicitly to eavesdrop on conversations that took place online. It seemed nothing was safe or private anymore, especially online. It was the exact reason Meshi insisted on Lex using burner phones to spread the word. At least then she could ditch it if the heat really got switched on, and it could never get traced back to either of them.

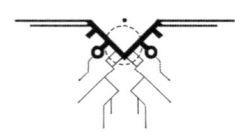

The clock on the wall ticked past their starting time and Meshi got up to close the door to the shop, making sure it was locked. As he got up to the front of the shop though, he spied Akoni and two of his ruffian subway gang coming up the stairs. He hadn't been made aware that they were interested in joining the meeting, and so he opened the door to try to drive them off. It wasn't the first time they'd come to his shop, and suffice it to say, the last time they did left much to be desired in terms of their actions and attitude.

"Go away. We're closed." Meshi said, waving his hand at them dismissively, trying to sound assertive.

"Quiet geezer," one of the ruffians said. "We're here for the meeting."

Meshi's face fell and his chest tightened. "What meeting? I don't know what you're talking about."

Akoni stepped forward. "Lex told us about it. It sounded interesting."

"I still don't know what you're talking about." Meshi insisted.

From inside the shop's backroom, Lex could see Meshi struggling with Akoni and some of his crew, realising she'd not told him that he'd be coming. She put her coffee down and wove her way through the sea of people into the front of the shop, coming up behind Meshi and trying to calm the situation.

"Sorry Meshi," she began. "I told Akoni to come."

"What? This reprobate?" Meshi replied. "You know he trashed my store once."

She paused. It was true, but if they were going to hope for any help at all in producing change from the government, everyone had to be involved, regardless of their former past actions and interactions with one another.

"I know." Lex said. "But we need as many people right now as we can get. Can't you let it go? Just for now?"

Meshi narrowed his eyes at Akoni and his cohorts. "I suppose. But one wrong move and I'll phone the police!"

"Yeah. Phoning the police to a resistance rally. Really smart, pops." Akoni said sarcastically, rolling his eyes and pushing past Meshi into the shop followed by the two who'd accompanied him. He winked at Lex as he passed her, making her want to smile back but she managed to resist. She didn't want Meshi thinking that Akoni and her were friends. Not that they were, not really anyway, but the whole thing wasn't something she thought Meshi would understand.

Inside the backroom people had taken their seats or were standing along the walls, trying to stay out of the way of one another. It was a tight squeeze to say the least, and with around twenty-five to thirty people, it was more than just slightly difficult to make sure you didn't knock into anyone or spill someone's coffee. Everyone managed though, and once they'd all taken their seats or made a spot for themselves amongst the sea of people, the meeting began with Lex and Meshi standing in front of the crowd.

"I know this might sound like something that we never thought we'd have to do in our day and age," Meshi began, "but it's also something that we really have to now that our government is getting carried away with what they can and cannot do."

"There doesn't seem to be any real line between the two anymore," someone called out. "I never used to be supportive of stuff like this, but lately I've had it up to here!"

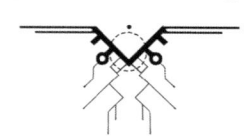

There was a murmur of approval from the rest of the room, a couple of claps and a lot of general agreement. It had been a growing problem with President Mason taking liberties for a while, with numerous benefits to life being slowly and methodically stripped away, never too quickly so as to alarm anyone, but likewise just quick enough to make people suddenly realise what was beginning to happen when it got too personal, like it had done with the Spots and access to Ascension – both the interface and the process itself.

"What we aren't sure of is what we can do to try and make our displeasure known." Lex said. She wasn't sure how far they should take their issues with the government. She didn't want anyone to get hurt, but likewise she knew that it could potentially come to that at some point, especially if Mason continued to take away things that the everyday person enjoyed or needed. First it was rainwater collection, solar panelling and making those things illegal, then it was growing your own food for profit, and now the issue with Ascension. There were other things that had happened in between all those, of course, but those were the main points of contention.

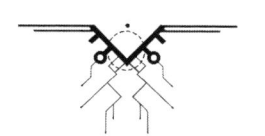

"Vandalise his office block!" someone else yelled out, while other people called out, "Let's catch him and make an example!" It was clear that tensions were running high and people really had various ideas and anger about the whole situation, but Lex knew they needed to be smart, concise and calculating in their execution of any plan. Not just for safety, but to ensure that even the smallest of actions would have the greatest impact. After all, people would be more likely to support or join their cause if they played by some type of rules and didn't allow themselves to get out of control. Striking for the sake of it and to inflict as much damage as possible simply wouldn't do, and they ran the risk of looking like a gang of miscreants – uneducated, uninformed, angry and out of control. That wouldn't help get anyone on side at all. As it was, they already ran the risk of looking like a gang of miscreants with the unexpected addition of Akoni and his crew.

"Look," Meshi began, growing irritated with the rambunctiousness of the crowd. "We can't just go off willy-nilly destroying things and make a bad name for ourselves. If we want to be taken seriously as a resistance group in the beginning, we should have a code of conduct. Way to behave."

"But what happens when they decide to play by their own rules?" Akoni suddenly asked. Everyone in the room turned to look at him, standing there in his dark, ripped clothes, shaggy, spiky hair with his bionic eye glowing an incandescent blue behind his bangs. He looked like something out of some not so distant futuristic comic book or film, a concept that some found disconcerting and others found riveting. He continued before anyone could answer him though. "People like President Mason don't have a code of conduct."

He was right. Lex knew he was, although she was trying to make things as ethical as possible in the beginning. She didn't want anyone to get hurt or go to great lengths to destroy property or lives, but she supposed that by this point lives had already been destroyed by the changes Mason had made to limit access to Spot interfaces amongst other things. Who was to say what was ethical really anymore? Things were becoming more convoluted by the day and it wouldn't be long before they were going to be forced to take some dirty steps to make their displeasure known, so why not begin the way they intended to carry on?

"He's right." Lex said quietly to Meshi. "Mason will never play by any rules of any kind except his own."

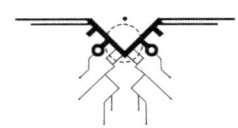

"And while I'm all for taking him down, I can't say I'm prepared to die for it." Akoni said, crossing his arms. His opinion was echoed around the room from several others, making it clear that there was no real discernible way that they could do what they needed to do without getting their own hands messy.

"Okay." Lex relented, admittedly not requiring much in the way of persuasion. It was clear they were going to have to play at least as dirty as Mason did in order to get through to him, or at least someone who would be able to have some sway in government policy in the future to hopefully get everything turned around in the near future. It was a bit of a long shot and could criminalise them to the everyday citizen as much as Mason was beginning to be, with Mason having the very obvious advantage of being the one in power. Many people tended to look the other way when the government was involved directly in criminality but less so when it was other ordinary citizens just trying to make life better for themselves and others. It was a catch twenty-two: ordinary citizens fighting to better the lives of everyone with the government working to better the lives of only their associates, but many of the citizens would turn in the 'freedom fighters', due to some kind of misplaced loyalty to a way of life long lost. Especially due to the fact that many people – mostly people who didn't use Ascension or Spots or anything of the sort – were generally happy with their lives. They had a vested interest in keeping their lives the way they were.

The room grew quiet, watching Lex and Meshi thinking about what to do and how to proceed with their plan. There was really only one real way that they could do what needed doing and achieve what they needed to and that was to ask the people themselves what they suggested. Lex turned back to Akoni then, glancing at the crowd of the other participants willing to get their hands dirty.

"Well, since you seem to know so much about getting under the skin of governments, what do you suggest?"

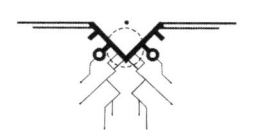

Chapter Eleven

It turned out that Akoni knew a lot.

Probably more than he should have, but with his background, it was hardly surprising. Within an hour Lex had been introduced to concepts she never expected to need to know about, including small time terrorist warfare, bomb making and hacking. Akoni said he knew a hacker who did good work and would be one hundred and ten percent on board with the whole plan, but she was out of town until the following weekend so he'd arrange a meet up when she was back. It suited Lex fine as she was going to have to take some down time to process everything that she'd had thrown at her, but it was for the best. Things were getting done and they'd soon begin seeing results. Or so she hoped.

She walked home slowly, avoiding the metro. She wanted a long walk to clear her head, even if it meant walking nearly two hours. It didn't matter. What mattered was getting her thought process straight with everything and getting to a place within herself where she'd be able to condone, help and even set off things like bombs herself. It was something she wasn't sure she could do. Walking towards home through the city, she looked at all the progress mankind had made to create such a vivid, new world and wondered at the cost they'd have to pay to make sure they retained their way of life. Was the price too high? She wasn't sure.

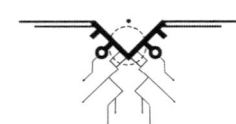

Eventually she arrived home, walking up the familiar street to Grandma Alice's house with the large garden that she used to play in as a kid with James while their parents drank cold lemonade in the shade with Grandma Alice and Grandpa, who was alive at that time. She remembered the fresh, clean taste of peas right from the vine, a welcome snack in the heat of the day and how refreshing they always tasted. She stopped and looked at the garden, leaves glinting in the late day sun and suddenly she really wanted some garden peas.

The vine was set at the back of the garden, behind peonies, sunflowers and other types of plants that Grandma Alice used for various things, including medicines. Coming from a Chinese background meant she knew all sorts of strange and wonderful remedies for different problems, and herbs were commonly at the forefront of almost every single solution to every single problem. One of Grandma Alice's concerns about EverDawn was that the old ways, the old stories, the world's folklore could be lost.

The scent of the herbs was heavy in the air, despite it cooling off and towards the end of the year. It was harvest time or would be shortly. Grandma Alice just hadn't got round to it yet, but when she did, Lex knew they'd enter the winter months with a barrage of canning, blending and creating tinctures, dried teas and other medicinal delights that could cure or at least help most things. That didn't help her unease now, though.

She crouched down and looked for the good pods – ones that were fatter than the rest and bright green. They sometimes hid beneath the vine and made you work for them. It didn't take long before she found a few, and gathering them off the vine and into her jacket pockets she sat back on her heels and looked up at the increasingly darkening sky. Night was on the horizon, creeping in like a bandit. It was a cleansing time of day and she decided to sit in the dirt of her childhood garden and eat the peas right from her pockets.

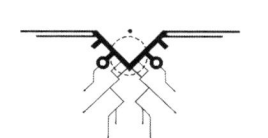

Halfway through her snack, bursting with flavour of what could be compared to a light grass taste, she got teary-eyed. Looking at the sky, hidden deep in the depths of Grandma Alice's garden, she began to feel lonely. She felt like she was the only one left of her whole family and even with Grandma Alice, she had no one. Except maybe Damian, but he was so busy with work and his own life that she didn't feel like she could unload to him like she used to. She suddenly got an intense pang of sadness in her stomach, a feeling like her family were actually somehow gone. They may as well have been. With access all but cut off there was no way she could do anything to speak to them, see them, or even send them a message. She wondered if it was the same on the inside – if they knew about the issues that were going on the outside and if they worried, were sad or struggled. Or were they just memories and words on a disk, like Grandma Alice described it? She began to ponder this deeply, but that of course, made her eyes well up.

She couldn't fight the tears. Truth be told, she'd been fighting them for a good long while by this point and it was bound to happen sooner or later. She was grateful that it happened there, in the dirt of Grandma Alice's garden somewhere between the peonies and the peas that the tears came. It wouldn't make a good impression if it happened in front of anyone that was supposed to be relying on her for at least some kind of leadership. She began to cry harder, sniffling as tears ran out of her eyes as she realised deeper and deeper down that this was the first time in a long time she actually felt truly alone. A paradox given the fact she had so many people rallying around her idea of finally standing up against President Mason, but it didn't help. She felt more alone now than ever before.

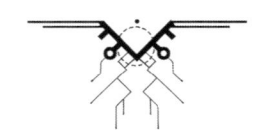

After a few moments of just letting the tears come, she decided to go inside and get some proper dinner. She wiped her face and took a few deep breaths. Grandma Alice was probably home and she didn't want to have to field any questions about why she had been crying – especially if Grandma Alice caught on that she'd been crying in the garden. It would look more than a little strange, something Lex aimed to avoid.

She stood up and brushed the cool, damp dirt from her clothes before gathering up her bag and a few extra pea pods and walking away from the vines. The sky was properly dark now, and the kitchen light had been flicked on from inside the house – a tell-tale sign that Grandma Alice was indeed home and was probably either halfway through or just starting dinner. The sudden image of Grandma Alice in the kitchen concocting some delicious treats made Lex realise she hadn't eaten a thing except the garden peas all day and was surprisingly ravenous, especially given the stress and nerves she'd experienced. She tried to put it all out of her head for the time being as she opened the door and stepped into the delicious aroma of some kind of stew with dumplings: a savoury blend of herbs and spices that made her feel comforted and warm. Maybe she wasn't as alone as she sometimes felt. At least not with Grandma Alice around.

"I wondered where you'd been." Grandma Alice said, poking her head around the wall and peering downstairs into the mudroom area. A north wind blew in from the door, sending a shiver down her spine, a foretelling of winter on the horizon, the darker and gloomier time of year that always got her a bit down.

"Sorry." Lex replied. "It's been a hectic day."

"Dinner will be ready in twenty minutes. Sweet and sour chicken tonight."

"Awesome. I have time for a shower then."

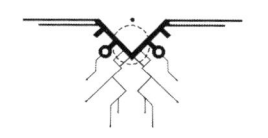

"If you're quick. I know you and your famous hour-long showers!"

"I'll be quick. I promise."

Lex went into her bedroom and closed the door almost all the way, peeking through the crack between the frame and the door itself down the hall to make sure Grandma Alice went back into the kitchen to finish dinner as stated. The smell of the sweet and sour chicken hung heavy on the air and made Lex salivate at the thought of tucking into one of her favourite meals after such a trying day. When she heard the clanging of pots and pans and Grandma Alice rummaging through the drawers she knew she was relatively safe; she took out the burner phone and checked the messages. She had over twenty.

'Tell me when and where and I'm up for anything.' read one.

'Willing to do what it takes to get this off the ground.' said another.

'Fuck Mason.'

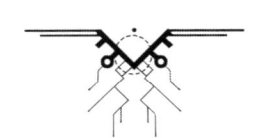

They were all of the same general idea: fuck President Mason and everything he stood for along with a very clear desire to do anything and what it took to get the message across to him that no one would stand for his bullshit any longer. They'd already had enough changes to life in general. The Ascension issue was just one step too far in a long line of problematic changes Mason had set out for some bizarre reason. A controlling of the masses? Trying to keep absolute control over everyone to quell any dissent or problematic uprisings that could question his power? It was probable – likely, even. Since he'd come to power, he'd banned rainwater collection, outlawed small scale subsistence private farming, and made it mandatory for all private gardens and farms to use pesticides in an apparent attempt to control the pest population.

Everyone knew the truth though. The pesticides weren't to keep a pest population down – there hadn't been any issues in that area in years once people were able to grow their own food, especially indoors with hydroponics. The pesticides were being enforced to hide the fact that Mason was using it as a cover to spray food with chemicals to keep people compliant. Or so was the rumour. Lex wasn't sure what she believed, but she knew that Grandma Alice didn't comply with regulations when it came to her garden and lied to officers when they came to inspect it, cleverly spraying only small bits in the earth where they were likely to take samples from.

Those were just a few things though. People weren't too overly concerned about either of those happenings, but when the Spots were made to be less accessible, there had been murmurings about growing unease in the general population. That was when the graffiti started, and not just in subways and metro stations, but on streets, busy pathways where it could be commonly seen by passers by on their commutes to and from work. A cheeky smile, often hidden behind a hand was common, and it was clear that people had begun to see Mason as something of an ogre. At least back then. The ogre had grown into something else now, causing a resistance movement to gain strength and speed.

She took her pyjamas into the bathroom, taking care to put the burner phone back in her purse so Grandma Alice didn't happen upon it if by chance she decided to come into her bedroom. Not that she made a habit of it, but she was known to, on occasion. The messages would wait, even until tomorrow but then she'd have to dump the phone somewhere. She had a couple of ideas as to where, but she'd orchestrate that with Meshi, so he knew she'd need a new one too.

Twenty minutes later and she'd finished her shower and went downstairs to find her grandmother was watering the hydroponic garden. A pang of sadness came over her again, but she managed to control it instead of bursting into tears. It was a palpable sadness – one that was deep and real, a concept that frightened her. It made her think more of her parents and brother and how worried she was that she'd never see them again.

Grandma Alice knew something was wrong though. Grandmothers always did. The minute Lex stepped into the room, Alice paused in her pottering and gave her that knowing look that said, 'I know something's up.'.

"What is it?" Grandma Alice asked, hands resting on the edge of the table height garden.

Lex's stomach tightened. She paused at the base of the stairs. She had been hoping looking at the plants might release some of the tension building up in her. "What?"

"You're up to something," Grandma Alice replied, narrowing her eyes. "I know. I've seen you look like that before."

"Nothing! I swear."

There was a palpable pause. Grandma Alice looked directly at Lex, who, by this point, was completely sure that she had been found out anyway and decided to spill the beans.

"Okay. Meshi and I got a little group of people together to try to protest the government and how they've cut off access to the Spots."

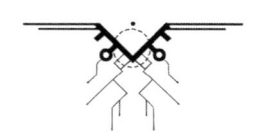

"That could be dangerous."

"I know, but…"

Grandma Alice put her hand up. "Don't worry. You don't need to explain."

"But…"

"I know you miss your parents and brother." Grandma Alice said. "I do too."

"Yeah." Lex said, her throat catching as she tried to fight back tears. "And we might never be able to see them again."

Grandma Alice looked down at the plants and sighed. She fussed with the system a moment longer, then shook her head. "I knew this day would come."

Lex cleared her throat. "What'd you mean?"

Grandma Alice made a broad gesture with one hand. Any other day, and it might have seemed like she was taking about the water-rot that had taken hold of at least half the crop. "The whole thing with Ascension. I could see the signs years ago, before I ever even retired."

"What? Mason cutting off access?" Lex asked, perplexed.

"That and more."

"Go on."

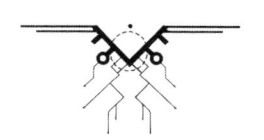

Alice knew that she shouldn't be telling anyone anything that she'd heard, especially not in recent years, but it was difficult when your own granddaughter had become so despondent and upset over the issue. She knew that she could get in serious trouble for sharing what she knew, as well as potentially getting those people she knew who still worked at EverDawn in serious trouble.

"Back when I worked at EverDawn there had been rumours that they were planning to close off access to certain classes of people. For the actual Ascension process, that is. They didn't want homeless people, poor people or anyone like that to get into the program, I don't know why." She paused. "Fear they might corrupt it with their supposed filth, I guess. Very few people agreed with it, but no one was really willing to risk their jobs. Plus, we all thought it would blow over. You know how it can be. Someone says something, it gets some backlash and it goes quiet."

"So, what happened?" Lex asked.

Alice shuffled her feet. She finally turned to face Lex, her gaze dark and serious. "I don't know. I retired about six months after the first murmurings were going around. In fact, your parents were some of the last people that got in before that little story started. I have to say, it was a bit too convenient that after it came out, even if it was a lie, the applications for Ascension dwindled almost overnight. We used to get easily thirty, maybe forty a day. It went to ten and under. A lot of people got laid off, but of course they didn't blame a lack of work. They didn't want anyone to know they'd purposely stopped taking applications from those of us who aren't 'elite'."

"So, what happened with my parents?"

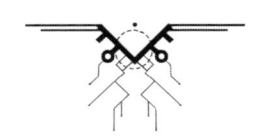

"Well. At the moment, probably nothing, except you being cut off from accessing Spots. But if you start playing little fire games, they could do something. They watch more than you know. Piss off Mason, and he'll piss off you." She paused again, this time much longer. "If you continue on with this, just be careful."

"What would you suggest?"

Alice's smile was wry and humourless. "Wait and see what their next move is. Now, come help me with this."

Lex swallowed hard. She moved to join her grandmother beside the hydroponic garden. "Yes, Grandma Alice."

Chapter Twelve

Lex felt a bit better after talking to Grandma Alice. She usually did. Grandmother's always had an innate way of making people feel better it seemed, and she'd helped massively. There were still questions Lex had about her time in EverDawn, but she didn't want to take liberties by outwardly asking questions and potentially getting Grandma Alice in trouble. As it happened, it was entirely possible that Grandma Alice had already said too much.

The stories Alice had told Lex hinted at some shady inner workings in the corporation as a whole. From about a year before Alice had retired there had been reports of people paying money to jump the Ascension queue. Normally you just applied, a process that was always approved regardless of the person, and then a date was set for the process and the whole thing was more or less done. Usually from the time an application was received it was about two to three weeks from submitting paperwork to becoming just a pure consciousness in the system. People had started buying their way in though, something that was banned, and before long the wait times were more like five weeks, maybe six. It was unheard of and when EverDawn was queried, they claimed that there had been an issue with the machinery that completed the Ascension process and so there was a backlog to get through.

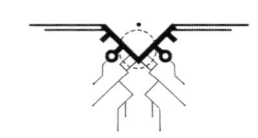

An internal memo had gone around though citing reasons that were only to be known to executive level employees and above, and that no one was to speak to any media sources. Of course, those, like Alice, knew the truth – or at least some of it. She processed the applications, after all and knew there was no backlog. Not in their department anyway, and once news of backlogs and issues with equipment hit the streets, people became less inclined to want to take advantage of the process and they found that fewer and fewer applications were coming in. That was when Alice chose to retire before she got laid off from a lack of work. She did worry about Jade, her replacement she'd started training when she announced her retirement, but Jade was young and if she ended up getting laid off, then it was going to be fairly easy for her to land another job quickly.

As it was though, Jade was fine. She picked up the job fine and stayed in the role for around a year. That was how Alice had found out that only elite members of the public and President Mason's inner circle were being allowed through to the Ascension process. For payment as well, which was even more unethical. There had been other stories too about how those people who were deemed 'undesirables' were having their information files shelved and access restricted so they couldn't move freely or be essentially 'awake' in the system. It was a way of quashing any kind of dissent from within the program itself, much like what Lin, Michael and James had mentioned when Lex had last used the Spot. People on the inside, as well as the outside knew what was happening and it was only a matter of time before both sets of people rose up and did something about it.

That thought though led to Lex feeling anxious about her brother and parents on the inside. What if their conversation had been being monitored and they ended up being shelved in some archive somewhere, never to be seen or heard from again? She wondered if she could get in touch with Jade to ask her to check, but wasn't sure if she should. It could cause problems for Grandma Alice – something she aimed to avoid. After all, if they were shelving people in the system for causing problems, what would they do to people on the outside?

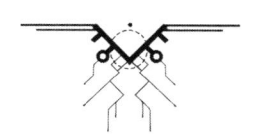

She rolled over in her bed and took her phone from her bedside table. She hadn't heard from Damian in a few days and wondered how he'd been. She pulled up his contact in her phone book and pressed the text icon.

'Been awhile. What you been up to?' she typed before putting the phone back on the night table. Within moments, it buzzed that tell-tale buzz of someone replying to a message. She picked it back up, thinking it strange that Damian would reply so quickly, given that it was a work night and he often got up at the crack of dawn.

'Busy as usual. Lunch tomorrow?' was the reply. She was definitely up for that.

'Where and when?'

'1:30, Martini's near my office?'

'Sounds good. See you there.'

She put the phone back in the drawer and put it on silent, not wanting to be disturbed by anything else. She had a lot on her mind and needed to sleep, and as she rolled over and faced the wall, the usual light draught coming from a crack between the window frame and the wall blowing lightly across her skin, she hoped she could sleep easily.

It turned out Lex had been more tired than she thought. Obviously, the long day of plotting and emotional upheaval had worn her out and she had dropped off easily. She slept soundly through the night and woke round nine in the morning, stretching and thinking to herself that she might have been in the same position in bed all night long.

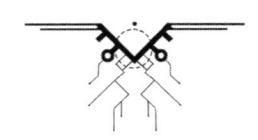

Her back, legs and shoulders were all stiff, so it was a possibility. The sun had been up for some time, and despite it being autumnal outside, the clouds had given way and allowed light to shine through brightly. It was the beams of light, pouring through her curtains that roused her from her sleep.

It was nearly ten and if she was going to make it for lunch with Damian, she had to get moving. She had to stop by Meshi's on the way to get a new burner phone, find a place to dump the old one and then go see Damian. It was shaping up to be a busy day indeed, and she still had a lot to come as their resistance movement gained momentum and started its onslaught of vandalism designed to antagonise President Mason, in the hopes he'd reinstate access to both Ascension and Spots.

She went into the kitchen, intending to grab a cup of coffee before heading out. She hadn't been sleeping well and caffeine was definitely needed. There was a pot of coffee still on the burner left from Grandma's morning routine. Lex wasn't certain where she'd gone but figured she'd be back before dinner that evening. In any event, she pulled out her phone and sent a quick text stating that she was going to meet Damian for lunch and then she had to 'run some errands' but would be back for dinner.

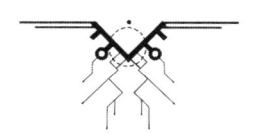

The coffee was hot, but tasted stale. It didn't matter though. It wasn't overly important at that point in time. She drank it as fast as she could, glancing at the clock on the wall every few moments. She was hoping to get the next bus down to the metro station instead of walking to save time. It was possible Meshi would want to chat about the previous day's turnout and what they intended to do from there, but she wasn't sure. Maybe he'd get cold feet over the whole thing. Maybe not. She had been unsure the previous night and the confusion lingered well into the morning. Even coffee wasn't helping clear things up, and coffee usually did.

She grabbed her keys from the key bowl on the counter and took her jacket from the hook on the wall that led down to the mudroom. She glanced outside. It was a damp and cool day with a bit of a breeze. It'd probably be fairly chilly and she contemplated taking her scarf that Grandma had knitted for her some time ago. It was purple with streaks of blue, two of her favourite colours and matched her jacket perfectly. She had matching mittens somewhere, but she wasn't entirely sure where and so she passed on them for the time being as she only had ten minutes to get to the bus stop and it was a short walk away.

As she locked the door, she felt her phone buzz in her handbag. She started walking down the steps and down the garden path towards the nearest bus stop and took the phone out to check the messages. It was from Grandma, just saying she was out with her old colleagues from EverDawn for lunch and she'd be back about four. She didn't comment on Lex's errands. Lex knew that Grandma Alice probably knew what she was up to when she said 'errands'. Just some light terrorism against a corrupt and tyrannical government for the good of the general populace. One of the errands would be disposing of the burner phone, but she assumed Meshi might have some ideas about that.

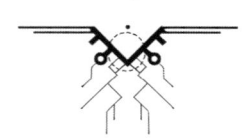

Turning the corner onto the main street, she saw the bus just up ahead, not quite at the stop yet. She quickened her pace and got to the bus stop just moments before it arrived, relieved that she wouldn't have to wait long. She put the fare into the fare box and received a small piece of paper to show she'd paid before sitting alone in a window seat, watching the dreary world go by as the bus moved through the city into the deeper neighbourhoods. It was only about twenty minutes by bus to the nearest metro station which would take her to Meshi's shop just outside Chinatown, which meant having to deal with Akoni and his gang again, but she wasn't overly worried. She seemed to be building up some strange, casual friendship with Akoni — something she never expected would happen with someone like him. But then again, everything about the last week or two were things she never expected she'd get into either, so it was all a bit surprising.

Or maybe not at all. People do strange things when they're put under pressure and the stakes are high. She was obviously just willing to do what it took to get things back to as normal as they could be.

The metro sign came into view and she pulled the cord to request the next stop. It wouldn't take long to get downtown now, maybe fifteen minutes. The bus pulled up and she hopped off, into a brisk wind that was rather refreshing, making her glad she'd taken her scarf. The traffic was quiet, so she didn't have to even wait to cross the street — something that was normally unheard of in that region of town. Thinking nothing of it, she reached the metro station and descended the fifty stairs or so to the main terminal area. Luckily her bus fare also allowed her on the metro without having to pay twice, so she walked right through the gates, showing the slip of paper she'd received from the bus driver to denote payment.

The train to Chinatown was five minutes away so she sat on one of the benches and took out her phone. She had no new messages but thought about texting Damian just for fun. There was probably no point since she'd be seeing him in just a few hours and he would be busy at his desk. She thought about it for a moment and then decided not to, opting instead to scroll through old messages on her phone and delete them to free up some space.

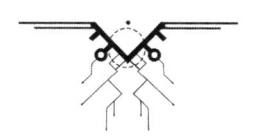

The PA system dinged and an announcement came on announcing the arrival of the train and its destination: South Station, a bus terminal ironically on the north end of town. It was the train she needed and would take her to the Chinatown station where Akoni and his buddies hung out in the depths of the station getting up to little if any good. The train was unusually empty for the direction it was heading in. Normally there'd be numerous people on the train at most times of day. Workers who worked downtown who were going in late, students going to later classes at one of the several universities, or people going shopping. Lex tried to think if it was a holiday or weekend, but it was neither, at least to her knowledge. Her days seemed to be running together, but that wasn't surprising. Her brain was preoccupied with more important things other than worrying whether it was a Friday or a Sunday.

Her mind wandered for what seemed to be only minutes as the train pulled away from the station and made its way downtown. She clearly had been stressed out and not paying attention as before she knew it, she was at Chinatown and needed to snap herself out of her daze and get off the train. Her eyes focused and she glanced around, looking for Akoni. She didn't want to admit that she was, but something still gave her the jitters about walking through the Chinatown metro without him around. She wondered if he'd have told all his little cronies to lay off of her. It was definitely safer with him around.

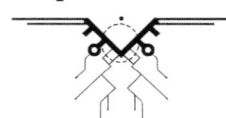

To her surprise though, she didn't encounter a single person aside from one other equally nervous looking metro rider getting off at the same stop. She began to wonder what was going on with the quietness in town, but chalked it up to it being a Friday or something. Many people had opted to have three-day weekends in the last fifty or sixty years. Some even went with four-day weekends. It was a nice option to have, and people seemed to be much happier for it. Damian usually had Mondays off, so it made sense he'd be in the office. The absence of Akoni though was highly unusual, but she wasn't going to question it as long as she could get out of the metro station unscathed.

To her relative surprise, her short trip through the Chinatown metro was entirely uneventful and she emerged safe and sound on the main street where people passed by giving her looks as though she were insane for ever being down there in the first place. Akoni's gang were known to be somewhat violent and picked their prey at random and so many people avoided the Chinatown metro and went just one block up to the next closest station, which was safe and peaceful. It beat having to take a risk every time you went down those steps at Chinatown.

She walked quickly along the familiar streets to Meshi's shop and took the steps up to the door two at a time. It didn't look open, but he had been clearing out the shop in recent days since he'd been visited by those unusual people that seemed to cause him some issues. They'd threatened him with something, and as a result he'd started clearing out his shop. Lex assumed it was something to do with some building violation – he'd had a lot of stuff crammed in that shop. It wasn't unusual but it didn't warrant a threat. She peered through the grimy glass on the door, trying to see inside but couldn't. She knocked three times lightly.

There was no real commotion from the inside, but she caught a glimpse of light coming from the back of the shop – from the room they'd held their little gathering in the day before. She knocked again, louder and harder this time and waited, looking through the glass for signs of life. Maybe Meshi had just forgotten to turn the light out when he was last there.

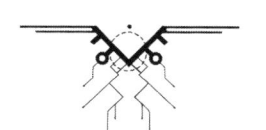

As it happened though, she saw Meshi poke his head around the door to the backroom.

"Meshi!" she called from outside and waved. She saw him nod and grab his keys from the counter-top that ran along the left-hand wall as he walked to the door to let her in. The large metallic lock thunked as the key turned three times to undo the deadbolt, with the shop bell above the door ringing out lightly as Meshi opened the door for Lex and let her in.

"What are you doing here?" Meshi asked.

"I came to get a new burner phone," Lex began, all too loudly. "If you have another."

"Well, you're just in time." Meshi replied. "I was going to phone you just now to come to the shop, but your timing is perfect." He locked the door again and motioned for her to head to the back room.

"Why? What's going on?" she asked, her chest tightening with fear that perhaps the cops were onto them already and were in the process of quashing their resistance movement before it even got off the ground.

"Just come to the back room." Meshi replied. "Trust me, it's fine."

Still nervous but feeling obliged to comply with Meshi's request, Lex walked to the back room and pushed the door open all the way in order to walk inside. From the doorway she immediately saw why Akoni hadn't been in the metro station. He was there, in Meshi's back room with some girl Lex had never seen before.

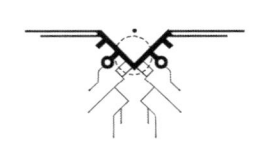

The girl was a lot like Akoni, she had shaggy hair that was just below her ears, some of which covered her face and had a slightly spiky quality to it. There were streaks of bright blue throughout it, but the majority of it was a dusky darker shade of blonde. She was wearing a blue PVC material bomber style jacket that shone in any form of light when she moved around. Her neck was laden with various chain necklaces, some of which had trinkets or lockets on them and some didn't. Lex noted that one of them did have what appeared to be a somewhat large padlock, perhaps worn as a joke of some kind. She was wearing tight, black trousers and a faded t-shirt of some obscure band under the jacket. Definitely an interesting number, Lex wondered who this girl was and why she was in Meshi's back room, but she assumed she wanted to be part of the resistance as well. She was right.

"Yo Lex, what's happening'?" Akoni asked in greeting.

"I missed you in the metro station today." Lex replied. "I'm good. How are you?"

"Never better." Akoni winked with his non-bionic eye. "This is Fade – the hacker I told you about."

Fade gave Lex an up nod in greeting. "How's it going?"

Lex smiled. "Good, you?"

"Same."

"Fade's been hacking since she was like twelve or some shit." Akoni said. "She's the best I know, and I know several."

"That's good. We'll need someone who knows their stuff." Lex replied. "Where did you learn how to hack?"

"Self-taught." Fade replied. "I used to hack into big corporate systems for fun and just to fuck with them. You ever heard of Serenity?"

Lex thought for a minute. "Serenity?"

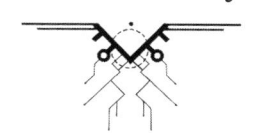

"Yeah, the hacker."

She had indeed. According to the press, Serenity had caused such bad problems for a bank that they needed to completely wipe their systems and use an ancient backup. They'd reportedly lost millions in manpower because they needed to put about a million accounts back into the system manually and even more of their clients had no access to their money for close to a week.

"Yeah – that's the one with the bank right?"

"Yup."

"What about them?"

"Not to boast, but that was me."

"What? No way!"

"Very way." Akoni chimed in.

"Why'd you do it?" Lex asked.

Fade tried to hide a rather proud grin. "Like I said. Just to fuck with them a bit."

"Fair enough."

Meshi moved from the door then, smiling. "Anyone want some tea?"

Akoni and Fade both agreed. Lex looked at her watch. It was already after twelve, but Damian's office wasn't far.

"Alright." she agreed, assuming one cup of tea and a chat wouldn't take long.

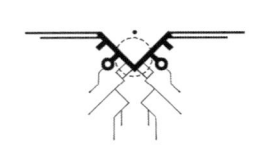

Chapter Thirteen

She was wrong though. Their conversation went on for over an hour and nearly caused her to be late for her lunch date with Damian. They talked about the general idea, how it came to pass and Akoni ended up learning more about Lex than he ever expected to. He had no idea she was so loyal to her family that she'd be willing to take on the President in order to set things right, but then again, who wouldn't? The guy was a fucking prick, with more and more people beginning to realise this fact, a resistance movement wasn't far behind at all.

It turned out that Fade knew a lot more than she let on about the whole thing. She'd obviously been talking about it with Akoni, but that wasn't an issue. The more people they got on their side the better. The only issue was with people talking freely about it with no real discernment. Kind of like someone giving away state secrets in a pub after he'd had too many shots of premium whisky kind of thing. People could flap their gums without planning to. That was the only concern.

Akoni was different though. He was quite careful about who he talked to about most things. As it was, he had felt uneasy that Lex knew so much about him and his family, purely by having met him briefly when they were kids, but that wasn't common. He kept to himself mostly in terms of who he shared what with and very few people knew the real Akoni. He preferred it that way. Something like the development of a resistance movement was along the same lines for him as telling people about himself. He just wouldn't do it – unless he had an extremely good reason.

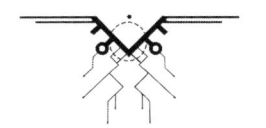

Lex was sure that getting Akoni on board had been a great idea. He seemed to know his stuff and was ridiculously street smart. But who wouldn't be if they'd lived the life Akoni did? He had to fend for himself at most every turn, so it was only natural that he'd be good at this kind of thing. He'd mentioned that he could get his hands on some tools and materials from which they could make small bombs. They'd be crude but effective and would get a couple of points across. The issue was selecting targets. What would make a good first target?

They pondered that question for some time with each of them having an idea about where to target but none of them could agree. Lex said they should target Mason himself, but Akoni and Fade, along with Meshi all agreed that would be too brazen for a first hit. They didn't necessarily want to target Mason to get their point across – they wanted to pressure him into changing his policies and he couldn't do that if he wound up injured or dead, and rumour had it that his potential replacement-in-waiting was twice as bad as he was. Maybe worse.

The agreement they reached was that they'd meet again the next day with all those who expressed an interest in helping with the whole plan. They'd take a vote on what the first target would be and then they'd go from there. Akoni promised to get as many materials as possible before the meeting so they could start fashioning the bombs.

"How do you know where to get this kind of stuff?" Lex asked, mildly horrified.

"Hey. When you live like I do, you know how to get a lot of things." Akoni replied. "Besides. It's not the first time and I have my ways."

"What, so you've done this before then?"

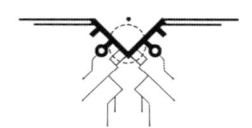

"No. I didn't say that. Just because I bought the stuff before doesn't mean I've made a bomb out of it. Some of those ingredients are common household things, you know."

"So, what? You bought bleach for the hell of it?" Lex asked, trying not to sound condescending.

"I do have a place I live in that I clean. I'm not a total bum."

He had a point. He did always appear to be wearing clean, or, well, clean-ish clothes and he seemed at least decently fed, so he must have had somewhere he went at night. He surely didn't spend every waking hour in the metro station hoping for some unsuspecting person to come through that he and his band of miscreants could shake them down for what could quite literally be pennies.

"What else do you need, out of curiosity?" Lex asked.

Akoni smiled a devilish grin. "Leave that to me."

"Why do I get the feeling you've done this before?"

"Maybe I have. Maybe I haven't."

That was enough for Lex. It was pushing onto nearly quarter past one anyway and she didn't want to keep Damian waiting.

"I have to go." she said.

"Where are you off to in such a hurry?" Akoni teased.

"I'm meeting a friend for lunch. If you must know."

"Boyfriend?"

"No, he's not my boyfriend."

Fade, Meshi and Akoni all laughed.

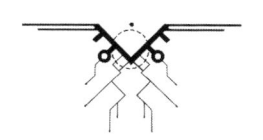

"Sure, sure," Akoni said.

"Ask Meshi." Lex replied, getting slightly annoyed with the inquisition. "He knows Damian."

Meshi nodded. "They're just friends. Have been for years."

"So knock it off." Lex said, trying not to blush. Things about boyfriends always made her blush and get shy. She wasn't even interested in anyone. Not really anyway.

"Fine. Boring," Akoni replied, winking at Fade. She just smiled and crossed her arms.

Lex gathered her stuff. "What time tomorrow then? And do you have a burner phone or not so I can text everyone?"

"Yes. Hang on." Meshi replied, going to a brown cardboard box with the word 'Misc.' scribbled across it in messy writing, one of many boxes he'd been packing up to take home for storage. He fished around for a moment and then came back over to Lex and handed her another phone, somewhat nicer than the previous one.

"It'll take you a while to send all those texts," he said. "Want some help? You do half the list and I'll do the other?"

"Sure," she replied. "I didn't really want to spend my entire evening sending texts but would have in the name of the cause."

"So I'm on explosive detail. You guys are texting. That leaves Fade needing a job." Akoni said, smiling a grin that could be considered somewhere between bad boyish and comical.

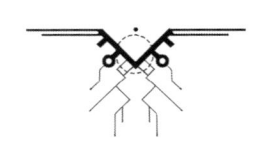

"Can you find somewhere for us to set up an HQ?" Meshi asked. "We can't keep meeting here. It's going to look suspicious with so many people suddenly coming and going in groups."

"True," Lex replied, remembering the unpleasantness that Meshi already occasionally dealt with from unknown toughs who seemed to intimidate him on the regular. "We need somewhere a bit more secretive."

"Don't worry," Fade began. "I know the perfect place."

Lex rushed up to the restaurant, 'Martinis' nearly ten minutes late, a fact that bothered her to no end. Being teased by Akoni wasn't exactly the excuse she wanted to have for being late and she was perturbed by the fact she'd allowed him to get under her skin about Damian. They weren't together but had some vague feelings for each other which neither had ever acted on due more to timing and life events than anything else. Lex wasn't sure she wanted a relationship with someone who travelled as much as Damian did, and he wasn't willing to give up his posting – not yet anyway. He was a driven businessman with something to prove, mainly to himself.

Damian was already sitting at the table when Lex got there, panting and obviously stressed out, muttering apologies about being late. She was regularly on time and the concept of being late made her stressed out, even though she knew Damian wouldn't overly mind, even if he was on a specific schedule and had to get back to the office.

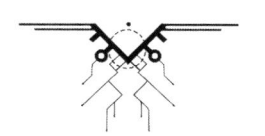

Lex sat down opposite Damian, grabbing the menu that had been placed casually on the table. "I'm so sorry I'm late," she began. He held up his hand .

"No need to apologise," he said. "I know how life is. Running around can get out of hand."

"You're telling me," she paused, catching her breath. "How's it going?"

"Eh, you know." he swished his red wine in his glass slowly. "The corporate world is going to the dogs."

"What'd you mean?" she opened the menu and began to look at the different options quickly, not overly reading them but feigning that she was.

"Oh, you know., he said. "Just the usual crap."

She didn't know though. She'd never really worked in a corporate environment and wasn't aware of just how difficult they could be to navigate and keep your head afloat. It was unlike Damian to express such outward disdain for the industry, so she figured something had happened. Perhaps he'd been given a chewing out by his manager over something or he'd failed to close a lucrative deal. Either way, he seemed stressed and bothered – two things that didn't suit his usual bubbly self at all.

"You're on the wine early," she noted, smirking.

"The way the day's going I'll be lucky if I'm not wasted by three," he replied.

Lex closed the menu then. "Okay, what's been going on? You've been surly since I got here. Are you pissed I'm late?"

Damian's eyes widened with innocence. "No!" he protested. "No, not at all! I'm sorry. I know I'm being a total downer. We got some bad news at work today and it's really getting to me."

"Oh no. What happened?"

"It sounds like they're downsizing. Something about losing a government contract and they don't need almost half the office anymore."

Lex's heart sank for Damian. "What's that mean for you? You're high up enough that you're fairly safe aren't you?"

Damian shrugged and took another, rather large sip of wine. "No idea yet. They said they need to wait to see how it plays out. I'm thinking of applying out now anyway. It can't be good. It almost never is when this happens."

Lex opened the menu again, anxiety rising in her chest. Damian's job meant the world to him and she knew that. He seemed very defeated, annoyed and generally hurt that a company that he'd given so much of his time and energy to could just line him up with the other to cast him aside when it suited them. It was one of the reasons she'd always steered clear of working for anything larger than fifty people or so. It seemed the smaller the operation, the more human they treated you.

It did start Lex's brain moving though, thinking that perhaps Damian might be interested in joining the resistance movement against the government. He did have motive, after all and he may know some insider kind of stuff that could come in handy, but Lex wasn't sure what he could possibly know. She knew he'd worked on several big contracts with EverDawn and other government agencies in the past, but to what extent she was unsure. He still could know something though. Even just knowing what coffee people drank in which offices could offer them an 'in' that they could exploit for their own gains.

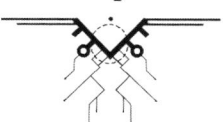

"Won't it reflect badly on you in this situation if you go back to work drunk?" Lex asked.

"I took the rest of the day off. I said I had an appointment." Damian replied. "Not exactly a lie. I was coming to see you. That's kind of an appointment."

Lex smiled. "How about I buy you lunch today?" she suggested, wanting to butter him up a bit. Despite the fact they were best friends, she wasn't sure how to broach the subject about Damian possibly joining the resistance movement and the possible charges of destruction of property, vandalism and even terrorism it could bring if they got caught.

"You don't have to do that." Damian said, sipping the wine again.

"Don't be silly," Lex replied. "You bought my dinner last time and I've suddenly come into a bit of money I won't be needing to use since I can't get online at any of the Spots."

Damian raised an eyebrow. "No? Why not?"

Lex went into the whole story about how the last time she used a Spot to get online she'd felt like she was under surveillance from doormen and even the bartenders. Not only that, but getting credits to get online had been difficult to say the least, with the only way to get them being through Meshi, who got them through strange means that were potentially illegal. She told him about the conversation she'd had with her parents and brother in hushed tones at the corner table in room seven, despite all the other rooms being empty and the fact that no one was much interested in the user experience anymore and how there was literally no one there when she turned up.

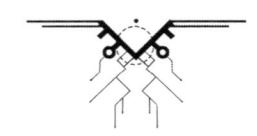

As she recounted the tale to Damian the memory suddenly flowed back to her that the receptionist had both been rather surprised and disgusted by the fact she'd been there to get online. It made sense now that she'd gathered more evidence from the likes of Grandma Alice as to the plans even a decade before to turn Ascension into essentially an elitist playground for the rich and famous. It was all starting to come together and it was impressive just how long they'd been phasing it out for. Sure, it had taken several years of slow and gradual work, but now that it was essentially completed, the absence of Ascension was palpable.

"Jeez." Damian said finally, finishing his wine. "How the hell did you figure all this out?"

"Well, Grandma used to work for EverDawn. She heard murmurings when she was still there. She gets together with some people who still work there and I guess she gets some of the latest gossip from them."

Damian was quiet for a moment, contemplating the problem. He had never really used the Spot interface. No one he knew had Ascended – or not yet, anyway. Many people were in the same boat, they planned to eventually once they reached a certain age or had completed or achieved certain goals in the 'outside' world, but by the time they'd done those things it was too late. Ascension was closed off to the common man, courtesy of the asshat-in-charge, President Mason.

"I guess people will get sick of his antics sooner or later and try to stop him somehow." Damian replied, still slightly incredulous that something like this could happen in the modern day. "I can see it happening."

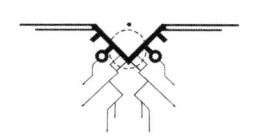

Lex saw her chance but didn't want to blurt out anything about their group or the plans. Instead she opted for a more covert way to tell Damian about the resistance movement that was gaining speed, and ask if he wanted to join up to help stop Mason before he could turn the world into a playground for the elite.

She took out her burner phone and started typing furiously under the table, including Damian's number in the recipient box, which she knew off the top of her head. She'd texted him enough times to know it by heart and while she never thought it'd come in useful, it sure did then.

"What are you doing?" he asked, peering over the table to see what she was doing in her lap as the waitress came over to take their orders.

"What can I get you guys?" she asked.

Lex kept texting while she stated her order: chicken Caesar salad, a glass of Sauvignon blanc and a glass of water.

"Another glass of wine for you, sir?" the waitress asked Damian.

"I think perhaps a bottle," he replied. "And the steak. May as well go out with a bang."

"What?" the waitress asked.

"Nothing. Never mind. It's not important," he replied, watching Lex, who looked up from her lap occasionally, a sheepish look on her face. She knew how bad it was to be texting when in the presence of others, a concept that was considered rude by many. The waitress gave her a bit of a look as it was, a look that suggested rude behaviour, but she just took the menus and walked away. Lex knew it was bad form, but far be it from her to suddenly verbally discuss the group.

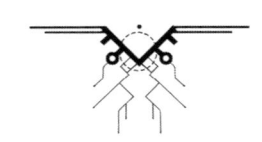

"Check your phone," she said to Damian, putting the burner back in her handbag.

"What? Why?"

"I've sent you a text."

Damian's face contorted in confusion. "A text? Now?"

"Just read the damn thing." Lex replied, getting impatient.

Damian rolled his eyes slightly. "Fine."

He reached for his phone from his jacket pocket and punched in his passcode. He recognised the tell-tale symbol of a received text message on his phone and glanced up at Lex who was decidedly avoiding eye contact. He opened the message, but saw it as a strange number and said "What number is that? That's not your number."

"I have a different phone," she said. "For sensitive conversations."

"What the fuck have you gotten yourself involved with?" Damian asked under his breath, opening the text and reading it silently. It was more of a rhetorical question than a demand for information.

After what felt like an eternity to Lex, he finally put his phone away, just as the waitress returned with their drinks. He waited until the waitress left again and was fully engaged with another table before he hissed across the table

"What the fuck are you on about?"

Lex looked around, suddenly aware that the restaurant seemed far fuller than she'd like it to.

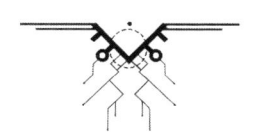

"Keep it down!" she whispered harshly.

Damian looked around and sheepishly read the message again. He tried to remain objective and open minded. It made sense, especially from Lex's point of view. Maybe it wasn't such a bad idea and was something that was necessary in order to incite change. He thought about his own position and how the government was involved in orchestrating the downfall of not just himself, but many, many others who had worked their way up through the ranks by sweating, shedding blood and choosing the bright fluorescent lights of the office for multiple hours per day rather than finding true life in hobbies, friends and family. It wasn't fair. Nothing about anything that was happening on either end of the spectrum was fair. It was difficult though because everyone had grown accustomed to fairness, equality and everyone having everything they could possibly need. It was only since President Mason came along that there'd been any inkling of issues in equality or fairness. Sure some people had it better or easier. But no one was ever denied anything they really needed – whether it was food, clothing, shelter or more.

"Okay. We'll talk about it," he said, putting his phone away. "So how's your Grandma?"

"Uh… yeah she's good." Lex replied. "Still as busy as ever. Her garden did really well this year."

"Awesome." Damian replied. "I miss her roast duck with orange sauce. That was always so succulent."

"Come over for dinner some night. She'd love it – and love cooking for you. I think she gets bored just cooking for the two of us."

"I'd like that." Damian said. "I haven't had a home cooked meal in so long thanks to work." he paused. "For all the good that did me."

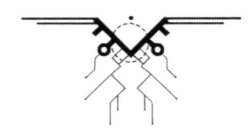

"You're talking like you've already lost your job." Lex said. "Have you?"

"No! No nothing like that. I guess I'm just pessimistic. And they made things seem pretty bad, so I'm not exactly hopeful." Damian replied. "Besides, better to be prepared."

"I suppose." Lex began, being interrupted by their lunch orders delivered by a different waitress than before.

Despite the fact they'd not said much verbally about anything to do with the resistance movement or anything to do with targeting the government, Lex couldn't shake the feeling they were being watched. She chalked it up to being paranoid, given the fact shit was about to get very real very fast, but tried to put it out of her head and enjoy her meal with Damian.

The rest of the lunch went off without a hitch, as it normally did. Damian had some reservations about what Lex was getting herself into, but he hoped that she knew what she was doing and she would get out before things got too hairy.

They walked out of Martini's and into the street just as one of Damian's bosses walked past, stopping and giving Damian a look.

"I thought you had an appointment?" the boss guy asked, a sour look on his face.

"I do." Damian replied levelly, hoping the smell of wine wasn't evident on his breath.

"Lunch isn't an appointment," the boss stated, glancing at Lex.

"I'm allowed to have a lunch hour, *especially* seeing as I left work at lunch, and I'm taking the rest of the day off."

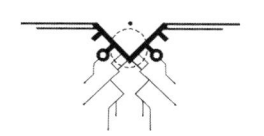

Damian stated back. "This is my time to do with what I want."

"Hmpf. We'll see how much freedom you have like that in the coming weeks," boss guy said before walking off. "I doubt you'll enjoy so many concessions."

Damian and Lex watched the boss man walk away, an air of arrogance and self-importance about him, evident in his swagger with his expensive suit and a demeanour that was more akin to a wet rag than a human being. Lex wondered how Damian could sell so much of himself to people like that, but never questioned him, nor tried to talk him out of it. She knew he was worth more than being treated as a workhorse for an already rich set of bosses, but something about the job had attracted him, so who was she to try and stop him?

"What a prick." Lex said matter-of-factly to no one in particular.

Damian just watched his boss go, a strange new sensation growing in his soul. Contempt? Anger? Some kind of loathing feeling that meant he was liable to not care if he was made redundant at this point. He remembered Lex's text then, and turned around simply and said,

"When do you need me?"

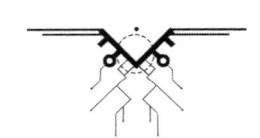

Chapter Fourteen

Lex returned home after lunch, half expecting to see Akoni in the subway and being surprised again when she didn't. It wasn't like him to not be around, but she supposed he'd set the record straight earlier on having a home to go to, so it wasn't overly shocking that he wasn't around. Maybe they'd shaken down all the people there were to shake down, done all the things they could for money and were having a day or two off. It worked for her. Despite her casual acquaintanceship with Akoni she still wasn't going to make the assumption that his crew would leave her alone in his absence. It was definitely better to be safe than sorry.

Grandma was hard at work at the stove when she got there, cooking something that smelled amazing for dinner. It wasn't even halfway done yet, but it was already smelling delectable. Grandma Alice heard someone coming in the door and popped her head around the wall, looking down at Lex in the mudroom as she came into the house.

"Oh good, you're back," Grandma Alice said. "There's someone here I want you to meet."

"Meet? Who?" Lex asked, looking up at Grandma, curious and slightly anxious at who she wanted her to meet.

Lex took off her boots and climbed the stairs into the kitchen, stopping to hug Grandma Alice before she went into the living room to see who was there. The kettle in the kitchen was on and steaming away with a couple of mugs set to one side on a tray, the good tea bags in a small glass bowl on the tray.

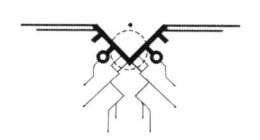

"Take that into the living room," Grandma Alice said, nodding at the tray. "I'll be in, in a minute with the kettle water."

Lex did as she was asked, her curiosity almost driving her mad by the time she picked up the tray and began to move to the living room with it. The cups jingled slightly and the teaspoons clinked against the china making the tell-tale tinkling sound of tea soon to be had. As she rounded the corner, her feet moving from linoleum onto thick, almost shag rug, she looked up and saw a young woman sitting on the couch, looking slightly awkward with her hands clasped between her knees and a slightly worried look on her face, gazing out the window at the dying light of day.

The woman looked over as Lex entered the room and smiled a weak smile at Lex as she put the tray down on the coffee table.

Reaching over with her right hand, she stood up and said "Hi, I'm Jade. A friend of Alice's."

Lex took her hand and shook it. "I'm Lex."

"I figured," Jade said smiling and sitting back down. "She asked me over to talk to you."

"About what?" Lex asked, trying to sound confident and not at all alarmed. She hoped Grandma hadn't said anything she shouldn't have to anyone, but then again, Lex knew Grandma. She was certain she wouldn't have.

Alice came around the corner then, carrying a teapot and a plate of small tea biscuits. "She doesn't know yet. Not everything. I only told her about the problems with using Spots."

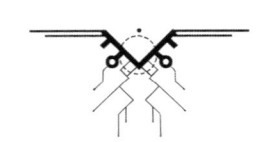

"Oh," Lex replied, pulling her scarf off and putting it on the back of Grandpa's old armchair before sitting down and preparing to pour Jade a cup of tea. "How do you take it?"

"Just milk."

Lex poured a cup of tea from the warm pot; the hot steam washing over her hands and warming them against the chill of the evening air since she'd forgotten her mittens earlier that day. She put the kettle down as Grandma Alice took a seat on the couch next to Jade.

"Tea Grandma?" she asked.

"Not for the moment, dear."

She handed Jade the milk before pouring herself a cup of tea and settling in on Grandad's chair properly. There was a long pause, something that Lex was eager to end. The problem was that she didn't know how. Whatever Jade had to say was going to be important, but she didn't want to spook her. The woman looked as though she might get flighty. That was understandable though. There was probably a lot at stake for her. No, Lex wasn't going to coax it out of her, whatever it was. She just needed to be patient and let the woman speak. Thankfully, she soon found her voice as she nursed her cup.

"So," Jade said awkwardly. "I understand you've been having trouble accessing the Ascension interface from a user standpoint."

"You could say that."

"A lot of people have." Jade drank while gathering her thoughts. "But that's not the whole story. I think Alice filled you in on a lot of the actual story?"

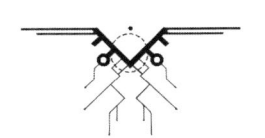

"I did," Grandma Alice said. "As much as I knew, but I know there's more."

"There is," Jade said, nervously looking from Alice to Lex. "What do you plan to do with this information anyway?"

Lex looked at Grandma Alice then, who just gave her a slight nod as though to confirm that Jade was safe and wasn't going to go ratting them out to the police or anything.

"Well, I might have kind of gone and started a bit of a resistance movement," Lex said. "Nothing too serious, yet, but we have about thirty members so far and counting."

Jade's eyes lit up. "That's amazing! I hope anything I give you will help you take down that snake Mason."

Snake Mason? That was interesting. Even people within the EverDawn corporation had begun to turn on President Mason and were willing to give information freely if it meant stopping him. Something was going on, and she had a feeling she was about to find out more than she ever thought possible.

"So you hate Mason?" Lex asked, hoping to push the idea a bit to see how much she could pry.

"He's a dick," Jade replied, with Alice agreeing. "He's gotten worse than before. He was always bad. I mean, he one hundred percent stopped people from having access to Ascension like it was meant to be, but now he's making us download all the file of those he says are undesirables in the system and shelve them in archives."

Lex was quiet as the news hit her. "Like my parents."

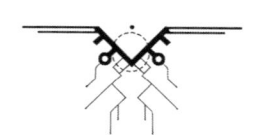

"Like everyone's parents," Jade said matter of factly. "Like anyone. If you haven't given ludicrous amounts of money to his personal 'charities' and charity foundations, you're considered someone he doesn't want around, clogging up the memory or something, so he is getting rid of all of them."

"Are my parents still in the system?" Lex asked.

"No idea. Sorry."

"Is there a way you can find out?"

"Well… maybe. But, it's difficult."

"How? I'll give anything a try at this point." Lex replied, sounding more and more desperate.

"I'll have to do it," Jade said. "At work. I'll see if I can get in tomorrow and maybe move them into a folder somewhere that the higher ups won't find." She paused. "Or make a backup of the files."

Lex thought for a moment. It sounded like a good idea, and likewise Jade sounded like she could be handy in their resistance movement.

"You sound like you know a bit about the inner workings of EverDawn," she said to Jade, who nodded.

"You could say that."

"We have a small group of people who are interested in trying to send a few messages to the government… if you're interested in joining up with us. Your knowledge could come in handy," Lex suggested.

"I dunno." Jade replied. "Sounds a bit sketchy."

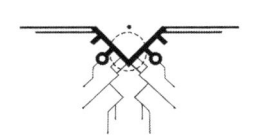

"Well you hate Mason as much as the rest of us do," Lex said, hopeful she could talk Jade around into being on their team. It would pay heavily to have someone well versed in EverDawn in the group – someone who still worked there to boot.

"What would I have to do?" Jade asked, slightly fearful of what her involvement in a group like that could do to her personally and professionally.

"Nothing much. You don't even need to meet the others if you don't want," Lex began. "You can retain total anonymity. If you have any details on the inner workings of EverDawn that we can use to our benefit, that would be perfect."

Jade thought about it for a minute. Of course there was some danger and risk involved, but it also could potentially help bring down President Mason, or at least stop him from making anything else elitist and out of bounds of the ordinary person. Sure, she'd never done anything like this before, but not only was there a first time for everything, but she'd be doing mankind a service by making sure things like Ascension remained free and for the people. The resistance would move forward regardless of whether Jade was on board or not, the only difference would be the speed at which they moved. Without her there would still be progress, sure, but they would be taking strides with her help.

Lex found herself holding her breath while Jade considered it. It was a big decision and she was entitled to a second or two, but that didn't make it any easier for Lex.

"I'll do it," she replied after some thought and relief washed over Lex like the clean beach waves of her childhood. "I want to stay anonymous though. No one can know I'm feeding you information from the inside."

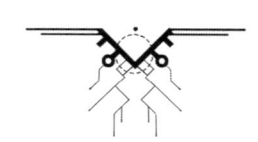

"That works for me." Lex said. "The fewer people that get caught up in the messy part of this the better."

"Don't do anything I wouldn't do." Grandma Alice said with a grin.

"From what I know about you," Jade began, smiling and half-laughing, "that doesn't leave much out."

Chapter Fifteen

The next morning, bright and early, the whole group of roughly thirty members of the resistance met in the back room of Meshi's shop. Crammed in like sardines once again, there was an air of excitement and anxiousness about the place which was palpable. Anyone could almost cut the tension in the air with a knife, especially considering there were several people scattered throughout the crowd who had histories with each other, not necessarily in the good way, and who were known for trying to start stuff. Luckily though it seemed that, at least for the time being, people were willing to put their individual differences aside in the name of camaraderie in taking down a common enemy.

"Can I have everyone's attention?" Meshi called into the crowd, clapping his hands as he did so. It took a moment or two before everyone turned to look at him and quit chattering amongst themselves, but when they did, Meshi continued.

"We have Akoni bringing us some equipment shortly that we can use to start up our coordinated attacks on various governmental and public targets. Do we have a list of targets yet?"

Someone Lex didn't recognise raised his hand. "Yeah, a couple of us came up with some."

"This is good," Meshi replied. "We're halfway there. Now we just need-"

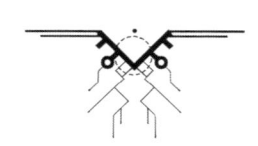

He was interrupted by Akoni banging on the door with a force that almost took it down. Lex rushed to the front of the shop, being careful to close the backroom door so no passers-by could peer in. She ripped the front door open and stepped to the side to let Akoni in, along with one of his usual subway cronies. Both were carrying very conspicuous duffel bags, making them look like drifters on a one-way ticket out of town.

"What's with the bags?" Lex asked.

"It's the stuff," Akoni said, pushing past her to the back room. "We're making CO_2 bombs."

"What're those?"

"You'll see."

Akoni walked into the backroom and threw one of the bags onto the table next to the coffee maker. He began to pull out smaller plastic bags filled with black powder, small pieces of rope that Lex assumed were fuses and something that looked like shotgun shells. He lined them up, enough for what looked like hundreds of bombs.

"Jesus Akoni. How many bombs are we making?" someone asked.

Akoni smiled, his bionic eye glowing. "That's the beauty of these bad boys. You make dozens and you can set them off in really inconspicuous places, enough to cause a whole lot of havoc and damage but with something the size of a lighter. Or thereabouts."

He opened all of the bags except the black powder ones, taking out what appeared to be a shotgun casing and a piece of fuse.

"This," he began "is how you fuck some shit up without getting too hairy. It's perfect for sending a message and making things highly inconvenient."

"What do you do with it?" someone else asked.

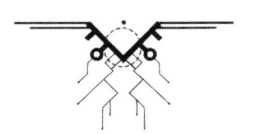

Akoni smiled and half laughed. "I'll get to that."

Lex crossed her arms, looking closer at the bags on the table and then Akoni who was fiddling with the casing and fuse. "Why do I get the feeling you've done this before?"

"What? Me?" he asked, feigning innocence. "Never."

It was the kind of humorous protest that read like he had done all this before a hundred times, and more. Lex was sure he had. You didn't live the life Akoni lived without getting your hands dirty occasionally, and that's exactly why he was the right person for the job of sourcing the materials as well as teaching others how to make bombs. He'd been in the position before, not just making bombs but placing them and also evading authorities – all traits and knowledge their motley crew needed at their disposal now and in the coming days.

"Anyone who wants to learn how to make bombs, join Akoni over here," Meshi called out. Numerous people got to their feet and crowded around Akoni and his collection of strange things that would be combined to make small bombs people could carry inconspicuously in things like pockets, inside shoes or even up their sleeves. The CO_2 bombs were a great starting point to be sure, something that was small and easily made on the go, easily hidden but packed a powerful punch. They didn't want to kill anyone, at least not yet and even then, only if it was necessary, but using small bombs powerful enough to wreck certain things, break windows, smash glass and the like was just what the doctor ordered.

Lex looked around at the crowd then, realising she didn't see Fade. Her heart skipped a beat as her anxiety tried to get the better of her, but managed to stay calm.

"Akoni, where's Fade?" she asked, trying to remain casual and chill.

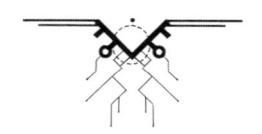

"She's finding a base," he replied, measuring out some of the black powder before taking a piece of fuse from his friend and inserting it in the shotgun casing. "Why?"

"No reason," Lex said, thinking a bigger base would be a great idea, hopefully something out of the way on an industrial estate or, even better, out of town.

"Don't worry," Akoni said, fastening the fuse into the casing tightly and looking up at Lex, half shrugging. "I'm on it."

She supposed he was. He did seem to know what he was doing, and while it was tempting to sit back and let Akoni take control of the whole operation if he wanted to, she wasn't sure about relinquishing control to someone that wasn't in on the ground floor, so to speak. While it wasn't about maintaining control out of a sense of wanting people to follow her, or view her as the leader of the resistance, she didn't want it to spiral into something akin to gangland warfare, tit for tat attacks or something that the movement was never meant to be. It wasn't that she thought Akoni would cause issues like this, but he could, so it was better to have him as more of a consultant than anything, even if there were no real 'official leader' of the resistance, at least not yet.

Lex left Akoni to his job of making bombs with several other people, Fade was finding a headquarters, so that left agreeing on targets. She collared Meshi and they went over to the guy who'd previously said they'd picked out some potentially decent targets that would, indeed, get the attention of President Mason and his pals. It turned out his name was Jer, but whether that was short for Jerry, Jerome or some other name starting with J remained to be seen. He just wanted to be called Jer.

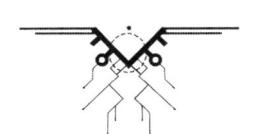

"You have some ideas?" Lex asked, hoping to make it fast. She was still feeling generally uneasy with the way things were turning out but was forcing herself to push on with the plan despite her misgivings about the whole concept. While it was something that would help many people in the end, she wasn't sure that she was the person to be partially spearheading the project, and so it was something of a point of anxiety for her. She just wanted to get the whole operation to a place where others could somewhat take control and she'd hopefully more or less fade into the background.

"Just a few," Jer said, pulling out his wallet and fishing around in the inner pockets. He clearly didn't want to be caught with a short list of potential bombing targets by anyone in any position of authority. Not that it had necessarily come to street patrols by police, indiscriminately searching civilians – yet – but it could. Very soon. There had been enough issues with restrictions of rainwater collection and solar panelling and whatnot that it was clear the freedoms that had been voted for in many past elections and reformed through many progressive governments were slowly being stripped away and it wouldn't take much for them to unleash the police to do random street checks just to keep the civilians in line.

Jer unfolded the piece of paper, putting his wallet on his lap. "Post offices would be a good place to start. Maybe bus or train stations too. You can put some of those little bombs they're making in backpacks in lockers and whatnot. Really blow a chunk of the place away."

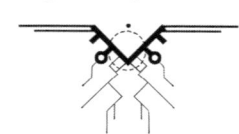

Lex could feel her anxiety rising at the thought of targeting a place that civilians could get caught up in the blast or the problems, but tried to remind herself that it's sometimes the cost of freedom. No one who was ever free got there without being complicit in a crime or two. It didn't mean they were bad people. Bad people did things without conscience or forethought for the consequences. This was totally different. She'd been thinking about the consequences, perhaps a bit too much.

She nodded in agreement, much to her own dismay. Meshi as well, who seemed much more stoic and steelier than she did about the whole operation. He'd been on the whisky again. She could smell it on him, but it didn't make him unreliable. In fact, if anything it got him slightly more riled, more energetic and braver, as drinking often did with people. With Meshi, it was all in the right ways though and never anything overboard in terms of aggression.

"I think the train station is a good idea," Meshi said. "And the post office. Both would interrupt the government in some ways for a bit. But what if we actually attacked EverDawn itself? Send the message right home that we aren't happy with their new 'policies'?"

"I like that idea." Lex began, immediately thinking of Jade. "I think I may know someone who can help us as well."

"Really? Who have you been meeting in secret without us?" Meshi teased lightly.

"No one in particular," Lex replied. "A friend of my Grandmother's."

"Which friend?" Meshi narrowed his eyes. "She has a lot of friends."

"No one you know. An old work friend."

Meshi's eyes lit up suddenly. "Any chance of some of her sweet and sour?"

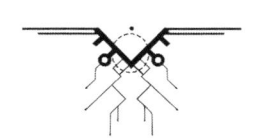

Lex smiled. "I'll see what I can do."

Jer tore up the piece of paper. "Sounds like we have a plan then."

Akoni heard them then from across the room and came over. "Where are we hitting?"

Lex looked at him sideways. "Nowhere. Yet."

"Aw come on. The bombs are almost done. We gotta get this show on the road."

"Maybe a thug, but he's right," Meshi replied looking at Lex. "We should do something as soon as possible. We can always build up to EverDawn after you talk to your contact."

More and more people turned to look at Lex expectantly, wanting some kind of guidance as to what they should do next and if they should draw straws for a small team of individuals to target somewhere in the next few hours. She looked around the room and realised that, like it or not, she was one of the supposed leaders of this motley crew of individuals who each had their own reasoning behind wanting to get vengeance on the government.

"Okay." She relented, knowing deep down that the sooner they got started, the better. "Who wants to volunteer?"

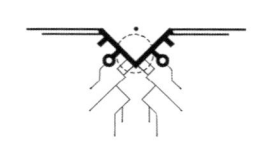

The group began to look around the room at each other, seeing who would volunteer themselves for the job first. No one seemed all that concerned about putting themselves forward, something that was surprising considering how many people were clearly on the side of hitting somewhere hard and fast. Even Jer was hesitant to put his hand up in the first instance, although when he saw no one else was willing, he thought he'd break the ice and raised his left hand.

"I'm in," he said gruffly. "And I vote we hit the train station."

"I'll join him," Akoni said, putting the bombs back into duffel bags. "It will be fun."

Jer turned to look at Akoni. "I don't know about fun, but it will be good to have someone of your knowledge on board with it."

"What's that supposed to mean?" Akoni asked, sounding offended.

"Nothing," Jer insisted. "Just you seem to know what you're doing is all."

Lex tried to hide a grin. Akoni did seem to know what he was doing and it was entirely likely he'd done things like this before, according to his checkered past and the fact he hung out in metro stations with people who probably should have been put in juvenile detention if not jail five years ago.

"I'd take that as a compliment," Meshi said to Akoni. "He means you actually know what you're doing with all this shit."

"Fine, fine." Akoni relented. "No harm done. Anyone else want to volunteer for this risky business?"

Numerous people exchanged nervous glances. One woman raised her hand as though she was still in school and asked "Is it truly risky? What *is* the risk?"

"As long as we keep it quiet and quick the risk should be minimal," Jer said in response, crossing his arms.

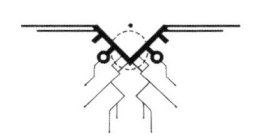

The woman pondered the answer for a moment before nodding in agreement. "I'm in then."

"That's three," Akoni mused. "A fourth would probably be a good idea. Two to set the bomb. Two for lookout."

"I'll go," Meshi said. "I'm keen to get everything started."

The whole room nodded in agreement, but whether it was actual agreement or more of a relief that people weren't being picked at random remained to be seen. Lex wasn't ready to get her hands dirty, and in her mind she was already taking a risk by getting Jade involved. If the heat really came down, the authorities could even implicate Grandma Alice in the plot, something Lex wanted to avoid. That many people willing to help was a strange notion, until she remembered that these were black market members and affiliates for the most part. Not to forget, Mason had it coming. Still, as appreciative as she was that they were there, she felt almost separate from them – like there was a divide between those who had already lost their innocence and her, Jade and Grandma Alice. She tried to remind herself that innocence wasn't a luxury that she could have access to, not since President Mason came into power and took away such basic rights. They were changing that though.

"You guys just be careful," Lex said. "We don't want anyone getting arrested at this early stage. And if you do you'll need to be prepared to take one for the team and not say anything to give anyone away. As far as anyone's concerned you're a crazy one man show. A lone wolf. Someone just doing it because they wanted to for their own ends."

"Chill out," Akoni replied. "I know what I'm doing. Pretty sure we all do." The others nodded in agreement.

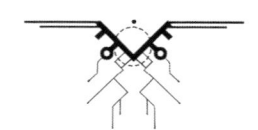

Lex looked at them, an air of worry rising in her. What else was new though? She sighed and nodded, knowing full well that the machine she and Meshi had put into being was quickly moving out of her control and there was little, if anything she could do.

Akoni grinned. "That's better. We're all in this shit together, right?"

Chapter Sixteen

It was already nearly half past two when Lex's burner phone buzzed with a message from Fade. *'Action group meeting 3pm.'* Nothing more. Lex knew it would be in the back room of Meshi's shop. The omission of the location was deliberate, although making messages clear enough without spilling any information had taken some getting used to for Lex and others unaccustomed to clandestine working conditions. The whole thing was like some big puzzle or a game show, although nobody seemed to be able to claim any prizes in life.

She grabbed her bag and bolted out, eager to get down there, but also keenly aware of whether or not she was being followed. In her area, like all of the poorer areas, she was used to checking over her shoulder and keeping a good grasp on her bag. It was just the way. In these times though, there was an extra reason to keep light footed – not that President Mason and his cronies really looked at the slums. It was people in the area dropping them in it that they really needed to worry about. Nobody liked a snitch, but nobody liked living in a place where the next meal wasn't guaranteed either. Sometimes, reporting to the President and his lackeys seemed like a safe bet on a better life.

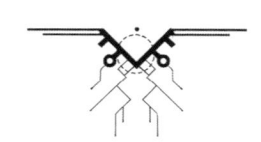

Lex made it to Meshi's just before three. Akoni had already turned up, so had Fade. Meshi had probably been there for some hours before, prepping the room and generally working around the shop, trying to retain some sense of normalcy about the place in case the cops decided to show up again. He needed it to look like it was at least somewhat normal – selling antiques and general supplies. Nothing at all out of the ordinary to attract unwanted attention. And there were so many people coming through that it might rouse suspicion. There were so many angles to consider. Honestly, she was starting to find a newfound respect for what Akoni did in a weird and twisted way. Her grandmother had always said that even bad fruits have their uses, even if that applied to jam, it kind of fitted Akoni and some of his crew.

Fade was sitting in the corner tinkering with her laptop, and had four bags with her. She had laid out the room like a small auditorium with chairs facing a large sheet that was hanging on a wall. The room felt much larger since Meshi had moved the last of his stock out. Fade had brought a projector from somewhere, and it looked like she was planning to present some information. Lex helped herself to tea, which seemed to have become a staple of their meetings since the coffee had proven to be unpalatable after a few sips. She found it comforting, in a strange way. A little bit of normalcy in an unusual environment.

Shortly, Jer and the woman, who Lex had learnt was named Cat, showed up too, quickly followed by a number of others. Fade walked across to the projector and plugged in her laptop. Switching it on, words appeared on the sheet: Accessing Restricted Areas. Fade walked to the front of the room, and the room took the hint and sat down. Akoni stayed standing at the back. He turned off the lights, leaving just the glow of his bionic eye in the darkness.

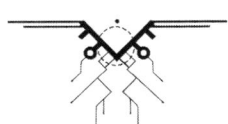

"Thank you for coming," said Fade, addressing the room. "I know you're all really keen to get moving, but I think there's some support that you need first." Lex was surprised at the confidence she suddenly seemed to have, but then remembered she'd heard Fade had been invited to talk at Black Hat conferences in the past. Fade continued, "I have done some research on our targets, and compiled some information on how their security operates." She pressed a button on a small device in her hand and another slide popped up: Access Cards. This one was accompanied by a map with some of the places Jer had picked out.

"All of these places, mostly rail stations, use RFID card readers. Akoni has been kind enough to run some recon with a hidden RFID reader and we've been able to harvest a significant number of staff passes, some of which I have cloned." Fade held up a blank white card, as if to demonstrate.

Cat raised her hand, her nerves kicking in slightly. "What if they don't work? Won't that be slightly awkward, and, well… dangerous?"

"They'll work," Fade grinned. "We have some of the best hackers in the field working on this kind of stuff, so don't you worry." She was clearly referring to herself in that category.

Cat went quiet, her question only somewhat answered. She had been concerned from day one when she'd heard about the whole plan – how exactly were they supposed to take down someone as seemingly untouchable as President Mason, EverDawn and the whole system in general? It was no small task and a harrowing feat, but she'd been talked around to it by Jer and some of his friends who had expressed a real sense of excitement and drive at the prospect of taking down the man. She had to admit, it was an intoxicating rush getting into something potentially so life-changing, not just for themselves, but for the world at large.

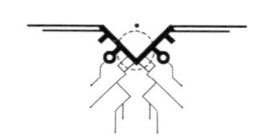

Fade went into a brief presentation around using the RFID cards to access a whole number of potentially brilliant places in which to place the CO_2 bombs and the like. They wouldn't do much damage – but it wasn't necessarily damage they were after. Not this early in the game. They were after getting their name out there, along with the message that no one would stop until they got access to Ascension and its interfacing back again. It had become far too elitist – but to what end? What could President Mason and his cronies possibly have to do in the program that was so significant that they wanted it all to themselves? It didn't make sense, but history has a way of repeating itself, and almost nothing any world leader did seemed to make sense when it came to wanting a stranglehold on one thing or another.

RFID card reader use was incredibly easy, and – as it turned out – incredibly easy to clone. Fade seemed to know exactly what she was doing when it came to this type of thing, which put many in the group at ease, at least somewhat. They needed a good tech person. Someone who really understood the ins and outs of everything because things were poised to get potentially very messy. No one wanted any undue problems to arise as a result of shoddy tech, especially since technology would be able to make or break their plans.

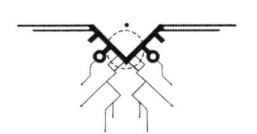

The presentation only took around thirty minutes to complete before Fade finished by asking if there were any questions. There weren't, but she insisted that if any arose that everyone could feel free to approach her at any time or send her an encrypted message with their query. Encryption was of paramount importance for obvious reasons, a point she stressed to everyone. They could take no risks once the first 'event' was underway and completed. From there on out, the authorities were sure to crack down on anyone who was remotely involved in any kind of possible insurrection or rebellion. With the new rules and laws that had already been put in place, it was likely new and arbitrary rules could be adopted – such as maximum numbers of people in public gatherings, a kind of vain attempt to control the further potential for uprisings.

The room began to empty out slowly, trying not to draw attention to a hugely popular, but nearly empty antiques store as would happen if droves of the rebellion group suddenly left the premises together. Only the few people who had volunteered for the first mission were asked to stay behind to get more information on the ins and outs of what they were going to be doing. The bombs were ready and now they just needed to discuss where to plant them. Luckily Fade had accessed a layout map of the train station they'd be targeting – the most popular and busy one in the whole city. It looked as though it was a straightforward type of deal, the final plans just needed smoothing over.

Akoni was unusually excited about the whole idea. He'd not been involved in something like this for a long period of time, often just getting up to no good in the Chinatown metro, often yearning to be a part of something more valuable to society as a whole, and here was his chance. Jer and Cat were more subdued in their anticipation of the mission, wanting it to go off without a hitch, but Akoni was somewhat more unbalanced in his desires. He revelled in the danger and excitement, letting it wash over him and energise him like nothing else could.

Once the room had cleared out and all the others had gone, Cat, Jer, Akoni, Lex and Meshi gathered around a large piece of paper onto which the plan had been roughly sketched out. There weren't many rules or suggestions, with Lex and Meshi generally being in agreement that they'd trust those in the field to follow their instincts when it came to where, how and when they did what they eventually would do. It made it not only easier, but insulated just about everyone else except those on the missions from the details, and so if anyone was ever picked up, they couldn't be pressed – or worse – for details.

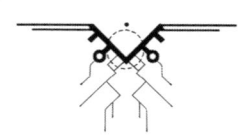

Rebellion's Martyr

With a rough plan in their heads, Meshi burned the paper so it couldn't ever be traced back to them. Akoni watched the flames grow and flicker before Meshi threw the flaming, smoking lump of paper into a nearby garbage bin.

"Shall we get started?" was all he asked, looking around the room. Everyone nodded. It was on.

Chapter Seventeen

It was a quarter past five when Akoni went strolling up to the window of a metro station and asked casually for a schedule of over ground trains from the central station. The metro stations all had them – they connected easily and so many who were travelling out of the city used metros to get to the central station and main train terminal. They were small, folded up pages, not very big and with writing so small many people joked that the pages were made for the eyes of ants. It didn't matter though – the headers were enough information for what they needed.

The fact was that they didn't want to harm anyone who was innocent and who had nothing to do with the government. They would consider it if it went down that road, as resistance movements often had to, but if they could avoid it at all, they would. That's what the train times were for – scoping out the quietest time in the station. It was a message they were sending and the message wasn't meant to be stamped by the Grim Reaper. Lex didn't want to think about those future times, whereas Akoni just didn't think about them. It was a dog-eat-dog world out there, and his priority was his survival: that and passing off anyone that dared to try stepping on him and his freedom. Survival was his priority, but revenge was his pleasure, and these mean streets? Those were his playground: his.

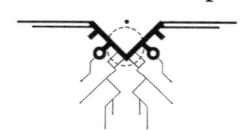

Akoni took the train schedule pamphlet from the woman behind the glass at the metro station ticket window and thanked her politely. Nothing out of the ordinary, except perhaps his appearance – a cyberpunk-come-steampunk kind of style – but even that was becoming more and more commonplace. The fashion was pretty cool, but more than that, the abundance of scrap and junk made for creative clothing choices. Making and wearing those sorts of things filled two gaps; getting cheap clothing so that they could afford to eat, and having something to do. He walked away from the station, his heart beginning to pound a bit in his chest as he revelled in the excitement of the moments to come and a wry smile finding its way across his face. He always loved getting revenge on people who'd wronged him – but this time it was a bit different. He'd be helping usher in a new world where the government didn't have such a stranglehold on the masses and it was exhilarating.

Jer, Meshi and the woman they'd come to know as Cat were waiting for him up the street and around the corner, milling about casually, acting as though they weren't together. Cat was having a pretend conversation on her phone, leaning against a light pole while Meshi was reading a paper and Jer was texting someone. Anyone who wasn't in the know would think they were just three random people on the street, with nothing in common between them at all.

Akoni walked by casually, being careful not to look at any of them for too long or give away anything in his expression that could be picked up by anyone watching. There were enough people around that if someone put two and two together later, it could have serious consequences. He wasn't stupid enough to get caught doing anything untoward. If he was, he'd have been caught by the authorities years ago.

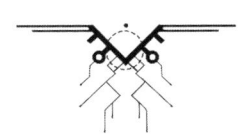

The plan was that they'd follow, slowly one by one, and reconvene in a park that wasn't far up the road where they'd discuss the next phase of the plan. Anyone that was around by that point would just see four friends hanging out in the park, meeting up, possibly going to see a show or out for dinner. The reality was that they'd head straight for the train station where they'd start with the next phase of the plan – blowing out the lockers and hopefully rattling a few cages.

Cat followed first, ending her phone call with an abrupt and loud "Fine! I'm on my way!" as though she had been fighting with someone and was off to see them to resolve the issue. People looked around at her, but more out of surprise from the sudden outburst than anything else, and it allowed her to begin following Akoni as he passed by without it looking suspect. Meshi gave her and Akoni a full minute before following suit and Jer did the same with Meshi. Each minute felt longer than the last with their hearts starting to beat, at least for Jer, Cat and Meshi. Akoni was practically as comfortable as he would have been at home with an ice-cold beer.

The park wasn't far, but far enough that anyone who had seen the four of them on the corner wouldn't put two and two together. It was lush, green and perfectly manicured with lots of hanging baskets sitting midway up vintage looking light posts, lending some bright shades of yellows, reds and pinks to the overall appearance of the park. The smell of fresh cut grass hung heavy in the air, and despite the lovely day it had been to that point, some clouds were gathering on the western horizon, obscuring the sun as it began to set, but only slightly.

Akoni walked to a nondescript bench and sat down casually, popping his right ankle on his left knee, leaning back into the bench and sighing while he waited for the others. He took out the train schedules and looked at them closely. There were a few times that the station would be insanely busy – something that could work for them. They could blend in with the crowd easier and stuff some lockers with the bombs they'd made to really make a statement. There could be casualties, but he was prepared for that. He was certain that Lex and Meshi were as well.

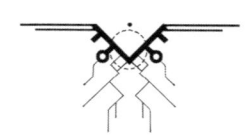

After all, people can't kick-start change without getting at least a little bit dirty.

Cat showed up about five minutes after he sat down. She'd fallen behind slightly when she had to take a real phone call from her mother asking about a dinner they were having on Saturday. Nothing serious, but annoying for the moment it came through. Meshi turned up shortly after Cat, followed by Jer only moments later. They all individually headed toward Akoni, with Cat getting there first, sitting down on the bench and taking a drink of water from the water bottle in her bag.

"You got a light?" she asked Akoni.

He shook his head. "That shit will kill you."

"Let me worry about that." Cat replied. "If we manage to pull this off that is."

"We will. Don't stress."

"Easy for you to say," she mumbled. "You're used to this kind of shit."

Akoni just grinned his devilish grin and crossed his arms. "We ready?"

"I am." Jer said. "Have been for ages. I can't fucking wait to get it started."

"Calm down." Akoni laughed. "There's lots of time."

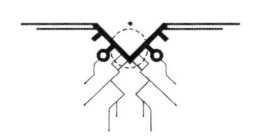

They all began walking toward the main train terminal, butterflies stirring in all of them at different levels. Akoni was the calmest in terms of anxiety about the plan. He was actually more excited than anything. Cat was apprehensive about it all going the way they needed it to go, while Jer was confident, but nervous, but it was to be expected. They *were* going to be doing something dangerous – perhaps not necessarily physically, but if they were caught, there'd be hell to pay in the form of potentially long prison terms or some kind of re-education system.

The train station was only a ten minute walk from the park and was visible from a bit of a distance, a fact that made Cat nearly panic. She was holding it together though, she had to. She knew it was only a matter of time before things got worse in the form of restricted civil liberties and she knew in her heart it was easiest to stop it before it got carried away than it would be to try to crush it later. It had to be done, and so she took a deep, shuddering breath and kept walking.

"You okay?" Akoni asked.

"I think so," she said, barely above a whisper.

"Don't worry," he began. "Just stick to the plan and everything will come out fine. We just need to get in there separately, go to the lockers toward the main platforms one at a time and put our individual bags in there, lock them up and leave. Nothing to it. We'll detonate the bombs from outside the station – after we've split up. Then we meet at the cafe on third street where Meshi will be with the car to take us to his shop to chill until the heat dies down a bit. Alright?"

Cat nodded. "Yeah."

"Let's go teach that asshole Mason a lesson then!" Akoni said excitedly. "I can't wait to see what happens."

The plan went down as well as it could, eventually given the circumstances. Cat had ended up getting detained by security at the train station, but it'd been her own fault.

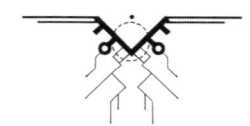

She had been seemingly on board until the final moment when it came time to put backpacks filled with bombs into the lockers when she started slowing her stride and looking overly suspicious, arousing the attention of the authorities who swooped in and collared her. Meshi, Jer and Akoni weren't able to do anything to help her, lest it jeopardise the rest of the mission, so they stuck to the plan that they'd agreed – if anyone fell behind, they got left behind. It was a bit of an unwritten code when dealing with actions of a rebellious nature. You didn't risk the crew to save one person. Not when so much was at stake.

The rest of the plan, however, went off without a hitch. The backpacks from Meshi, Akoni and Jer were in place, strategically placed for maximum impact. It wouldn't necessarily impede operations, although they hoped it would. They also weren't keen on killing anyone, but if it happened, it was a necessary sacrifice for the cause. After they'd put them in place in the lockers, one by one, they casually exited the train station through different avenues – except of course for Cat – and once clear of the train station, even just a bit, the plan was to take their cell phones and dial *666#, a bit of a joke as to the relevance of the number, which would then detonate the bombs in the bags, causing general chaos and panic in the station.

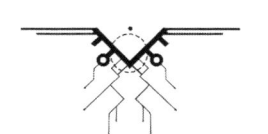

Akoni didn't stick around after he dialled the number. Without looking back toward the station he tried to walk at a normal pace toward a back road that he could use to cut through part of the city to third street. He could hear the explosion, dulled through the thick brick walls of the train station, accompanied by almost instantaneous screams of people who either had been in harm's way or who were just taken aback by the sudden insanity. Although he'd been well versed in questionable activity in the past, his heart was beating fast and he realised he was sweating. Perhaps this was just slightly more than he was used to. Normally it'd been small time stuff – vandalism, maybe some mild assault like muggings or roughing people up a bit, but never anything of this calibre. He had to admit to himself that perhaps, just maybe, he was a bit nervous about it all. Nervousness was definitely not something he was accustomed to; however, he did rather expect that he'd get over it quickly.

The walk to the cafe wasn't long, but he began to feel awkward about it all, especially as a dreary and fairly heavy rain began to fall, as it seemingly always did this time of year. He quickened his pace when he was far enough from the station that it wouldn't seem strange or out of place and he kept noticing that he was checking behind him frequently, as though he expected he'd just get caught. That was his past catching up to him slightly – the constant worry of getting picked up by the authorities after doing something deemed unacceptable by societal standards, despite the fact that it was all he, and many others like him knew. It still surprised him though that he'd be as affected by his recent actions as he was. After all, no one got hurt – necessarily. And the only person who fell by the wayside was Cat but a lot of that was of her own making and her nervous leanings. He'd expected from the start that she was going to be no good for any mission like this. She'd definitely have been better off staying back and working with the likes of Fade, behind the scenes. Some people just couldn't handle the heat.

He turned the corner onto third street and could see the intersection where the cafe sat, just two streets up. It was still a jaunt but he essentially had freedom in his sights – assuming that no one reported a tall male with dark, spiky styled hair, dressed like a cyber punk street bum with a bionic eye walking in a part of town in which he'd never been seen before. Those were his main concerns for the moment. Not Cat. Not any deaths caused by their plan.

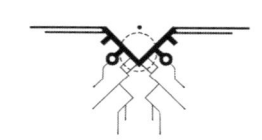

Nothing except getting to the cafe scot-free and getting the hell out of dodge.

The cafe on the corner of third street was just the kind of place three reprobates might meet up after pulling some kind of job of questionable ethics. It was run down, dingy and dirty to say the least. Two of the four windows on one side of the building were broken and taped up with clear packing tape and the door had a bit of a trick to getting it to cooperate. The wood throughout had seen better days and was cracked, mouldy or missing chunks altogether where the integrity had finally given up the ghost and pieces had fallen away to reveal the old, damp wood beneath. The air hung heavy, a combination of the wet wood caused by the almost perpetual and incessant rain and what could have been decades of old spilled ales and beers, soaked into the decrepit old carpet. The stale smell of old beer was almost offensive, as it sometimes is in old bars that were due an update twenty years ago.

Akoni stepped into the threshold, shaking his coat casually, as though he had walked into this place a thousand times before. He scanned the room for any sign of Jer or Meshi but realised he must have been the first to arrive as he spied neither one and so to look as casual as possible, he strolled slowly up to the bar as though he was a patron from out of town passing through and ordered the cheapest lager the barkeep had. It looked a bit like piss as Akoni watched the rather surly bartender pour it from a bar tap that had seen better days, but he said nothing and slapped down what little money he had to pay.

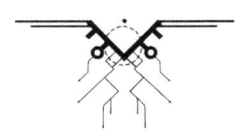

He turned to look into the cafe itself, holding the dingy glass that had seen better days, his fingers quickly getting cold from the icy lager that had been poured. It might be shitty and cheap, but at least it was frosty. There wasn't much to the cafe, it was more like a bar than anything. A few circular tables dotted the room, mainly pressed against one wall and an old TV was playing some news channel on silent. The idea of a news channel playing in the bar made Akoni's stomach flip. He definitely didn't want to listen to the news. Not right now.

He turned away from the TV, precariously positioned on the wall, above head height and looked for the darkest corner where he could drink in peace while he waited for Meshi and Jer to show their faces.

It was at least another twenty minutes before either of them did, in the end. Akoni had realised he had more or less drained the pint he'd purchased, partially through nerves causing him to drink far faster than he normally would. It was unusual for him to put a pint away so quickly, and truth be told, it had affected him slightly, so by the time Jer and Meshi pulled up a chair or two, Akoni was feeling the effects of the cheap, shitty lager.

"What took you so fucking long?" he asked, not exactly being quiet. Jer looked at him with a sharp stare.

"Keep it quiet," Jer replied, waving down a hand. "Got caught up. That's all."

"We took a longer way," Meshi explained in a hushed tone. "For safety."

Akoni was silent. Sure, he could have been up in arms about it, but it would cause them more harm than good at that point. It was better to keep it quiet and just play it as casual and cool as possible. Have another drink – maybe a half, since he was already feeling it pretty hard.

"Okay. Sorry," Akoni relented. "I was just getting a bit skittish. That's all." Then under his breath, leaning over the table, almost knocking his nearly empty glass over with his chest as he did so.

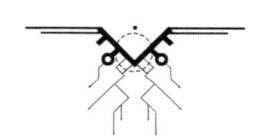

"Shall we have one more to keep up appearances?"

Jer and Meshi agreed. It would look like three friends meeting for a drink. Nothing unusual. Nothing out of the ordinary. Everything calm, cool, collected and normal. Meshi put in a text on a burner phone as the second round of drinks arrived at the table, indicating they needed a pickup around back in about twenty minutes. Someone from the group would come with, presumably, a van with blackened windows so as not to draw attention to the occupants. Or so he hoped.

"Cat didn't make it out, huh?" Jer said, more to himself than to anyone else.

"Not that I saw," Meshi replied. "I had a bad feeling about her from the start."

"Me too," Akoni said. "She was way too anxious and concerned for this kind of role. We should have seen it."

"Now all we can do is hope she doesn't rat us out to the authorities." Jer scratched his chin. "Or the government."

"Hopefully not," Meshi agreed. "That would be bad."

Akoni sipped his beer, trying not to drink it too quickly so as to exacerbate his obvious drunkenness, and nodded in agreement. They all sat in relative silence for a moment, each quietly reflecting on the day's events, being careful not to mention Cat again nor the fact that she was probably being ungraciously questioned by the authorities, to say the very least. There was nothing they could really do except drink their drinks in feigned camaraderie and wait for their ride so they could get back to Meshi's shop and lay low for the next while.

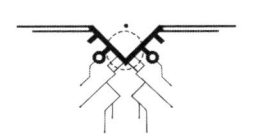

Chapter Eighteen

The fallout from the bombing of the train station ended up being significant. Various news outlets were all over it and wouldn't stop speculating who was behind the first bombing in what was around twenty-five or thirty years. Since things had become more utopian, people hadn't needed an outlet to voice their concerns or frustrations, such as bombing a government building or a significant place of business. In general, things had been good. Maybe too good for too long that the masses had become complacent in their utopia, although that was unlikely. After all, that was the goal – a utopian society where everyone was equal and the constructs of the day in technology and the like were designed to support said society. What was happening with the sudden lack of access to the Ascension programming was certainly not, nor ever was, part of the plan. The people's plan at least, clearly, President Mason had other ideas.

The people by and large weren't stupid though, and they knew exactly what had led to the pandemonium. Things had always been good and with the added potential of upgrading your existence into the Ascension program, the world was on the brink of being better than ever. It almost seemed that once the access to Ascension was restricted and then finally cut off entirely that the people realised that it wasn't a world as utopian as they'd been led to believe by their leaders, and now more and more were having their eyes opened to the issues that these so-called leaders were causing the masses.

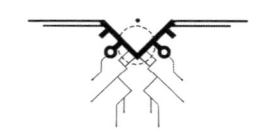

It wasn't just the access to Ascension though. It was a lot of little things with restricted access to Ascension just the latest in a long line of things that the government under the very shady President Mason had been responsible for doing. First it was limiting supplies of fresh produce, claiming that the cost to ship it was too great. Then it was a fuel shortage that never seemed to go away, causing people to have to resort to very strange solutions to heat their homes. Thirdly was a cut to education and healthcare and the axing of thousands of jobs on the proviso that the money was being funded back into the fuel crisis. It had been, but not to help the people. Instead it went into the pockets of big wig executives who would scratch Mason's back in return for fat corporate kickbacks and pay-outs for doing essentially nothing except contributing to a social decline and further economic class division – two things that had not existed under previous governments.

There were only a handful of the crew hanging out at Meshi's shop when Jer, Akoni and Meshi turned up from their mission to the train station. They were huddled around a small, rather old television set in the back room, watching as one of the more popular and controversial reporters of the day reported and speculated on the cause and reasoning behind the attacks. As Akoni entered the room he heard her clearly say:

"*- Police are still unsure of who is beyond this particular attack, but if recent governmental policy changes and cutbacks are anything to go by, it's anyone's guess as almost anyone who's been affected is a potential suspect.*"

"She knows her stuff," Akoni mused, sitting down on the far side of the room.

Jer nodded. "If she isn't careful she's going to get picked up by the feds."

"Why? Because she tells it how it is?" Akoni asked, getting defiant. "That's what a reporter is supposed to do, you know."

"Maybe. But not in this climate." "Fuck the climate. We need people like that more than ever," he said, gesturing toward the TV with an upward not of his head. "Not cry-babies like Cat."

Jer sullenly dropped into a chair on the opposite side of the room from Akoni. "Leave Cat out of it."

"Jer is right, Akoni," Meshi interrupted. "Let's leave it."

There was an awkward silence in the room amongst the three of them and those who had been watching the news. Meshi was clearly perturbed by everything as he suddenly snapped and said to those who hadn't been on the mission

"Make yourselves useful and get us some supplies. We're going to need to lay low here for a while."

They were clearly startled by his sudden brash tone and jumped up, almost clamouring over each other to get to the door of the backroom, which they more or less slammed behind them in their haste as they left. Jer, Akoni and Meshi heard the front door to the shop open and close just as hastily, with the bell above the door ringing out rather violently as the two stragglers rushed out. Meshi finally sat down, after what seemed to him to be forever.

"I'm so glad to be back here," he relented, after a minute or two of uncomfortable silence.

Akoni hesitated. He was supposed to be the guy with the experience, but he had to admit that even he'd been somewhat rattled by what they'd just done. Finally though, he nodded and agreed.

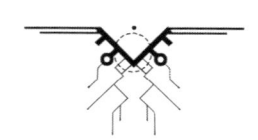

"Same," Jer said, looking down at the floor, the news still replaying the report from the train station, almost on a continuous loop, repeating the same information over and over, with no change or deviation. Finally Akoni had enough and angrily stood up and switched it off in a huff.

Meshi and Jer looked at him strangely. "You alright?" Meshi asked as Akoni sat back down and stretched his legs out, trying to be casual and relaxed.

"Yeah, it was just driving me nuts. We know what happened."

Silence filled the room again, each of the three still thinking on the activities they'd participated in that day, all knowing that sooner or later there would be another set of actions orchestrated by another of their cellular groups, but that they didn't know when, where or what. They only hoped that everyone adhered to the general rules that they'd all agreed in advance – that anyone who fell behind got left behind and that you never give away the information of the collective. All they could do was wait and see what happened next and go from there.

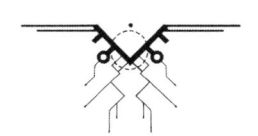

While all of this had been happening, Fade, Lex and a few others had set up a sort of headquarters in an old abandoned warehouse on the edge of town. Luckily for Fade, the internet and power hook-ups were decent, if not excellent, allowing her the ability to hack into certain systems with ease. Her computers were fairly top of the line – at least for the moment, so she needed some primo power sources to ensure she'd be able to run them so it was a good spot. There wasn't much in the way of furniture in the room, but they made do with what they had: some old boxes that worked for desks and tables as long as they didn't overload them too much, and a sofa so worn out that it may as well have not had any upholstery on it in the first place. It was strangely comfortable, the material just so thin you could almost see the bare cushioning beneath it.

Lex had been busying herself by finding a coffee maker at a nearby shop and setting it up so they at least had caffeine to sustain them throughout the coming days. Tea just wasn't going to give them the buzz this kind of thing might demand, not like she was any kind of expert on it. They'd likely be needing it – especially Fade, who was likely to be working around the clock to try and get into various governmental computer systems to try and take them down from the inside. She hoped she could cause them a bit of inconvenience at the least, and at the very most potentially destroy what they had been doing with policies and the like. She also hoped she could somehow hack into the Ascension system, gain control, and reverse the rules about who was able to access it, either through ascending themselves or through the Spots. If they controlled the program in its entirety, they could essentially return it to the people.

They were also on the lookout for a potential list of targets: secret government installations, names of people who were higher up in President Mason's list of friends and associates and things of that nature. If they could start targeting the government directly, it would help them send a message home sooner rather than later. Sure, the existing cells could focus on their individual jobs, but those at headquarters could go after the big guns: Mason and all his buddies. That's where the biggest impact was likely to be.

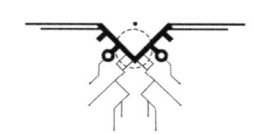

"I got coffee if anyone wants it!" Lex called out to several people doing various odd jobs that would help make the room more comfortable. They all stopped what they were doing and came over to her, taking mugs from a shoddy, haphazard collection of mismatched drinking vessels, some of which may not have been ideal for hot liquids.

"Thank God," one of them said, taking a sip of the strong coffee that she had purchased to replace the bitter blend that Meshi had. "I've been dying for one all day."

"Not literally, I hope." Lex joked. The reply was general nervous chuckles and weak smiles followed by each of the individuals going back to whatever it was they were doing. One of them, a blonde-haired girl around Lex's age had found a map of the city and had pinned it up behind Fade.

"Nice map," Fade remarked, turning around from her place behind an old desk she'd managed to find and dust off for the heavier of her computer equipment. "What's it for?"

Lex came over then. "We could use it to map next targets?" she suggested.

The blonde-haired girl nodded. "Just what I was thinking."

"You know where I wish we could target like, right now?" Fade asked, standing up and making a handgun motion with her hands, closing one eye as though she were focusing on a target.

"Where?" Lex asked, putting a cup of coffee on Fade's desk.

"Mason's mansion," Fade replied, upbeat, in an almost carefree, yet confrontational manner, her eyes gleaming" That boogie fucking mansion of his where he entertains all his buddies with money. Take 'em all out at once."

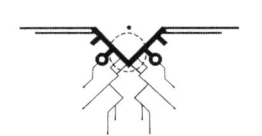

Lex laughed. "That's the dream. Too bad we don't have the ability."

"Maybe later." Fade put her arms down and winked before grabbing the mug Lex had put on her desk and taking a huge gulp of coffee. "This is nice. Just what the doctor ordered."

Lex took a sip of her own coffee. It was nice indeed. It had been a while since she had a proper cup of coffee, even the places she frequented with Damian were sometimes disappointing, and he was a guy who knew his coffee, but also preferred to look cool while drinking it, something that often didn't jive well with a good cup of java. Trendy cafes aren't always the best when it comes to that kind of thing – something Damian still had to learn, apparently.

She got lost in her own thoughts for a period of time, thinking about Damian and what he might be up to, if he was on another business trip or if he was holed up in his office, working away for the man, a job he wasn't thrilled about on occasion, and wondered why he didn't give it up to work a job he was more aligned with. He'd be happier, certainly, and he'd have more time to do things with friends or even have a romantic relationship with someone. The thought of Damian having a romantic relationship with someone sent a pang through Lex. Maybe – just maybe – she liked him as a bit more than a friend, but it was something she'd tried to ignore for a while. The thought of texting him crossed her mind, but was interrupted by someone calling her and Fade over to where they had switched on an old TV they'd found in one of the offices.

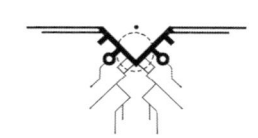

Fade and Lex walked quickly over to where the blonde-haired girl and another, older woman, were watching the news. It was the controversial reporter, in front of the train station reporting on what was obviously the day's events, but this time with a difference.

"Turn it up," Fade demanded, sitting on the arm of the old, dilapidated couch. The blonde-haired girl reached over and twisted the volume dial. The words of the reporter sprang to life, crackling through the old speakers of the TV, almost sounding like they were echoing through a tin can, but it got the job done. Better than nothing, anyway.

Below the reporter, in bold lettering across the bottom of the screen read the words "Breaking News". It couldn't have possibly been about the bombing itself as they had been broadcasting that more or less since it happened.

"I hope this breaking news isn't that they caught whoever was responsible for this," Fade began. "Or we're in big freakin' trouble."

"I seriously hope not." Lex agreed.

"To recap our story at the top of the hour," the reporter began. *"One person is in custody after a bombing today at the central train station where three people have been killed and a dozen seriously injured."*

"Oh fuck." Fade whispered.

"It's alright, it's fine." Lex said, her stomach starting to churn with anxiety.

"While the person in custody isn't cooperating with authorities at this time, police are confident that they know who is behind this terror plot. President Mason has vowed to find the culprits and bring them to justice. However, fuelling speculation that this bombing was in response to recent economic and liberty interruptions as a result of some of President Mason's policies, he's indicated

that he will give a live, televised speech tonight at eight o'clock to address these issues."

"Set your watch," Fade said, standing up from her spot on the arm of the couch and stretching casually, acting like there was nothing at all out of the ordinary happening. "We need to see that shit."

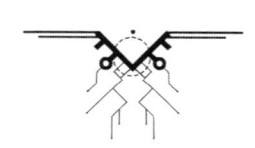

Chapter Nineteen

The clock seemed to be going slower than it ever had before. Lex paced the floor, waiting for eight o'clock to strike so they could tune into President Mason's speech about the bombing and who knew what else. It sounded pretty official, and possibly huge, so it was imperative that they listened in. Lex knew that it was wishful thinking to hope that maybe one bombing and a couple deaths were enough to sway Mason's thinking and make him reverse the policies he'd put in place in terms of problems that were arising with access to Ascension and Spots, along with other various issues such as the cost of food, distribution of electrical supplies and more. It was more likely he'd call for someone's blood – especially with how things had been going.

It was seven forty-five and Fade looked up from her computer screen, her eyes clearly tired.

"Dude, you gotta stop pacing that floor, you're gonna wear it right through and you'll end up in the basement."

"I'm just nervous is all." Lex replied quietly. "I've never actually done anything like this before."

"None of us have. Relax. We're all in this together."

"What about the one they got in custody?" Lex asked. "What if it's Meshi?"

"So text him and check?" Fade gave a shrug.

"No! What if it is him and they have his burner and then we inadvertently give away the whole thing?" Lex was starting to flap then. "That puts like forty people potentially at risk."

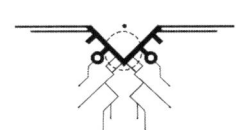

"Hm. Good point. I hadn't thought of that." Fade was clearly over this conversation, and put her headphones back on, singing under her breath, then getting louder. "I prefer soups and stews to crackers and tofu. You know you wanna-"

Lex spun around. "I know that from somewhere."

"You should, it's a classic."

Before they could say anything else, Lex's phone buzzed. She whipped it out of her pocket – just the weekly update.

"I'll go to his shop later and check on them." Lex said. "After the broadcast." She looked at the clock. Only two minutes had passed. "God damn it."

Fade laughed. "I told you. Relax. Time goes by." She returned to whatever she was doing at her computer that was making her eyes tired. "I think I need glasses."

"Why?"

"Eye strain."

"Take more breaks." Lex suggested.

"Mob justice waits for no man. Or woman. Or whatever," Fade said, half-laughing. "Besides. I'm almost done."

"What are you doing anyway?"

"Just running some preliminary programs to test security features. Nothing too hectic. Yet."

Lex crossed her arms and sat on the worn couch. "I need a drink."

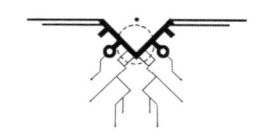

"Well there's that old coffee from earlier."

"I meant an alcoholic drink."

"Well, that I can't help you with, I'm afraid." Fade replied. "At least not right this minute. I think you've been hanging around Meshi too much."

The Nixie clock Fade had installed read seven fifty-eight. Lex leaned forward and turned the TV on. She didn't want to miss a second of this news report, but likewise she didn't want to have the news on all evening, reliving what they'd put in motion time and again, a perpetual reminder that any of them could potentially get picked up for their roles in the pandemonium and deaths they'd caused because of their disenchantment at what was quickly becoming seen to be a governmental regime of some kind.

The TV flashed to life, on the same channel as earlier. It seemed to be a press conference room, but instead of a podium there was only a large projector screen. Journalists milled around, but there definitely weren't many. Not as many as there should have been, not by far.

"That's weird." Fade said, having looked up from the computer again. "Where are all the journalists?"

"I don't know." Lex said. "There should be at least twice that number."

"Exactly what I was thinking."

The door to the warehouse blew open in a storm that had started up, making both Fade and Lex jump out of their skin.

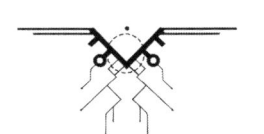

"Jesus freaking Christ!" Fade said, putting her hand on her chest and getting up from the computer desk. "That scared the shit out of me."

"Me too." Lex agreed, her heartbeat only slowly beginning to return to normal after the fright. She turned back to the TV, still puzzling over the apparent lack of people at the press conference.

Fade, meanwhile, made her way to the door, shivering against the autumn wind. She reached out for the door handle to close it when suddenly Akoni burst into the room, making Fade scream – again.

"Yo, shut the hell up," Akoni said. "You don't want to attract attention." He grabbed the door and closed it behind him as the wind picked up further and lightning flashed in the darkened sky.

"Me shut up? Who the fuck makes an entrance like that when they're meant to be laying low, asshole?" Fade spat.

"People like me. Now get over to the couch, sit down and listen."

Lex could tell by the look on the hacker's face that Fade thought about getting up in Akoni's about how he was talking to her, but decided against it. It wasn't going to solve anything or help the cause or do anything to adjust Akoni's attitude. She did as he had more or less demanded of her, without a word.

Akoni pointed at the TV. "I have a little story about that," he said, pouring a cup of the stale, old coffee from that afternoon. "Turns out only certain journalists were allowed into that."

"How the hell do you know that?" Lex asked, watching him drink the coffee.

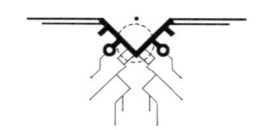

"Christ how old is this?" he asked, throwing it off to the side from the cup and putting the cup back on the table with the coffee maker.

"Thanks for messing up the joint," Fade remarked. "Not like we didn't spend all day setting this dive up."

Akoni ignored her. "You know that controversial reporter? The one that actually tells is how it is and gets in shit a lot?"

"Yeah?" Lex asked.

"She wasn't allowed in."

"Well I'm not surprised to be honest. But how did you find this out?"

"I have a friend who works for a news outlet. Not a good friend, more of an acquaintance really, but I had been texting him and he said he wasn't allowed in either and then gave me a whole list of different journalists who weren't allowed. For obvious reasons I thought this information should be shared and for further obvious reasons I thought it should be shared in person and not over something that can be traced, even a burner phone." He pulled a piece of damp, folded up paper from his chest pocket and handed it to Lex who made a face as she unfolded it. "It's just rain," he said. "Calm down."

Sure enough, it was a list of media outlets – more libertarian and liberal than right wing or centre ones that would have been disallowed from the press conference. It suddenly dawned on Lex.

"Oh my god. He's trying to control the media."

"Exactly." Akoni agreed, taking the soggy paper and trying to burn it with a lighter.

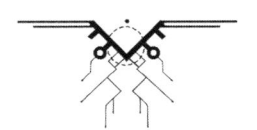

"This means war." Fade suddenly chimed in, expression as white hot as smoking metal in a furnace.

Akoni turned to look at her as the paper struggled to light. "Calm down over there John Wayne."

"You calm down."

"Everybody calm down." Lex sighed, exasperated by their fighting. "Or just fuck already and get it over with."

That seemed to take the wind out of both of their sails. For some reason Fade and Akoni didn't get along very well, but they were so similar that it was probably the fact they saw themselves in each other and weren't particularly keen on that fact which was a driving factor in the attitudes they had toward each other. Almost like they were trying to outdo one another all the time. It was comedic – occasionally. When things weren't quite so serious.

Before any of them could say anything else, the press conference started on the TV. A tall, lanky man came out and addressed the crowd of selected journalists and said that while President Mason wasn't able to be there in person due to safety concerns, he'd be joining them digitally and wouldn't be fielding questions. He seemed to want to get out of the limelight as soon as possible and generally wasn't very informative at all. He more or less introduced President Mason and got out of dodge, so it seemed, off to hide away from the cameras and lights of the questioning press, avoiding as much contact with them as he was able.

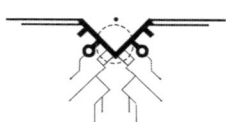

Akoni, Lex and Fade all crowded around the TV, wondering exactly what was going to be said. It was the first time any such thing had happened since President Mason had been in power, and, truth be told, it was the first time anything like this had ever happened since any of them had been born. President Mason had always kept a bit of a low profile, opting to send various goons of his to do dirty work than do it himself, so actually seeing him – in the flesh or not – was a rare occurrence.

The screen flashed and showed static before finally an image of President Mason himself came into view. He was silent for a moment or two, as though he were waiting for cues from someone to begin talking. When he did though, he sounded very odd, kind of like the voice equipment on his end was malfunctioning. He didn't address it, and instead just kept talking.

"The events of today should not go unpunished," he said at one point, failing to indicate that they'd taken Cat into custody. "We must stand up against violence in our society and crush it with stern and affirmative action."

"That's the pot calling the kettle black a little bit there, don't you think?" Akoni mused. Neither Fade nor Lex replied and just kept watching the broadcast.

"There are people in our society who would want us to suffer at their hands."

"That's rich, coming from him," Fade remarked.

"No kidding." Lex agreed. Akoni looked at them both sideways. He wasn't sure what they meant as he'd always led a bit of a rougher life so he hadn't taken much notice of things going south in the social welfare or wellness department.

"I don't know who he could be referring to when he says that," Akoni said. "Who the heck is going after anyone except US after HIM?"

"Exactly." Lex agreed.

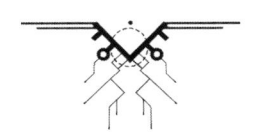

"Why isn't he actually mentioning the bombing?" Fade asked. "You'd think he would mention it specifically by now."

The broadcast continued in its vague way, with no mention of the bombing specifically, an odd omission considering that was the main reason the press conference had been called. Something about the whole situation just reeked of some kind of – what? A cover up? It couldn't have been because Lex, Meshi, Fade, Akoni and the others all knew they were responsible, so what would Mason be covering up? Or avoiding? Or maybe he was avoiding mentioning it because it was pretty obvious that he'd been partially to blame thanks to his cuts, changes and general messing up of policies, procedures and institutions that had been in existence since anyone could remember.

As the video of Mason moved on the screen, Fade moved from her place on the couch next to Akoni and got closer to the TV, inspecting it closely. The picture wasn't the best by any sense of the word, but she was sure something was out of the ordinary.

"Didn't you ever hear about how if you get too close to a TV it will wreck your eyes?" Akoni asked, teasingly.

"Oh, relax," Fade replied, still focusing on the image. "I'm not going to be here for the rest of my life."

"What are you doing anyway?" Lex asked.

"There's something about that video," she said. "It's weird. Look at it. I mean, it's not a great image on this shitty TV, but the way he's moving is kind of unnatural, like there's the smallest delay. And the colouring is kind of off. You see in the corner?" she pointed to the bottom right-hand corner of the screen. "It's got a weird hue to it, like this is a recording of a recording or something."

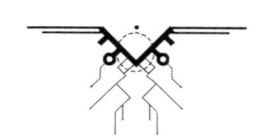

"But why would they play a recording of a recording?" Akoni asked, genuinely puzzled.

Fade paused. "Why indeed?"

"Maybe he was busy?" Lex suggested. "Or he wanted to get it out quickly."

"Yeah but that doesn't explain why he's not specifically mentioned the bombing at the train station." Fade looked up at Lex from her place on the floor next to the TV. "Something's fishy."

"Not only that, but didn't he have some weird scar on his face before?" Akoni suddenly chimed in. He was right. There had been a distinctly noticeable scar under Mason's left eye, cause unknown, that seemed to have vanished.

"You're right," Lex said, moving to get a closer look at the video. "It's totally gone."

Fade got up in a hurry and stalked over to her computer setup. "I bet I know what the deal is."

"What?" Lex and Akoni asked, almost in unison, turning to watch Fade sit behind her myriad of screens and electrical equipment.

"I bet that motherfucker has already Ascended." she said. "But there's only one way to know."

Akoni and Lex glanced at each other, then back at Fade.

"We need a list of everyone who's ever Ascended." Fade said, typing something into her computer. "And while we're at it, a list of his associates, partners, close friends, investors and the like. I'll wager if he's ascended, they have as well."

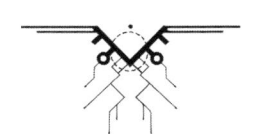

Lists of people of this nature? It wouldn't be easy. Where exactly were they supposed to get all that information?

"Can't you just hack it?" Akoni asked. "That is, after all, while you're here."

"No kidding genius," Fade replied sarcastically. "What do you think I'm trying to do? But I'll tell you now it won't be easy and it wouldn't hurt to have a hard copy of that information from somewhere."

Akoni and Lex were quiet for a minute, trying to think how they could help Fade find the information – if the information even existed. Chances were that if Mason and his buddies had ascended, the information might have been kept hidden, but there had to be records somewhere. Records of any kind that could give them a hint.

Suddenly Lex had a thought. "Hey. My grandma worked for EverDawn. And I know she still knows people who work there now. Maybe we can get someone on the inside."

"There's thinking with your head," Fade said from behind her computer screens which illuminated her face in an eerie green shade coming from the various programs running on the screen.

"What?" Akoni started. "As opposed to your ass?"

She ignored him. "Follow up on that lead and let's see where that goes because it wouldn't hurt to get a bit of insider info on other things too."

"What can I do in the meantime?" Akoni piped up.

Fade wasted no time in relaying a sarcastic reply. "Sit there and look pretty. At least you're good at that much."

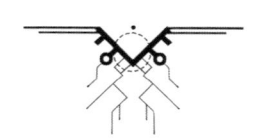

Chapter Twenty

It was going for nearly ten in the evening when Lex walked through the garden gate of her grandmother's house and through the garden. The kitchen light was on, indicating that Grandma Alice was still up and about, which was ideal as Lex needed to ask her about getting details out of EverDawn through her colleagues, if possible. She hoped she wouldn't be putting her grandma into an awkward position, but if it meant they could change things for the better, some temporary discomfort was worth it. Besides, she was sure that Grandma Alice would want to see her daughter and other family members through the Ascension program again, too. She had been the one to bring Jade in and she hadn't exactly punished Lex for her involvement. If there was anyone that could (and would) help, it would be Alice. Besides, it wasn't as though she had much of a choice. They had come too far, buried themselves far too deep; all of them.

Lex walked up the steps and into the house, trying to rehearse in her head what she was planning to say to her grandma. She needed to get her to speak to someone she knew at EverDawn to try and get the information they needed. Fade had mulled it over a bit more before Lex had left the warehouse and asked if it was possible to get blueprints for the Ascension machine itself – the actual device they used to remove the consciousness from the human body and put it into the computer system. Lex wasn't sure why Fade wanted it, but presumably it was to study it and to understand the inner workings of the system better. She was the computer genius. She knew what she was doing, after all.

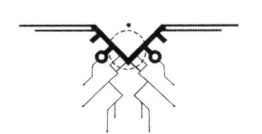

Grandma Alice was sitting in the living room, watching TV. It was some kind of old soap opera type of show, Lex recognised it from years of Grandma Alice watching it as she had been growing up. She had never paid attention so couldn't begin to say what it was about, but as soap operas go it was along the same lines of them all: some sappy love story with a lot of drama. Lex walked into the room, taking off her scarf and woolly hat and setting them down on the back of one of the armchairs before sitting down and leaning back into it, trying to relax and play it cool, like nothing had been happening that day.

"You're late," Grandma Alice commented, not even turning her head much.

"I was out with friends," Lex replied. "You know. Time gets away sometimes."

They sat in silence for a bit before Lex decided to just bite the bullet and come right out with it.

"You still see your old colleagues from EverDawn, don't you?" she asked, trying to sound as casual as possible, fiddling with part of her scarf that hung down alongside her arm.

"Yes. On occasion." Grandma Alice replied. "Why do you ask?"

"Was just curious when you're seeing them again."

It was at this point Grandma Alice turned the TV down and got serious. "You need something don't you?"

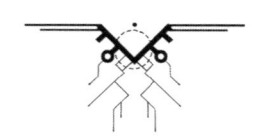

Lex didn't want to lie to her grandmother, but also didn't want to jeopardize anything by admitting what she and the others were up to. She certainly wasn't about to admit that she was remotely even the tiniest bit involved with the bombings. She decided that it was probably going to be best to just admit what she needed and at least somewhat why. She hoped Grandma Alice would understand and agree to get in touch with her colleagues who might have been pissed off enough at some of what had been going on that they'd agree to help.

She started explaining everything to Grandma Alice as planned, leaving out the parts about the bombing. Much to her surprise, Grandma Alice seemed to understand, at least to some degree. The conversation was primarily one sided, with Lex mainly doing the talking and trying to share how she felt about being unfairly kept from the Spots and her family because the government was led by some greedy old man who wanted to keep everything for himself and his friends, essentially causing the Ascension program to become a membership only, elitist club.

Grandma Alice nodded at that description of the program. It certainly had been turning into that kind of thing, even when she was still working at EverDawn. She began to notice more and more that people who didn't meet certain 'criteria' were being denied and told that the system was too busy and they'd be put on the bottom of some waiting list − which didn't exist − and they would have to hold on for several months, if not a year, before they'd be able to ascend. The whole thing was a farce, of course, orchestrated by EverDawn higher ups, who, of course, were controlled by President Mason. Anything Mason wanted, they would do, and he wanted Ascension all to himself and his special friends.

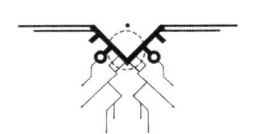

Lex finished explaining the story − the parts she needed to share, anyway. Grandma Alice didn't immediately say anything and sat in contemplative silence for a short while. Lex's heart began to tick on louder and louder as she began to worry that she'd overstepped her bounds and asked too much of her Grandmother and was about to open her mouth in apology when, much to her surprise, Grandma Alice replied with,

"I always knew it was going to come down to this."

Lex was taken aback slightly. She definitely didn't expect that kind of reaction. Grandparents could be rather nosy and ask a lot of questions but Grandma Alice seemed less concerned about what, who and why and was more concerned about what she could do to help. It was definitely a step in the right direction.

"What?" Lex asked, trying to hold her jaw from gaping like a fish.

"Don't look so surprised." Grandma Alice said to Lex. "I may seem old and like I don't know what's going on, but I've been around for a while, and I've worked at EverDawn when all this was starting to go down."

"So… you'll help us get the information we need?" Lex asked, still not believing her incredibly good luck that her grandmother had people on the inside of one of the organisations they were trying to get information from.

"Sure I will. In the morning. I'll give the ladies a call. They will be in on it too. I know they will. But for now, it's past my bedtime." She switched off the TV and stood up from her usual place in her favourite armchair. "I left your dinner in the fridge for you."

"Thank you, Grandma." Lex wasn't sure which part she was thanking her grandmother for – the dinner, the help, just being herself – everything?

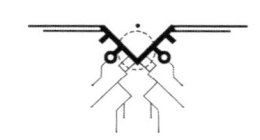

She patted Lex on the shoulder as she shuffled past, out the door and down the hall to her bedroom. Lex could hear her close the door and the familiar creak of the bed as she climbed into it. Lex breathed a sigh of relief and sat

back in her chair, her anxiety over asking for Grandma Alice's help melting away, giving way to anticipation and a bit of excitement.

The next morning Lex woke late. Much later than normal. She opened her eyes and realised that her room was far more bright than usual due to the sun being higher in the sky. She wasn't concerned. She clearly had needed the rest after the last few days she'd had. She laid in bed, relaxing and slightly dozing, not quite falling back asleep but not fully in the process of properly getting up. The sound of the old clock on the wall ticking was all that broke the monotonous silence of her room – ideal for sleeping, but too long with a silence that heavy and it could drive you mad.

There was one other noise though: the occasional sound of Grandma Alice's voice. She was talking to someone, presumably on the phone as Lex could make out anyone else's voice in the house, unless they were talking incredibly softly. She laid as still as she could, trying to listen to what was being said but couldn't make it out. She could hear the occasional laugh and the rise or fall of the pitch in Grandma Alice's voice, but aside from that, no discernible words were audible.

The thought of a hot cup of coffee and hopefully an update on what Grandma Alice had been able to organise is what got Lex moving eventually. She looked at the clock, which read 10:31. Not horrible, but not her usual time of around 8. She thought about getting dressed but decided against it and instead opened her bedroom door and poked her head out into the hallway, listening closer to Grandma Alice and whoever she was on the phone with.

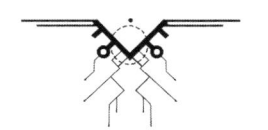

"Okay," Grandma Alice said to whoever it was. "I'll see you at three. I hope they have that carrot cake again. It was delicious last time." There was a pause for a moment as presumably the other person commented on the desire for this supposedly amazing carrot cake before Grandma Alice bid them farewell and hung up the phone.

Lex waited for a moment before coming casually out of her room and down the hall, still in her two-piece long pyjamas and bare feet. She rounded the corner into the kitchen where Grandma Alice was sitting at the table, finishing a cup of tea and a muffin of some kind.

"Morning," Lex said.

"You're up late." Grandma Alice sipped her tea.

"Yeah. Took awhile to doze off." The reality was that she wasn't sure if it did or not. She couldn't even remember going to bed.

"That was one of my old colleagues on the phone."

"Yeah?" Lex asked, walking to the coffee maker and starting to work on making a pot. "What did they want?"

"I phoned her," Grandma Alice said. "To ask her to meet me to discuss what you were talking about."

"I figured." Lex lingered on the thought. "I assume she said yes to meeting."

"She did. Today. At three. I'll ask her then about getting the information you need."

Lex turned on the coffee maker. "Thanks. I really appreciate it. And, I know it's dangerous for everyone to get involved like this."

"Don't worry, dear," Grandma Alice said. "You don't know Shelley. She's a bit of a dark horse like that."

"Really?"

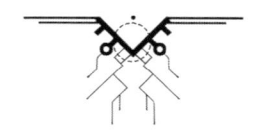

"Yeah. And she has been there longer than I have. It was getting bad when I left five years ago. It's even worse now, obviously. She was pissed off about it back then but stayed because she actually enjoyed her job."

"Hopefully she's pissed enough to be OK with losing her job, if she gets caught smuggling plans and lists out of the place." Lex mused.

"We'll see, I guess." Grandma Alice commented. "It can't hurt to try, anyway."

"That logic is how I got into this," Lex gave a half laugh, reciprocated by Alice.

"I always knew you were my favourite." Alice winked.

"Grandma!"

Chapter Twenty-One

Fade was sitting on the old couch, watching some cartoon show from her childhood, her legs up on the cushions next to her, stretched out and a hand behind her head. Her laughter echoed through the building, bringing a twinge of light to an otherwise dreary place. Akoni was wandering around, rather anxious and trying to distract himself by reading old timecards and reports from the factory that had been present in the building sometime in the not-so-distant past. It was the least he could do to keep from going insane. Normally he'd have shaken down thirty people for money, jewellery or other goods by that point in the day and the lack of his old routine was starting to bother him. He at least had some kind of structure. He did well with structure. Without it, he had a tendency to get into other types of trouble that were more difficult to get out of.

Not that he could do much this time. He was supposed to lay low after his part in bombing the train station but laying low without much to do was beginning to wear thin. Fade laughed again, a deep belly laugh, at something that happened in her show. It made Akoni smile, the way that when someone gives a giggle it's easy to tell they are truly laughing in a genuine way, it's almost infectious.

The cartoon show was coming to an end when it was interrupted by breaking news. There had been another bombing, this time at a post office on the west side of town. The whole thing reeked of an operation by one of their splinter groups, which was good: it meant people were dedicated to the cause. Fade watched with interest at first, with Akoni coming over and watching for a moment too.

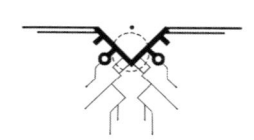

"Sounds like one of ours." he mused.

"Agreed," Fade replied. "That's good though. Means people are dedicated."

"I suppose," Akoni said, slightly sullenly. He was bowing his head and his body was slumped in all sorts of ways, more than usual in fact. Fade couldn't deal with that. Cartoons were one thing, but a full-grown man, and a gangster at that, sulking like a spoiled brat. It just wasn't cool. Her voice exploded about as loud as the Post Office bomb.

"What's your problem?"

"Nothing!"

Fade looked at him. "Why do you have such a sour face all the time?"

"Hey, I–" he began, but was interrupted by Lex coming in through a metal side door which clanged and banged every time someone used it to enter or exit the building.

"We really should stop using this thing," she said as she walked in, looking at the TV while she took off her jacket. "What's going on?"

"Another bombing," Fade replied, pointing at the TV with her thumb. "Pretty sure it's one of ours."

"Cool." Lex said, sitting next to Fade on the couch and reading the headlines.

"Not what Captain Bringdown here says," Fade replied, motioning toward Akoni.

"Oh, whatever." Akoni said, turning and walking away from them.

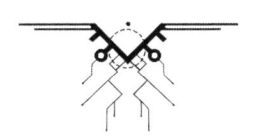

195

"What's his problem? Lex asked.

"Who knows?" Fade asked. "What isn't his problem?"

Lex watched Akoni stalk off like a pissed off panther into a rainy night, wondering what his deal was. He hadn't really been the same since the day before when they bombed the train station, and she wondered if he was feeling some guilt or regret, especially since a few people had fallen victim to the process. It was unusual for him, to be sure, but it wasn't entirely out of the question. He was, after all, still human, even if it was easy to occasionally forget, what with that glowing bionic eye. Maybe, she considered, that was projection; just her trying to put her own feelings on him. Akoni was uppity like that sometimes, it wasn't like he was known for his chilled-out attitude and polite charm. Lex blew out a long breath, wiping the thoughts from her mind and turning towards the hacker.

"Anyway, I spoke to my Grandma," Lex began, sitting on the arm of the couch as Fade switched the TV off.

"Oh yeah?" Fade replied. "About getting that info?"

"Yeah."

"What'd she say?"

"She's in."

"No way!" Fade exclaimed. She was surprised that anyone over a certain age would be down for a little chaos and anarchy considering their upbringings focusing on peace and being good, law abiding citizens. "When do we get it?"

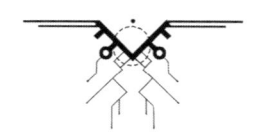

"She went to see her colleague today. So I guess any time. She is going to text me when she's home so I can head over and get the details." Lex replied. "My guess though is that it will still be a couple days. Maybe as much as a week."

"That's alright," Fade said, crossing her arms with a grin. "There's lots of fuckery we can still cause without that information."

It was true. There were still a lot of splinter cells at work, possibly planning more bombings and the hacking that Fade had been playing with could cause a lot of problems for some people.

"What have you been up to?" Lex asked.

Fade uncrossed her arms and walked over to the desk. "Well come and have a look. Nothing too serious right now. I have managed to get into some phone systems, some emails and a couple of data files for some people who work for the government. This is just small-time fun stuff I do to mess around and test security features. There's a few other things I have in mind but they're taking some time." She motioned to another computer screen that seemed to be trying to decode a password.

"What's that?" Lex asked.

"That," Fade began, not able to hide her grin "is hopefully going to tell us the password to our dear friend President Mason's personal computer drive."

"No way!" The words practically burst from Lex's mouth.

"Way. And if we can get into that and have a good snoop around we can get an idea of what's going on. If he's ascended. Not ascended. If he's still around. You know. All that pertinent info."

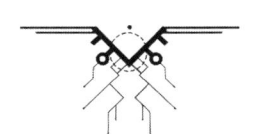

"That's so cool. You're so smart."

Fade crossed her arms and spun around in her chair theatrically. "I know."

It was pretty impressive to say the least. Lex knew nothing about that kind of thing, and had no idea where Fade would have picked it up. She was a bit strange though. Kind of tomboyish with a roguish, sometimes devil-may-care attitude. It was something Lex admired, considering she normally played by the rules. In fact, the whole situation she found herself in now was something of an abnormality. Normally she'd just sit back and listen to the government and never get involved. Being cut off from contacting her family in the Ascension program, though, was more than she was willing to put up with, and she knew she had to do something. Not just for herself, but for everyone else who was in the same situation – and there were literally thousands of people just like her.

"I found out that some government workers like to whet their appetites around the office," Fade said, clicking a folder and opening it up. It seemed to be an archive of old emails. "This guy clearly doesn't realise that an organisation like the government is going to keep backup files of emails. Check it out."

She opened one email. It was short and to the point. Essentially the man in question, a fellow named George, had been having an affair with one of his colleagues and mentioned in the email that he'd fed his wife a bit of a lie so they'd have more time for that evening's rendezvous.

"That's not all. I mean look, there's easily a hundred of those," Fade said, chuckling.

"That's hilarious." Lex said, giggling. "Anything else that might be good? Or that we could use? I mean, blackmailing someone seems a bit pointless."

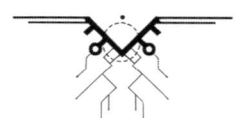

"I'm still going through what I've unearthed, but these guys are all pretty small fish. I doubt we'll find anything in here, but you never know," Fade replied. "I'm gonna get some fresh air and some java and I'll be back to go through more of this. Maybe I'll send Akoni on a food run." She grinned.

"He won't like that."

"Exactly."

Lex joined her in a beaming smile. It was pretty hilarious the way Fade and Akoni got on each other's nerves. It breathed new life into the situation and added a light-hearted feeling on occasion which was much appreciated, especially when things got heavy. Lex wasn't sure how much heavier things were going to get, but she envisioned that things certainly were poised to get worse before they got better. It was challenging to be sure, but she tried to remind herself that everything was for the greater good, even if it was all rather dark and horrendous in the first instances.

Fade busied herself with her hacking, monitoring the computer screen where she was trying to get into President Mason's personal information. She wasn't getting overly far, but she was confident it wouldn't be long before she was in and they could get to the bottom of whether he'd already ascended. She wondered if it would be easier to take care of him if he had. She supposed they could just delete his file and he'd be gone. But would it be that easy? These were the questions they needed answers to, and she hoped that when they got information from inside EverDawn these were the answers they'd get.

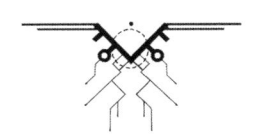

Lex, meanwhile, went to go see what Akoni was doing. He had been acting unusual for him, but she figured had she been on the team that did the bombings and someone had died unnecessarily, she'd struggle too. She walked across the floor of the warehouse to the office – the last place she'd seen him heading to. He wasn't in the office, but she heard a sound coming from further down a hallway toward a break room and followed the noise. Sure enough she found Akoni playing some game of crumpling up balls of paper and seeing how many he could get into a garbage can several feet away. Judging by the lack of paper balls on the floor, he was doing quite well and had only missed twice.

"What's up?" Lex asked casually, trying not to sound like she cared too much one way or the other.

"Nothing," he replied, not looking over and throwing another paper ball. "Bored."

"Yeah. These lulls when there isn't much to do can be annoying. But my grandma is working on getting some information from inside EverDawn. That's pretty cool."

"That is," he agreed, crumpling another piece of paper in his hands.

Lex wasn't sure how to proceed with him. She didn't want to make him uncomfortable, but she also didn't want him sulking around when there was shit that needed doing.

"You alright?" she asked, hoping it wasn't too forward.

"Yes," he replied, levelly, almost coldly. "Fine."

"Are you sure?" she asked, trying to drag it out of him a bit to try to get him back to his usual self. "You've been kind of moping around here since the train station."

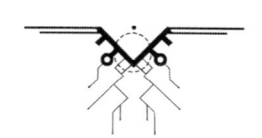

He was quiet for a second, and instead of crumpling another piece of paper, he idly ran his fingers along one of the edges with his left hand while holding it with his right, almost willing himself to get a paper cut. To Lex it seemed like it was forever before he said anything else, the tension in the room growing thicker by the moment.

"I know," he finally relented. "I'm sorry."

"What's wrong?"

He paused and took a breath. "I guess it just was different to how I expected it to be."

Lex completely understood. She'd got herself involved thinking that they were somehow going to save the world from the elitist views of President Mason and his cronies, but instead they were bombing train stations and hurting innocent people. It wasn't ideal, but it was what happened in cases like this.

"I know it sucks that people got hurt," Lex began "but you can't blame yourself for that."

"I can perfectly blame myself," Akoni replied. "I'm the one who planted those bombs. I had a hand in it."

"Well, how do Jer and Meshi feel about it?" Lex asked. "Have you talked to them?"

"No."

"Maybe you should. You might be surprised. They probably feel similar."

"Maybe," he said, not actually sure of that suggestion at all. Jer especially seemed particularly stoic about it all. And Meshi just seemed mad as hell and willing to do what it takes. Akoni thought about it for a minute and pondered why he didn't feel more passionate about the cause. It wasn't rocket science of course. People often tend to be indifferent to issues that don't directly affect them. Akoni

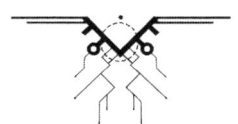

201

had never had problems with being denied access to Spots or Ascension because the type of life he had been living didn't really lend itself to ever caring about that kind of thing. Not only that, but when EverDawn had introduced paying for ascending several years ago, much to the annoyance and anger of the general populace, he knew it was a world he'd never experience due to his personal situation. He never cared because he knew he'd never be affected because it was out of reach economically for him. At least after money got involved.

All that probably shouldn't have mattered to him, but it did. At least somewhat. He was struggling with connecting the violence he'd had a hand in creating and marrying it up to a cause he struggled to identify with and relate to. He decided to keep that under wraps for now, but did admit to Lex that he'd felt kind of disconnected with everything since the train station bombing.

"Hey, that's alright," Lex said, sitting down across the table from him. "I'd say that's fairly normal. I mean, none of us ever expected to be in this situation."

"True," he agreed, feeling slightly better about everything.

"And if you don't feel like you want to do any more hands-on stuff there's lots of stuff that you can help with around here," Lex began, smiling. "For example, Fade wants someone to be her food bitch."

Akoni laughed and looked at Lex properly. "Of course she does."

They grinned at each other for a moment or two before Akoni broke the silence. "Thanks for talking to me."

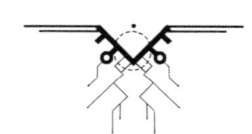

"No problem. I know how it is sometimes." Lex reached for some paper and crumpled it into a ball before trying to land it in the garbage can as Akoni had been doing. It bounced hard off the back and went rolling across the floor.

"I'm clearly bad at this," she chuckled. Akoni agreed and they both howled with laughter, a welcome respite from the stress and concern that had been plaguing them over the previous few days.

Lex wiped a tear away from her eye and caught her breath just as her phone beeped in her pocket. She took it out and looked at who it was. It was from Grandma Alice just telling her that dinner would be at six and to not be late. Lex figured she had some important news because she almost never told her not to be late. She'd just put the food to the side and Lex would have it when she got home.

She put her phone back in her pocket and looked at Akoni, sitting low in the chair, his arms crossed over his chest.

"Hey. You wanna come to my grandma's for dinner?" she asked. The idea seemed to have come from nowhere, but he didn't reject it right away. Eventually, he shrugged.

"Why not?" he replied. "A home cooked meal might be nice for a change. And we can bring back a doggy bag for Fade." he laughed.

"Good idea," Lex replied. "Let's go."

Chapter Twenty-Two

Dinner at Grandma Alice's was delicious. It was the first time in probably months, if not years, that Akoni had eaten something as nutritious as the meal Grandma had cooked: fresh fish, a lush green salad made from her own garden vegetables, along with potatoes, peas and other veggies she'd picked by hand just that afternoon. It was an amazing dinner to say the least, and it showed in the speed at which Akoni cleared his plate, prompting Grandma Alice to offer him seconds, then thirds, all of which he finished. Lex wasn't sure which part of that was the most endearing, or the strangest; an old lady's glee at having someone to doll out her delicious delights with, or a guy like Akoni taking such pleasure in cleaning his plate. At the end of the day, it was a poignant reminder of the humanity that they all held in common. Sitting around that table, they must have looked like the strangest bunch of misfits ever to have rolled out of Chinatown. It worked though, and they all smiled the same.

They ate primarily in silence, Lex bursting to know what Grandma Alice had found out from her colleague, but decided dinner probably wasn't the best time to bring it up. She could wait until after, when they were having tea and coffee with dessert. It wasn't too urgent anyway – or if it was, she was certain Grandma Alice would have said something the moment she and Akoni walked through the door. Instead, a lovely meal had awaited them and they'd been dining as though nothing was out of the ordinary – except, perhaps, for Akoni's obviously ravenous appetite. That could have put street dogs to shame.

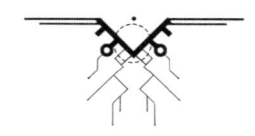

Lex began to clear the table but Akoni stopped her and insisted that he do it in payment for one of the most delicious meals of his adult life. That took her aback. The last time a grip that firm had locked onto her from a member of the Wu gang, it had resulted in being threatened at knife point. Then again, there was one thing that gang members understood – respect. Lex wondered if this was something she had misjudged, limited with her privileged scope.

Grandma Alice was pleased that he had enjoyed it so thoroughly, so she and Lex let Akoni do whatever he wanted as he seemed immensely grateful and wanted to show his appreciation. A far cry from the rough kid that used to lurk in subways shaking people down for small change or electronics to sell. He was actually a really nice person when he wasn't in the subways.

Lex set to making coffee and tea to accompany dessert while Grandma Alice took a phone call in the living room. Lex tilted her head and pinned her ears as she tried to listen, but Grandma Alice was being her usual, quiet self and she couldn't hear over the sound of Akoni doing the dishes, nor the kettle beginning to boil. She decided to wait and see if Grandma Alice said anything. Maybe it wasn't even related to the whole situation anyway.

Akoni finished cleaning the last plate and put it in the strainer on the side of the sink. "Man, I haven't eaten like that in years."

Lex smiled. "I'm glad you liked it. Grandma definitely likes feeding people. I think most Grandmas do." She paused for a minute. "Do you want tea or coffee?"

"Tea, please."

"Regular or green?"

He snorted, halfway between mockery and truth. "Wow, this place is like the Ritz. Green, I guess."

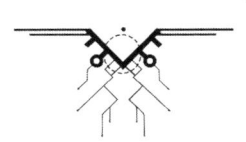

Lex laughed. She supposed he wasn't used to so many options or so much selection when it came to food. She wasn't sure if he actually had a home. He always seemed to have been in the subways, so she figured he lived on what little he could afford to beg, borrow, cadge or steal from people or shops. She suddenly was extremely glad she'd invited him to dinner. It filled her with a warmth she'd not felt in a long time to be able to provide Akoni a nice dinner.

Grandma Alice came in from the living room, putting her phone into her pocket. "Oh, thank you Lex for making the tea."

"No problem," Lex replied, pouring hot water over the green tea bags in two mugs for Akoni and Grandma Alice, scenting the room with an earthy waft. She knew Grandma Alice always had green after dinner to help digestion. She brought the mugs to the table and grabbed the sugar bowl for Akoni and Grandma Alice before making herself a cup of coffee.

The tension in the room began to build, especially considering Lex knew Grandma Alice had something to tell them but the cat hadn't been let out of the bag yet. She sat at the table between Akoni and Grandma and sipped her coffee, almost willing Grandma Alice to break the silence, which she did.

"I saw Shelley today," she began. "As you know."

"Yeah?" Lex replied, wanting her to continue.

"I told her what you told me, and what you needed. She's more than happy to help in any way she can."

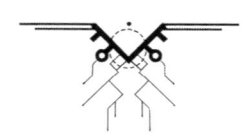

The knot in Lex's stomach suddenly gave way and a wave of relief washed over her. They were playing a dangerous game getting people on the outside involved, but it was a risk they had to take. It was imperative they got the information from inside EverDawn, otherwise they wouldn't have much to go on without Fade hacking the hell into the place, and that was risky and tricky on its own.

"She said she can probably have the things you need in a day or two." Grandma Alice continued, "But-"

"But?" Lex asked, the tension in her body building again.

"She wants some kind of danger pay. Which I agree with. I mean, she's putting herself in a precarious position doing what she's doing," Grandma Alice replied. The woman had a point, danger pay was a cheap alternative to getting sold out. Still, it sounded like she had been at EverDawn long enough to splash her feet in the toxic pool of capitalism.

"What's she want?" Akoni asked, getting intrigued and more interested by the minute.

"Three thousand dollars. To be shared among those who are helping her."

Lex tensed. "What the hell? We don't have that kind of money just laying around." Lex replied. "It might take a while to get that together."

Grandma Alice held up her hand. "Don't worry. This is where I come in. I have the money. I just want you to do everything you can to fix the situation. Whatever it takes, you should do it. For the greater good."

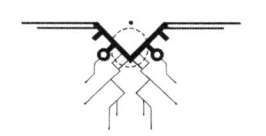

It was a peculiar problem. They could be branded terrorists at the very least and here was kindly Grandma Alice, purveyor of fine sweet and sour pork being willing to fund potential terrorists and conduct shady back room deals from her single-storey house with an extensive garden. It was both perfect and yet weird. No one would ever suspect anything, it was so devious and ideal.

"I'll take care of everything." Grandma Alice continued. "I'll pick up the stuff and bring it home here. But when I text you that everything's ready, you'll have to come straight over to get it. We're doing a dance with some shady people, I think, and the less time I have that stuff in my house, the better."

"Agreed," Akoni said. "That's fucking amazing."

Lex sucked in her breath sharply and gave Akoni a look for swearing in front of her grandma. Grandma Alice didn't seem to mind though and in fact she smiled a smile Lex had never seen before and simply said,

"Indeed, it fucking is, my boy."

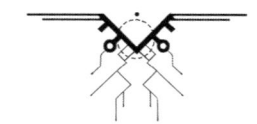

Fade meanwhile was sitting behind her computer reading through different people's chat logs that she'd come across. She hadn't found anything too juicy, not yet anyway. There was the occasional mention of someone planning to Ascend, or various details that someone had submitted to the program for consideration to ascend, and all sorts of random work-related stuff. The deeper she dug, though, the more she found pieces of information, albeit sporadically, that she thought could be useful. She saved these bits to a specific flash drive. The information contained data like lists of names, procedural changes to the technology, and even the occasional blueprint change that had been sent from engineering to production as they improved the technology. It was a pretty decent collection and Fade began to wonder what would happen if they could create their own version of the technology. Would all of the violence and resistance be necessary?

One of the lists of names was a combination of people who had already ascended and those who were waiting in line, along with the dates that they'd gone through the process, proposed dates for those not yet ascended and the procedures for disposing of the bodies after the consciousness had ascended. Fade was unconvinced that the bodies had to be disposed of, and suspected that there could be a way for the consciousness to pass from the ascension program and system and back into the "blank" brain after someone had essentially ascended. She presumed the risk of failure was the reason they'd chosen not to advertise the possibility: nobody wanted to be lost in a data buffer like in some Star Trek transporter malfunction.

She continued the somewhat laborious process of saving the documentation she came across while on her other desk her hacking program was only one number shy of figuring out the password that would let her into Mason's own private hard drive. She hoped that she didn't get caught before then so she could get a few minutes of snooping around before they caught onto her. She had a distinct feeling that she was going to find a treasure trove of different things in there, if only she could get in. And Fade wasn't the sort of girl to give up on a gut feeling; something that she had been heavily rewarded for in the past. This particular program, "hashcat", was fairly good for cracking passwords and passcodes, but it had let her down in the past. She was hopeful that since it had got so far, it would go all the way and let her in.

Fade perused the list of names of people who had ascended in the last six months. Nothing unusual, a few people she had heard of in passing in her own circles of friends and associates, but nothing that stood out such as

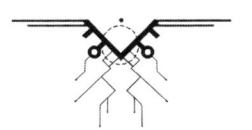

President Mason. She wasn't expecting to find him on a normal list though, if he had ascended. But why would he keep it a secret when it should have supposedly been accessible to all? But maybe that was the point – keep it secret that he and all his elitist buddies had gained access while the waitlist was miles long with no end in sight, dating back years with no movement at all. That could cause a lot of issues among the masses, especially for those who were in danger of passing away while they waited, which of course there were several.

Her coffee was getting cold, so she grabbed it, sat back in her chair and took a long sip of it. It was nice and strong, a medium dark roast from Guatemala, just as she liked it. No sugar, almost black but with a splash of the lightest milk you could find. None of that two percent crap, that was way too much. Strong coffee was definitely preferable as she was beginning to feel the effects of being up for extended periods to run various programs and generally keep an eye on things around the warehouse.

She stretched in her chair, moving around a bit, trying to exercise her back when a pinging sound from her computer running the program trying to hack into Mason's hard drive alerted her. She looked over, almost in shock or surprise. She wasn't expecting it to be done quite as quickly as it was, but sure enough. She was in.

She pushed her chair over to the desk and looked closely at what had been exposed, her eyes widening as she looked closer at what was in front of her. It was the mother lode of information on that slimy fucker that they'd been waiting for. It was all there, organised into neat folders and lists, names, phone numbers, birthdays and personal details of his associates. She rushed to save all the information she could before her security breach was discovered.

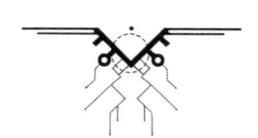

Rebellion's Martyr

In the meantime though, she couldn't keep this to herself. Reaching for her burner phone, she tapped the number to Lex's burner in. There was hardly one full ring before Lex picked up on the other end.

"Hello?"

"It's Fade. You gotta get over here. You need to see this."

Chapter Twenty-Three

Lex had never run so fast in her life, not even in the dark alleys where she felt like she was being followed. Truth be told, she probably was. She had to get back to find out what was going on, and rushed like a demented dog chasing its prey. Once she got there she went right up to Fade – not even stopping for a mug of coffee.

"What is it?" Lex panted and wiped sweat off her brow.

"Nice," Fade teased, spinning the monitor in Lex's direction. Page after page came up. They were all pictures of people's faces, government officials by the look of it.

Lex twigged. "These are EverDawn?"

"Not just EverDawn, lots of government areas."

"Should we be looking at this?"

"Don't worry. This is a copy. I wiped my footprint clean. You're getting better at this stuff though, you know?"

"Thanks." Lex couldn't help but smile.

"Are these potential targets?"

"Better. I've found a way to get into the entire mainframe. We can take them down from the inside out."

"You're amazing, you know that right?"

"Don't make a girl blush."

"How did you do it? How did you get in?"

"Well, we haven't – yet. I noticed there were a lot of specific staff members on these files."

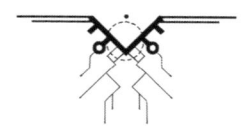

"You're telling me."

"So, I noticed something weird as I went through. A lot of them have qualifications that focus on quantum computing and quantum physics, as well as the expected medical research degrees. That's how Ascension must work."

"There's a direct link to the other side then?"

"Yes, but it's heavily guarded."

"But, you know how to get past that?"

"I've figured it out, we need a quantum computer."

"A what?" Lex looked at her as blankly as a passer-by in the street.

"It's a matter of quantum computing."

"Should I know what that is?"

Fade tried hard to hide her eye roll, clearly reminding herself that not everyone was quite so technologically advanced, or appreciative.

"Quantum computing is the use of quantum phenomena, like superposition and entanglement to perform computation for our benefit."

Lex had no idea what Fade had just said. To be totally honest she didn't even think she could repeat it. It was just a lot of long words that Lex wasn't even sure that she had ever heard before – apart from 'computer' – but that was about it. Quite suddenly, she managed to get a firmer grasp on Meshi's understanding of the world: that outdated feeling that is utterly confusing, but that she was not sure she actually wanted to be a part of anyway.

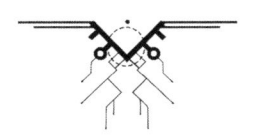

"Quantum computing is the use of quantum phenomena – you know, like superposition and entanglement – to perform computation. Computers that perform quantum computations are known as quantum computers," Fade repeated the sentence again but this time slower, as if that might make it any easier.

Lex put her arms up at her side with a shrug of her shoulders. As far as she was concerned the hacker was speaking a foreign language. And this was the expression that she would have given in a foreign bar when they asked her something about a drink order, establishing that she was practically an alien in their area. The only difference was this was the other way around, Lex felt decidedly human. Everything Fade was talking about was distinctly out of this world.

"I'm sorry," Lex tried. Not really sure what she was supposed to say, she opted for an apology. That usually worked, although she wasn't sure what she was apologising for.

"It's based on the principles of quantum theory."

"And that's?"

"The theory that explains the behaviour of energy and material but on a minute scale, on the atomic and subatomic levels. But that hasn't got much to do with what you need to know right now."

"So, what do I need to know?"

Lex was about to wish she hadn't asked.

"The kind of computers that we use today, each and every day, can only encode information in bits that take the value of ones or zeros. That's called binary."

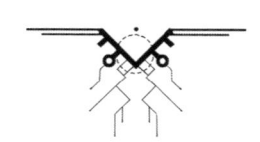

"And that's the code?"

"Technically, no. It's encoding, but close enough. So this limitation of ones and zeros restricts their ability to do some of the heavier work. That's where quantum computing comes in."

"I think I'm following. You need a smaller measure, because the pieces of the puzzle you're trying to remember aren't so simple."

"Right! It'd be like trying to identically replicate a modern digital movie in 8-bit 80s computer graphics. It just doesn't fit. You can't get the whole picture on the right scale."

Lex nodded, that kind of made sense. "Okay."

"So, the computer we need uses quantum bits – they're called qubits. It harnesses the unique ability of subatomic participles to exist in more than one state concurrently."

"Whoa, whoa, whoa. You're losing me again." Poor Fade was struggling but she pushed on.

"It means that a bit can be both a one and a zero. It's like the Schroedinger's cat of computing."

"Whose cat?"

"You know, where you put a cat in a box and it's both alive and dead until it's opened?"

"Why would someone do that?" Lex asked, horrified.

"Ha! It's not a real cat. It's- let me just get back to the computer."

"Couldn't you just-"

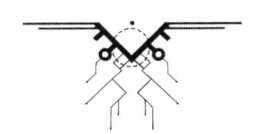

Fade cut her off. "Superposition and entanglement are two features of quantum physics. These supercomputers are based on those characteristics."

"Let's just say science wasn't my strong point."

"Superposition is where two or more waves cross at a point. Not water waves but the kind you can't see with the naked eye."

"Like gamma waves?" Lex proffered.

"Bingo! But not so dangerous. The displacement at the point where they cross over is equal to the sum of the displacements of the individual waves, meaning they occupy the same space. You can see it with Chandi plates more easily, but we don't have the equipment to go through that right now."

"Shame," said Lex, flatly. This lecture was giving her a headache. She was relieved not to have a practical to do too. There were only two things keeping her hanging on; the promise of good news and Fade's excitement.

"So, as for entanglement – this is where objects have to be described with reference to one another, even though the individual objects are often spatially separated – not that they have to be."

"That... kind of sounds like the same thing."

Fade shook her head. "Similar in context, different in application. This entanglement leads to correlations – that's regularly repeating patterns – between observable physical properties of the systems."

"And the system is the computer?"

"In this case, yes."

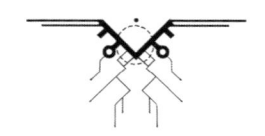

"So, you have a computer based on those two, cross particle thingies."

"No, I don't have one. I need one. The combination of these two, and a whole host of things we won't go into today, are what empowers quantum computers to handle operations at speeds exponentially higher than the conventional computers you've seen me working on, and at much lower energy consumption."

"Making us harder to spot on the grid but getting a better picture?"

"Yes. And that picture is of a mind."

Lex's eyes lit up. "Ascension!"

"Yes! High five girl!" Fade raised her hand in the air and there was a clap as their palms met.

"You worked out how they do it? And that's somehow going to help us."

"The only thing I can't quite work out is how they actually get the memories out. I mean, sure, the brain lights up, but it's hard to see an actual picture, let alone millions of them." She tapped her lip. "I can work on that though, when I get a quantum computer."

"Sure, I can go pick one up."

Fade laughed. "It's not going to be quite that simple. You can't just get these things at a store."

"Where am I supposed to get one?"

"… EverDawn."

"Jesus! How are we meant to do that?"

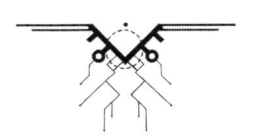

"You'll find a way. I'm sure Akoni or Alice will be able to come up with something."

"Well, it can't get much worse. May as well get it over with."

There was a long pause.

"That's the thing I need to talk to you about. We need a virtual cat." Fade didn't sound half as confident then. In fact, she was rubbing the back of her neck.

"Spit it out."

"So the cat is both alive and dead, yeah? Kind of like the people in Ascension."

Lex inhaled sharply. "We need someone to Ascend?"

"It's the only way to get around there safely. Don't get me wrong, I've dabbled before. It's virtually impenetrable beyond the lounge though, unless you're on the system."

"And you can't make a fake account?"

"No, not with the amount of tech at their disposal. There's just too much risk. Sending in a cat to help us catch all of the rats is the safest bet."

A chill chased its way over Lex's skin. "Who?"

"We need to think about who we can trust, really trust. I need to be here for the tech side, Akoni has the power in the streets. Reasonably, it comes down to you and Meshi."

Lex sighed. That virtual cat was going to be as reluctant as a real one on it's way to the vet.

"Then, it's likely going to fall on me. Meshi has too many contacts we might need. And I started all of this. I don't want that though."

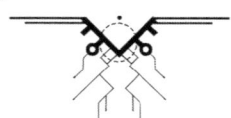

"No," said Fade sternly. "EverDawn and that shit bag Mason did."

"Well, I'm ending it." Lex nodded with conviction. "I'll get your quantum computer, and then we'll talk about whether I can Ascend. First, I need to do something much more frightening."

Fade tipped her head to the side. "This is kind of critical. What could be worse?"

"I have to talk to Grandma Alice about it."

Chapter Twenty-Four

Lex had never realized just how little she wanted to Ascend before the decision had been thrust upon her. She still had a choice, that was the main thing. And she clung to it.

Lex didn't want to Ascend. Far from it. Her first thought when Fade had mentioned it was going to talk to her grandmother, not because she wanted to let her know the details, but so she could find some logical reason for her not to go ahead. All of the arguments Lex had were selfish. They were all about her and her family. As she passed one of the beggar kids on the street, tossing a coin his way, she could barely look at his gleeful smile as he received it. He was just one example of who Lex would be betraying if she didn't do it.

For a fleeting moment she hoped Meshi would go ahead. He was old, didn't really have any family. Ascension would afford him some luxuries that he had never even seen in his physical life, let alone had. Didn't James say he got to partake in some awesome hobbies? And without the concern of aching joints. Meshi probably had a few aches and pains he would like to be rid of.

"Stop being ridiculous," Lex told herself. Meshi didn't want to Ascend either. One of them was going to have to – or maybe Jer, or Cat? Though, Cat had been nowhere to be seen since the train station. Lex had heard on the grape vine that she was free, but clearly her commitment to the cause wasn't as staunch as they had thought. Well, hoped. Akoni and Meshi had doubts from the start. They had never said anything about Jer though. She could ask him.

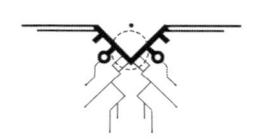

Lex took out her burner phone and punched in her pin, giving him a call. He picked up right away.

"What's up?"

"We need to get something, and I'm going to need backup, you in?"

"Sure, anything for the cause."

"Get Fade to send you the details."

With that he hung up. He had said anything for the cause – so, that was settled, right? As soon as they had the computer, she would ask him.

When she reached Grandma Alice's house, there was soft music flitting out through the cracked open windows. It was a hauntingly familiar tune.

"Hi grandma," Lex called as she wandered inside. The door fell shut behind her with a click, and she inhaled deeply. Her grandmother's house had a very unique scent to it. The musk of incense burning, the faint wetness of the garden permeating through all of the rooms, and the particular brand of cleaner that Alice had used Lex's entire life.

It occurred to Lex that there was no scent in the world that could be better than that – or in Ascension, not that Lex was going there. It was already set in her mind. It was to be Jer or, if not, as a last resort Meshi.

Alice, humming, stepped out of the back room. She was carrying a soft rag, meant for cleaning glass collectibles. "There you are! Just in time. Come help me with this shelf."

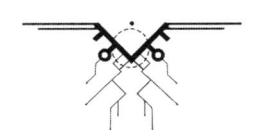

And then she was vanishing into the back room again, and Alice had to rush after her. This was exactly why she couldn't go. Her grandmother needed her.

The back room was mostly for storage. There was a large cabinet on the back shelf with glass doors, filled up with all that Alice had collected over the years. The doors were sitting open, the shelves half cleaned.

Alice gave Lex a rag and a glass cat. Lex started to clean.

Lex decided to bring up the subject of Ascension as casually as possible. The response was less relaxed.

"I was thinking, maybe the best way to get in the system is to be in the system."

"Excuse me? You better not be saying what I think you are." She had paused, a glass duck held in one hand. Her mouth twisted into a frown.

"I'm not saying I am, I'm just saying it would be the right thing to do."

"Good, because you're worth more than that. Now, do you remember how I got that cat?"

"Yes. I remember. You don't need to tell me every time I help with this."

Alice huffed and went back to her own cleaning.

"Everyone thinks that about their own family." Lex said after a while. She wasn't looking at her grandmother as she said it. She couldn't bring herself to.

"Not everyone has the privilege of deciding."

"Grandma!" Her eyes were on her then.

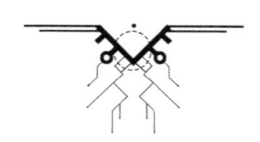

"Lex, it's the way the world works. The rich do well, I didn't work years at that place so you could become a bunch of ones and zeros."

Every muscle in Lex's body tightened up. Her grandmother had always been her moral compass. She had raised her right. Now, she was throwing all that away? Just because they had some money?

"Actually, they're bits."

"I don't need the technicalities. After everything you have learned, why would you even consider it?"

"Because of everything I've learned." Lex didn't know why she was arguing. She didn't want to Ascend. There was something about someone, even someone she loved so dearly, trying to take the choice away that made her skin crawl. "I have choices! President Mason might not think so, but I do."

"I dislike him as much as you-"

"Clearly not."

Alice was taken aback by that. It wasn't like her granddaughter to be confrontational.

"Well, if you want to Ascend so badly. Forget these!" She pulled the cat away, shoving it back onto the shelf. She placed her duck down as well. It landed with an angry clack.

Like a petulant child, Lex snatched up a different collectible and started to wipe it down, too. "I'm not."

"Well, then why are you bringing up such nonsense?"

"Because if I needed to-"

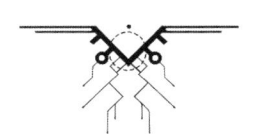

"Don't expect me to be there!"

Lex took a few breaths and shoved the cloth and the glass figurine onto the shelf. "I'm going to meet Jer, I don't want to be late."

"Who is Jer?"

"None of your business." Lex left, trying hard to hold in her tears and anger. Things were too important to be hung up on a bit of disappointment. Her grandmother would understand one day, and she wasn't going to Ascend anyway. Jer was. Lex knew he would. As soon as the mission was done, she would talk to him and they would all be set.

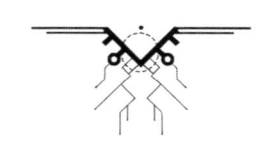

Chapter Twenty-Five

"This feels like such a bad idea," Lex said as she and Jer stood outside EverDawn. The building was remarkably grand and stretched into the sky like a school yard bully towering over his next victim.

"Then let me go ahead."

"No, I'm coming. We have Fade's key cards, they'll get us access."

"She only made one. Doesn't that seem weird to you?""

"She has bigger things to deal with. And one is all we need if we stick together, right?"

"I suppose. Something just seems off."

"It's EverDawn."

Jer chuckled. "I suppose so. There's no pressure to do this. I'm happy to slip inside myself."

"No, two pairs of eyes are better than one."

"Alright, let's do this."

"What are we going to do? Just walk right on in?" She said sarcastically.

"Actually, yeah. That's how all the best thieves do it."

"How would you- oh wait, yeah."

"Head held high and confident."

Sneaking into the building was actually a lot easier than they had expected. That was probably thanks to the

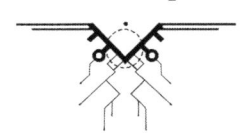

EverDawn arrogance. After all, who would go after such a big company with so much money? They probably thought that they were safe. That attitude had made them weak, and not just in that regard.

The building was made of pure white marble, which seemed to be blasphemous beyond anything else. There was certainly nothing pure about EverDawn.

Regardless, it was quite the impressive building. To think that this was where Alice had once worked was quite amazing. Lex had become used to the finer things in life, thanks to her grandmother's wealthy pension, but it took her by surprise just how much opulence there was in the simple office. To be quite frank, it made it look like Grandma Alice had been severely underpaid.

Her hand ran across the stonework wall. Just one side of that room would be enough to fund Chinatown for an entire week of eating and education. That didn't matter to the fat cats though. Why would they bother to look after the next generation if they could have beautiful decorations like this instead? And why would they educate them, when that would lead to people who ask questions? It was far better to keep them oppressed and willing, rather than give them free will like any human being should deserve.

Needless to say, they sauntered right in, after telling the receptionist that they had a meeting with Dave. Of course, they didn't know a Dave, but every building had one.

Getting in was not the problem, getting out was. They should have seen it coming, given that the only room with a lock on was the one that held the quantum computers. Fade's custom-made security card had worked there, but it had still been all too easy.

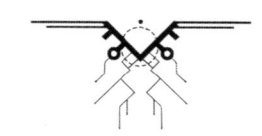

The moment they walked into the computer lab, a deafening alarm sounded. It made an announcement first; "Uncarded member in the computer lab. Uncarded member in the computer lab". The corridor was illuminated with red light, screeching to everyone and anyone within the building.

"Shit!" Lex felt her heart constrict as the sound went on and on. She desperately wanted to cover her ears, but that would mean dropping the price of a piece of equipment she had just ripped out of the wall.

"It knew there were two of us!" Jer said, grasping the other piece they needed and darting out of the room.

"But one card. Oh God, I'm so sorry."

"Be sorry later!"

Even over the rumble of the alarm system, they could hear footsteps thundering down the corridor.

"Take this!" Jer dumped his half of the equipment in her arms. For a moment Lex thought that he was going to run and leave her. That would never happen though and deep down she knew it.

"What are you going to do? I can't run and carry these at the same time!"

"Get in there!" Jer shoved her roughly into a double-doored utility closet. "And whatever you do, don't get caught."

Before Lex could protest the door was shut on her. There was nothing but a thin line of light in front of her, where she could watch the horror unfold.

"Key card!" Demanded one of the guards as they circled Jer.

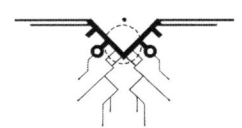

"Sure, I was just about to do the update with the quantums for the Spot system change when some guy ran in there." He dug into his pocket and handed over the card.

"Looks legit. Which way did he go?" The other said, handing it back.

"That way, I think." Jer nodded behind him.

Lex couldn't believe their luck, maybe her stupidity hadn't cost them everything! Hope rose in her chest for all but a second.

Another group joined. "Did you get them? The guy and the girl?"

"It's two guys. This one's with us and the other went that way." A guard nodded.

The other squinted. "But it smells of perfume."

Lex froze, but Jer was cool.

He said, "Well this is embarrassing, but I-" Jer balled his fist behind him in preparation.

"And there's a computer missing!"

At that moment Jer swung his fist around and punched one of the guards square in the gut. The guard doubled over, crying out in pain, while another two piled on top of Jer.

Lex didn't have room to put the computer down. She had to decide what to give up − the computer, or her comrade. Lex knew that this would be one of the most important decisions she would ever have to make. It was a defining moment, one that would shape her for her entire future.

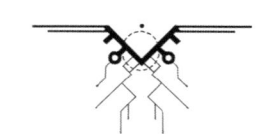

There were only two options.

She could stay there in that cupboard and sneak away after the drama, leaving Jer to a beating, and possibly a prison sentence. Or she could drop the computer and dive in to help Jer. If she did that, there was no way of getting one. EverDawn would be locked up as tight as President Mason's wallet after this.

The fight was still going on. Jer had managed to wriggle free and stood up before taking a punch to the face. He swung back. "EverDawn bastards! I'll teach you to charge me to see my little girl!"

Lex gasped, she had never really questioned what people's motives were. She had assumed they were all there for some kind of hatred at the rising prices. If Jer's little girl was in there, she had to have been sick.

"If you ever wanted to see her again, you shouldn't have broken in here!"

It hit Lex like a thousand falling bricks. If she didn't help him, that little girl would be stuck in the system for eternity, wondering why her father had stopped coming.

She had to drop the computer and get out.

She would find another way – somehow. She had no idea how, but she would. It was her mess to clean up.

She let go, feeling the tech slide down the door, ready to push. She hoped she could hit one of the goons as it spilled open. And she was right! It took one of them down, splitting his face open.

"I told you to hide!" Jer shouted, kicking back at another.

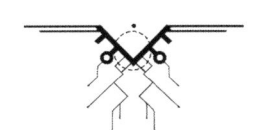

"Change of plan!" Lex joined the fray. The guards were strong, incredibly so. The computer fell to the floor, cracking on the side and it's monitor shattering.

"I can handle them! Get another and go!"

"I won't leave you" She dodged a punch.

"Then you'll be leaving everyone else."

Lex still didn't run. Their eyes met and he could tell. He yanked away from the nearest guard and raised his hands.

"Let her go, and I'll go with you. She's just a girl. I dragged her into this."

"What are you doing?"

"Get out!" He dropped to his knees.

Lex was torn, so much that she felt like a rag being dragged apart in two directions. He was doing it to save her. Maybe she could have stayed, but more were coming – thanks to her hesitation.

"Go!" He shouted, hard and cruel.

"I'm sorry." She snatched up the broken pieces and ran. The guards didn't stop her, they were too busy, dragging Jer away.

On the way back Lex crumpled into a pile. She had left a man to face God only knows what, just because she couldn't follow a simple instruction. He would have been fine – maybe. Fuck! She didn't know.

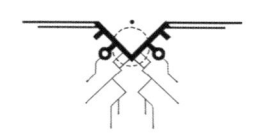

"Yaaahh!" She booted a fence, sending the rotten panel across the yard in a series of splinters. Screaming was all she could do. What if she had just listened? What if he was going to be locked up for all of time now? Away from his daughter? She screamed into the blackness of the night. What had she dragged him into? What had she really got him involved in? And what did she have to show for it? A broken computer and blood on her hands, that was what.

Heat blistered at her skin – a burning rage, swallowing her up from the inside out.

"The hell did you do, Lex?" She kicked, again, and again, until there was nothing but fence posts left.

The rain began to spit – her unholy baptism into the person that she had thrown herself into becoming. The stupid, stupid girl. How was she ever supposed to protect her grandmother if she couldn't even protect herself? If she took innocent people into the jaws of EverDawn just because she wanted to see in there? Maybe he wasn't innocent, but it wasn't his fault.

Lex had to salvage something. She pulled the pieces of the computer together, knowing it wasn't enough. Not for the cost, but it might be, if she told Fade that she was ready for Ascension.

Realising that the rain was starting to fall harder she made her way back to the warehouse, clinging to the dry shadows as much as she could. Hopefully, there would still be something to rescue, because Lex didn't feel like she was worth it.

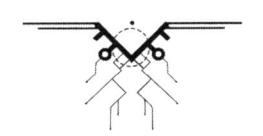

When she got back, Fade was ecstatic. There wasn't too much damage to the main unit, and she had already set up the seating for it to be attached to. A meeting was being held between old members and the new ones. Lex didn't give a damn that she was interrupting. The only thing Lex could ask though, was:

"How soon before I can Ascend?"

"You're the reason we're here."

"And I'm the reason others aren't." She looked at the her friends. "And I should be the one to do it."

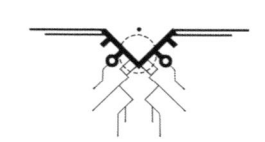

Chapter Twenty-Six

Lex was starting to realise why she had never wanted to train as a scientist, or a computer programmer for that matter. The things that Fade was doing with all those wires and circuits and God knows what, were beginning to make her brain fry – and she wasn't even the one plugging them in. There were some parts that she could understand, like the chair and the caging around the head that would undoubtedly be what took out the information. She figured that was what was held in the brain anyway, her consciousness. With what Fade was doing she could have told her that all of the information was stored in her big toe and she might have believed her. Some things were just too complex to get her head around – this being one of them.

"I don't understand this one bit," Lex said as she turned to look at Meshi.

"I don't either, but I have a way to make it fathomable in my head. I think a bit like your grandma's cooking, it's something you have to have special skill in. Like sweet and sour pork, selling antiques, or making black-market contacts."

Fade got down on her knees, tinkering with something at the back of the chair: a wire of some sort. All Lex could have told someone about it was that it was blue. She wasn't too happy about hearing Meshi mention her grandmother either.

Fade gave an exasperated huff, then flicked the wires together.

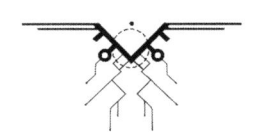

"Speaking of-" Fade made a small spark by putting the two bits of metal together after peeling off the case, as if she was trying to hotwire a car – which was probably child's play to her. Lex figured that it was the sort of thing that her spunky comrade could do in her sleep. "-any chance you could get hold of those black-market contacts?"

Meshi nodded. "I can get a burner phone now and ring. What do you need?"

She tapped her lip, lost in concentration for a moment but looking like a viper that was about to strike. Clearly something was up. Perhaps that should have made Lex feel uncomfortable, but far from it. It actually made her feel better. If Fade, the legendary Serenity among other names, was finding something difficult to rig, then surely it was the safe bet that EverDawn would struggle to catch them out. The things that Fade did were as close to anything that Lex had ever seen to magic – and that included uploading people's consciousness into the Cloud. EverDawn would have nothing on her skills.

"It should be easy enough."

"Easy for you to say," Lex muttered, just loud enough to be heard and to receive a raised eyebrow for a moment.

"I only need one part, aside from the neurotrophic electrodes, which are, annoyingly, already programmed. My Nally-Stakhov gold-crypter can handle scrambling and IP obfuscation, and the Lister cracking module is fast enough to compensate for sniffing on the fly, so there's only one thing left. I mean, I could also use some kind of highly parallelized secondary processor to boost the packet encode/decode rates, a GPU would do. We could hook that into the power supply running off the-"

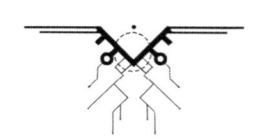

"Stop." Meshi raised his hands. "I already learnt English, I don't need to know another language this late in my life, especially not without a glass of whiskey in my hand. Tell me the name of the thing you need."

"Oh, that's simple. I just need a router, the beefier the better. With the data we're handling an enterprise grade core-capable router would be ideal, but a commercial office one would work well enough as a backplane. This one's as burnt out as a fast-food worker on a twelve-hour shift on double burger day. Oh – and an SFP media converter."

Meshi blinked, then looked over to Lex, who looked back at him and blinked. There were a couple of words she recognised, but not enough to understand them. Fade was an awesome woman, the kind of person that Lex would have wanted around if she had ever had a little girl – not that there was ever going to be an opportunity for that now. She was strong and independent, pretty but also intelligent, and to be quite frank she totally kicked ass. Sometimes though, Fade just didn't understand that the rest of the world didn't speak computer jargon. To be quite truthful Lex wouldn't be surprised if the other woman started talking in binary, greeting her with ones and zeros instead of English.

There was no way that she or Meshi would be able to correctly translate her shopping list, even if it did only have one item.

"Why don't you give Fade the burner phone and the number?"

Meshi let out a long sigh of relief. "A good idea."

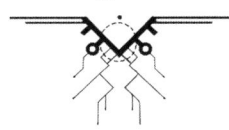

He took a phone out of his pocket, punched in the number for one of his many contacts, and handed it over. Fade held onto it as it rang for a short time, just long enough to give Lex concern that the contact of the other end might have other things to do, or worse, they might have been arrested.

Don't be stupid, she told herself, scolding herself with a paranoia. They had already come this far, why would things be getting more difficult? Even if they were, this contact didn't know that Meshi was going to ring them today, and on top of that they had already had an incident of one of their ranks getting captured. Cat hadn't brought them down, had she? Or Jer. She hadn't heard. It was going to be okay, she told herself, they'll pick up any second now.

And thank goodness they did, because if she'd have held her breath any longer, she might well have fainted.

Fade took the call in the other room – no doubt walking away from them, so she didn't entirely scramble their brains.

In the five minutes that she was gone, Lex managed to calm herself down. Why was she getting so worked up now? They were nearly there. The next phase of the plan was within reaching distance. Maybe that was the problem. It was like Christmas Eve back in the days when people actually had the money to celebrate. Through all of December she would take down her advent calendar and eat a little chocolate each and every day, knowing that Christmas was right around the corner. When it came to Christmas Eve however, it was so close her excitement seemed to boil over. Once the idea of the big day was within touching distance, she found that she couldn't sleep, her mind would go into overdrive and instead of dreams it would become a wash with scenarios that could have could occurred playing out in front of her. What toys would you get? When will Santa arrive? Would she get to see him even for the break this moment?

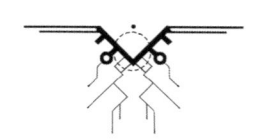

Building up the device was her Christmas this year, and once again questions flooded into her head like a torrent. When would it be ready? What would it feel like? How safe was it really? Would it be enough?

"I think I need a drink," said Lex, flopping down into a spare seat. The one that would be used for the device was much closer, but she wasn't about to sit in that. For one thing it seems like the end, and she definitely wasn't ready for that – technologically or mentally speaking. And for another, perhaps more frighteningly, she was scared of what Fade would do to her if she broke something else. The project was her baby, not her first child for sure, but 100 percent her baby.

"I think that's something we can all understand. I'll pour a whiskey," said Meshi, tottering off without being told twice.

Lex called after him, "Make mine a double."

"Fuck that. I'm pouring us both a full glass each."

Lex burst out laughing. She had heard the old Chinese man swear before. It wasn't uncommon. After all, she had been just like him in her youth. Whenever a person gets a grasp on a new language, they want to learn the swear words first. It seems like an inbuilt need; a glimmer of childish glee that rises and everybody. Hearing Meshi so freely and eloquently use the word "fuck" though, that was exactly what she needed. It was the perfect thing to brush away the darkness at the moment, and remind everyone of the kind of world that was worth fighting for – one where everyone could have a laugh and revel in friends and family, not having to become a millionaire and buy tokens to a Spot machine.

"I love you, Meshi," she chuckled.

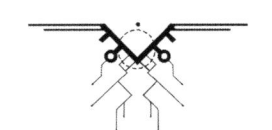

The old man looked back with a sparkle in his eye that was better suited to a youth sneaking out of the house to visit young love.

He gave her a proud grin. "And you're like a daughter I always wanted… And at least you can handle your drink."

It was not long before they were all in the room again, but Fade wasn't going to allow the others the courtesy of finishing off a drink before she filled them in on the phone call.

"I have a girl who can get the part, good call on which contact to ring. We'll make a hacker of you yet." She patted Meshi on the shoulder, who was most perturbed that it almost made him spill his drink.

"No, no. I deal with antiques for a reason. The old ways like me, and I like them."

He had a point, Lex thought. What they were fighting were in many ways the old ways, technologically advanced or not. They needed those old-fashioned socialist values, communities that cared about each other, looked out for the elderly and were safe for kids to play in nature.

"It seems to me like we're all after the same thing, we're just taking different paths together." Lex downed half of her glass, feeling the burn on her throat and relishing it.

Meshi laughed. "You are definitely Chinese my girl, nowhere else comes out with proverbs that true."

"That's all well and good," Fade said. "But there's a bit of an issue with the part."

Lex's heart sank in her chest. She tried to drown it out with a swallow of whiskey but that just seemed to stir things up more. She shuddered, preparing herself.

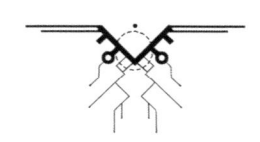

"So, what's the problem?" Lex scraped the words from her mouth.

"This contact is already under surveillance. She's managed to reroute all of her electronic devices, but she thinks there's still eyes on her."

"Meaning one of us needs to do a pick up, without raising suspicion."

Fade snapped her fingers, pointing at Lex with a grin as wide as President Mason's ego. "You got it."

"Luckily, she needs to get some groceries. She says she'll make the drop in the Asian supermarket. She's going to put the part underneath the packet mixes for squid dumplings."

"Takoyaki."

"Yes. Then you can get the last component and I can keep hacking these damn electrodes."

"Can you hack an electrode?"

"If I can't, none of us are getting in your head. Just focus on the drop off, okay?"

Lex stood up and put her glass down. "I should be the one to go, I started this whole thing."

Meshi grunted. "But we need you for the upload."

Lex didn't want to think about that. "Consider it my last meal on real air."

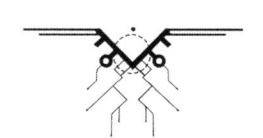

There was no arguing with that. Honestly, she just needed to be able to do something. Having Fade do all the work was starting to make her feel out of control. Throughout the entire thing there had been something for her to do. It might have been small, but it was still enough to keep her anxiety tied up in a neat little bow so that the rest of her could function.

Meshi, ever the businessman, raised a question. "What payment does she want? I like her, but she overcharges almost as much as EverDawn."

"That's the best part." Fade sat on the chair with one foot up on the arm. "She said she'll take our victory as payment."

That warmed Lex's heart and a smile chased across her face. "So, it's free?"

"Just like we will all be."

"Just one thing," Lex started. "What is this SFB thingy?"

Fade fell back in the seat, her whole body slumping into it like a toasted marshmallow being pressed into a gram cracker. "S. F. P! Don't they teach you anything? Okay, let me explain."

Lex made it to the Asian supermarket with a hood over her head. Luckily, it was raining, so she didn't seem entirely out of place. That was unusual, actually enjoying the rain that seemed to never stop falling. It was almost as though nature itself was conspiring against President Mason and his material driven ways. Each drop seemed to say "you banned rainwater collection, huh? Well, Mr President we're still here for the people, and we'll rain on every fucking avenue to help your enemies get through without a trace."

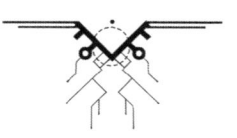

As Lex walked along, the centimetre of rain that had already slung itself down in protest of the unnatural ways of the world, sealed away her footprints within a second. There was no trace of her – too hazy for a camera to pick up and no tracks to follow.

The walk felt longer than it should have, as Lex drudged on through the poor, yet glorious, weather. By the time she got to the toxic yellow of the Asian supermarket sign, she was iced to the bones.

Walking inside, she wrapped her arms tightly around herself, shuddering. At least she wouldn't have to lower her hood.

All she had to do then was find the takoyaki mix. That would be in the Japanese section. It wasn't one that she was too well acquainted with, but the heady scent of black garlic, soy and ginger were homely. It was like getting a hug from Grandma Alice as she infused her food – because that wasn't happening any time soon. Lex hadn't faced her since making her decision. The smell was where the similarities ended though. Japanese cuisine had a more umami taste, whereas Chinese, especially Cantonese cooking was richer, more often fried than barbecued. Perhaps, before the waters had become so polluted and the industry had over-fished the remaining population, the two would have shared more culinary commonalities. Fish eating was a long-passed luxury, although there were a couple of seriously overpriced lobsters swimming about in a tank. Then again, can there be a reasonable price to pay on an animal that is close to extinct? Just so it can be boiled, slopped on a plate with some lemon butter and shit out a day later?

"Takoyaki, takoyaki…" Lex reminded herself, looking around.

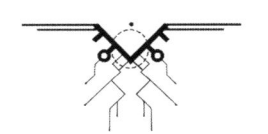

If Leena was being watched, Lex knew that she had to be careful. She looped the store a couple of times, waiting for people to clear out.

The thing was, they weren't moving – and they were right in front of where she needed to be. The hairs on the back of her neck pricked up like heckles on a cat. Maybe they were just there to pick up supplies themselves? She couldn't be the only one who took ages to find things.

A text buzzed in her pocket and she checked it.

New message: *'Did you pick up dinner yet?'*

At least that looked fairly inconspicuous. Lex replied quickly, saying that she was almost done, and then decided it was time to make her move. She couldn't keep standing around and not arouse suspicion.

Lex walked over and grabbed a bag, she could feel the cable with the adapter on the end. It was curled up tight, just as Fade had said.

She pulled her hand back, but was stopped. The fine fingers of another woman clasped her wrist.

"Sorry, did you need a bag of-"

"No."

Lex's heart dropped so hard that her knees almost gave way.

"You're Leena? Why are you meeting me? Do you know how risky this is?" Lex tried to keep her voice low. When she had run in Akoni in the metro all that time ago, he had called her the amateur for carrying around her poster. At the time, that had seemed a little harsh. Now, she understood his frustration.

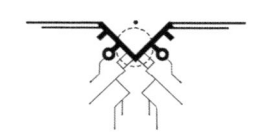

"Because I wanted to tell you in person that I'm sorry."

Lex's heart just about stopped beating. "What?"

"I had to, my little girl, she's sick. Ascension is the only thing that can help her."

Lex stared at her slack jawed. She knew as well as anybody that there were going to be people that EverDawn manipulated.

"Come with me, miss," said a voice from behind.

Leena leant into Lex, whispering: "I threw out the phone, Meshi is safe."

With that, Lex was in the back of a van with no idea what would happen to her. The cable and the bag of octopus dumpling mix were still in her hand as they slammed the back door shut, leaving her in a daze.

Chapter Twenty-Seven

Her mouth was dry, her skin like ice, but still sweat settled on her brow. The van had rolled on for what was probably only a mile, and as it did, the man opposite her hadn't taken his eyes off her. That made sense, she supposed. After all, she was a criminal – a terrorist, in their eyes.

The man opposite her was in his late 60s, and had long, black hair in a ponytail that hung down to his waist. His eyes were like marbles, cold and blue. Their glass refused to look away from her. The man's thin lips were pressed together as tight as the Ethernet in her hand. She needed to throw that away. The question was, how? The longest time she got without his eyes on her was as he blinked.

Getting caught wasn't her biggest fear, but maybe that was the shock. What really struck her was that the EverDawn goons might work out what she was doing if they saw that lead. Lex knew that she could keep her mouth shut, there were no two ways about that. Nobody that had helped her would suffer because of her tongue. They would suffer though, if all eyes were turning towards computer hardware. All EverDawn would have to do would be to trace the pieces and check who was buying them. They might even be able to work out what Fade was attempting to do. They could set a trap. That would be the end of everything. And someone else would need to Ascend.

"What are you staring at?" Lex asked the man. His eyes scanned her then he spoke in a withered tone.

"There's something familiar about you."

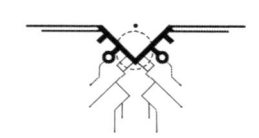

"Is there?" Lex tried to remain nonchalant.

"Yes."

And that was the end of that conversation.

Lex kept twisting the wire in her hand. She considered her options. Maybe she could drop it behind her seat? They would find it eventually, hopefully long enough for Fade and the others to work out what was happening and get a replacement. EverDawn would still know that they were trying to connect though. There was also the option of tossing it when they got to their location, whatever that was. Probably cameras though, Lex thought. Her only option was to keep it on her and hope she could ditch it somewhere at EverDawn, if that was where they were heading. If she could just throw it by a computer or something there, it wouldn't rouse too much suspicion. Seeing something like that lying around a computer system was fairly standard. It shouldn't be a problem – if she could get near one. For all Lex knew, she might be going straight to the gallows; a rebellion crushed without so much as a whisper to inspire a further uprising. Her palms were growing clammy, and like her chances at escape, the cable was slipping in her hands.

"What I wouldn't give for some sweet and sour pork." Lex tried to get them to pull over, half hoping that she could run. "I'm actually starting to feel faint."

The man leaned forward, eyes narrowed. "You think we are going to stop for sweet and sour pork? I haven't heard something so ridiculous since Alice…"

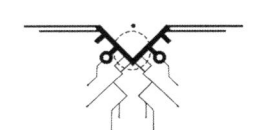

Lex gasped, and though she choked it down, it was clear that his suspicions were rising. She couldn't let him know her connection to her Grandmother, she just couldn't. There was a chance that he was talking about someone else, of course. Something told Lex that this was more than coincidence though. She had to throw him off.

"Who is Alice?"

He crossed his legs, placing his hands on his knees and weighing up the question.

"A woman I used to work with. A good woman."

"Where did you work?"

"EverDawn, but you already knew that."

"Right." Lex hung her head briefly, fears confirmed. Silence followed and they turned a corner, van swaying. Lex had to wonder if this is what prisoners of pirate ships had felt like back in the day. Her stomach was swaying about as much.

"She was Chinese too," he said after a while. "And made excellent sweet and sour pork."

"She still does." Lex didn't know why she had said that. It had just sort of blurted out.

"Last I heard, she had a grandson called James. He Ascended. And a granddaughter who didn't, Lex. I suppose that she never did."

Lex swallowed, trying to find what strength she had and channelling her inner Akoni.

"And who does that make you?"

"Doctor Takahashi."

"Sorry, I haven't heard of you."

He inhaled, nostrils nipping tight. "Not surprising. She broke my heart that girl."

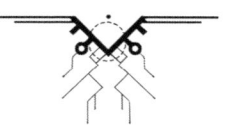

Lex let out a whimper. That was not what she needed to hear. Her heart plummeted in her chest. Had she just pointed out her grandmother's involvement? And from there Jade's?

Lex did not have long to think about it.

"Pull the van over," said Takahashi. "Next time you get a quiet spot – away from prying eyes."

Fuck.

The van turned onto bumpy ground shortly after. Lex could barely breathe, and between the time the van stopped and the bang of the driver's door closing, she was blank.

The man opposite her stood up. He reached out for a box, flipped open the clasp and drew out a handful of small items. Each of them consisted of a hollow glass cone attached to several gold wires.

"These," said Dr. Takahashi, taking a small box from his bag, "are neurotrophic electrodes. They were invented by Dr. Philip Kennedy around the turn of the century, designed to read the electrical signals that the brain uses to process information."

"I won't give up my friends, even to that," she said firmly.

"You wouldn't have a choice. We could upload you – or at least what we needed of you – and from there, you would be left a drooling mess. That, or you could fully Ascend."

"And be at President Mason's mercy? He'd hit the delete key the moment I got in."

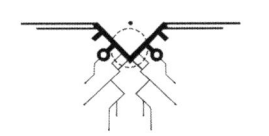

The back door opened.

Takahashi snorted. "You aren't that special, small fry. Now, get out."

Lex stood, walking as if she was a ghost on the path she was forced to walk every night for centuries. Her feet just followed, pacing on without thought.

The place they had come to was sheltered, but thick with mud from where the rain pooled off the back of abandoned buildings. The rain beat down so hard from the guttering that nobody would hear them. The driver, a chunky man with a vile sneer, had a gun holstered on his pudgy hip, and Takahashi had something in his hand. When he clicked it, it lit up the air with a spark – illuminating his face. It was a taser.

"You don't have to do this!" Lex shouted over the noise as he sparked it on and off, coming closer.

"Oh, I think I do. I owe it to your grandmother. All of those years of pain."

The two men moved in, backing her into a tight corner until they were all pressed into a hidden triangle.

"Just zap her!" demanded the driver, smacking his lips like a dog.

"I think she should hear a story or two first," Takahashi said. "Let's start with a lesson of what you'll be missing out on. Listen carefully."

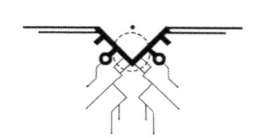

Takahashi held up the neurotrophic electrodes, careful not to take the taser away from its target. "These electrically conductive gold wires are what allow the electrodes to get into your brain, not the most pleasant feeling I imagine. Dr. Kennedy was the first person to have them successfully implanted for the first time, but the experience nearly drove him out of his mind. It took him months to recover. But we've moved on a lot from those days – though maintaining a body remains difficult, not that many choose to hold on to such things. The cost of cryogenics is enormous."

Lex looked down. The patch she had been backed into was hard rock. She cursed herself, inwardly kicking herself for not dropping the cable as they passed the mud. She could have stood on it then, smashed it into the filth and grime while he got on with his stupid story. That was nobody would have been caught apart from her.

"Are you going to get on with it?" Lex asked.

The driver put a hand on his gun.

"Wait," demanded Takahashi.

"You better not be going soft on me," the other grumped.

"Not at all, there's one more story to tell."

He chuckled. "You always were the sadist. Go on, bore the bitch to death if you must."

After a moment's breath, Takahashi cleared his throat. "This story concerns your dear grandma. Alice."

"Don't talk about her."

"You are in no position to make demands. I suggest you listen. It might make things easier."

Lex wasn't sure what he meant by that. She was about to die. Did he mean he would torture her if she didn't listen? Or... would it be worse for Alice? That was a risk she just couldn't take. So, she listened intently.

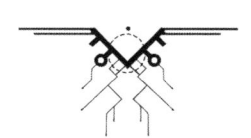

"I worked with Alice, she was a wonderful woman. Smart, beautiful – the best cook in the area, especially sweet and sour pork," he said, making Lex really wish that she hadn't brought it up. "I spent nearly a year building up the courage to ask her to dinner. And what did she do? Reject me. She was all about those grand babies – and they weren't even babies! A year later, her family Ascended anyway! All but one." He directed the taser at Lex again, giving it a click.

"Me."

"Correct. Now, when she had family commitments, I could understand. That was an honourable thing to do. In fact, it made me adore her more. So, when the time came that everyone else was Ascending, I knew my chance had come. She had no ties! I had skipped Ascension myself for… several reasons; but she had kept me hanging on. So, I readied to ask her again. I got to her office and what did I find? Her desk; cleared out. She was done, gone to spend the rest of her days with little Lex." There was venom in his voice, like the spit of a cobra.

"That's not my fault." Lex was starting to lose her strength. Her voice was faltering. She felt like a little girl. It was as though he was telling her a bedtime story, and after she would be left alone with the monster under the bed. Except, once his story was over, she would be facing the real monsters of the world – capitalism, greed, cruelty, death.

"And after she left, I found myself in counselling. That was where I found my true love, my true purpose."

The driver turned to look at him. "Hang on, didn't you marry your councillor?"

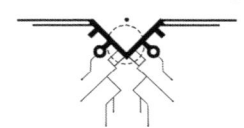

No sooner had he asked it that the taser was activated. Lex dropped to the floor, but nothing touched her. There was no pain, no revulsion, no burning from the point going in.

There was a bang.

Her head snapped up.

Takahashi stood over the driver with the gun smoking in his hand. A taze mark was fresh on the drivers neck as his chest pooled with deep red.

"And for that," Takahashi said. "I will be forever thankful. Your Grandma Alice opened my eyes to EverDawn." He wiped the gun on his shirt and tossed it in the mud in front of her.

Lex blinked. "Are you saying…" What was she asking? She had no idea. The thoughts were coming together in her head, slowly.

"I was too deep, but there has to be someone on the front line. Remember this, Lex, some of us have to leave for our families, and some of us have to stay for the same reasons."

"You're staying to protect your wife?"

"And kids. There is nowhere safe in this world, not anymore."

Lex swallowed. "I need those." She pointed at the golden wires in his hand.

"And I need you to hit me."

"… what?"

"I need this to look like an escape gone bad."

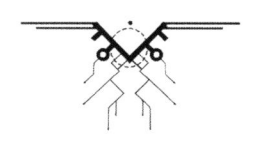

Lex didn't want to hit an old man. Her hand quivered and she stood with her lip shaking.

"For God's sake." He shoved his sleeve over his hand, picked up the gun and shoved it in her pocket along with the neurotrophic electrodes, and stood.

"I can't make every strike for you. The rain will drown out the van recording, but you need to save my skin. Save it, or even as Alice's granddaughter, I'll have to take you in."

"Thank you," Lex nodded.

"Thank me by hitting me and ending the nightmare that is Ascension."

There was no choice. She swung her first, cracking him in the face. He fell on all fours, looking back at her with a grin on his already flushed face; split lip pouring red.

"Just as strong as your grandmother. Go."

As instructed, Lex ran. She ran and ran and ran until her feet hurt and then she kept on going. When she returned to the warehouse she burst through the door, and slumped.

That had been a close one.

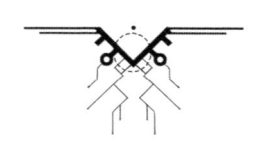

Chapter Twenty-Eight

By the time Lex woke up, she had almost forgotten about the events that had unfolded. Almost, but not entirely. The dry mud on the hem of her clothes was a reminder. Part of her wanted to ask Alice about Takahashi, but that meant broaching the subject of Ascension again. That wasn't how she wanted to spend her last conversation with her grandmother. Then again, did she want to have a last conversation? Of course, she wanted to talk to her, but not in a negative mood.

"It's not our last," Lex reminded herself. "Just the last for a while. It's not like-" A painful thought cut off her sentence, gripping her tongue so hard that it felt as if it had been cut off to halt her from saying it.

Keeping the thought tucked to herself, Lex got changed into something loose and comfortable. The thought refused to leave her though. It was something that her grandmother had hinted at. Yet, the bigger part of Lex had refused to hear it. She was going to be leaving her grandmother. It didn't matter that her consciousness was somewhere else. Alice would never get to hug her again, and she would never get to taste her cooking. All of the little but important things would be lost. Those, it occurred to her, were the very things that made the human experience... well... human.

They had all the parts now, and the equipment was starting to come together. That was almost done, and with the delivery of the Ethernet and the neurotrophic electrodes, they were minutes from done. Maybe not even that much. Normally it was trained agents who carried out what was known as Ingress. People would walk through a door and simply move somewhere else. This time it was

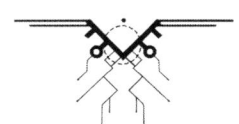

253

Fade. It wasn't that Lex doubted Fade, the things she could do with a few keys were borderline godly in themselves. The thing was, she wasn't just being godly, Fade was going to have to play god here. It was no more than what President Mason was doing. Still, that seemed further away, even with his presence hanging over them like a shadow.

Lex wandered around, catching Fade next to Akoni and watching some terrible cartoon. As soon as she came in the Wu gang leader moved away, giving Lex a nod and muttering something about needing to pee.

"One sec, one sec," Fade laughed hard, even before the punch line. She had seen that show probably a hundred times, but it never failed to spark joy.

As the credits rolled, Lex sat next to her. "Fade, I need to ask you something."

"About those parts? Girl, you were amazing, literally a-maz-ing. I was having such a bitch of a time getting hold of similar technology and then boom! Here you are with the real deal, already unlocked."

"Thanks." Lex knew that her heart should be warming at the praise. It was pretty amazing that she had been able to help Fade with her magic and mayhem.

"You alright?"

"I don't know how to answer that."

Fade nodded slowly. "Right. Well, why don't you start by telling me how you got those babies. I hadn't told her we needed new ones, only that I was struggling."

Lex hadn't been able to tell Fade that the meeting had gone bad.

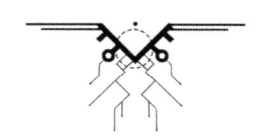

"Maybe it's something EverDawn has locked hard." Lex began before filling Fade in on the whole story. It began with a few lines, then tumbled on and on with Fade only interjecting the occasional "no!" and "oh?"

When Lex finished, she could have fainted all over again.

Fade only had one thing to say. "Well fuck me."

Weakly, Lex chuckled. "I'm not Akoni."

"Hey!" He had just come back in.

"Oh, you should be so lucky – where are you going?"

"To get Alice. If this is happening, she deserves to know."

"No," Lex said. "I don't want her to see me... die."

"She's going to want to be here."

Lex shook her head. "I want her to see me with a smile on my face. If that has to be Ascension, so be it."

Akoni started walking. "That's so disrespectful."

Fade stood up. "Where are you going?"

"To get something to eat. I don't want to be a part of this... don't worry, I'm still in. I just think you should tell Alice."

"I can't."

"Then I can't be here."

The door fell shut with a bang. Fade gave Lex a squeeze on the shoulder.

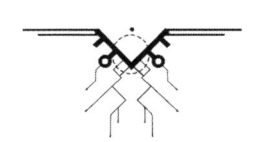

255

"He's got a point. Are you sure?"

"I want to say goodbye. I don't want her to see it though."

"I'll make sure."

"She's totally against this."

"There's still time to say no." Fade tried to sound convincing, not that either of them believed her.

"I've made my decision. It's the same one my parents and brother made, she can't stay mad at me forever."

"Thank God." Fade slumped back. "I mean, no offence, but this is the high point in my career."

The first thought floated back to Lex then. "So, um, what is going to happen to me?"

"Well, the device will take out your consciousness. That's all of your memories, and the essence of who you are, everything that makes you, you."

"That's not what I meant. I meant… what's left of me."

"Ah," Fade hesitated.

With EverDawn Ascension, there were no funerals, no burials. The body was just "dealt with" – if the person had consented, their organs would be used for donation, and then cremation. It was easier for people to deal with it that way – their loved ones were still 'alive', just somewhere else. This would be different. They weren't in a sanctioned environment now, and they were soon going to have a corpse to deal with; Lex's corpse.

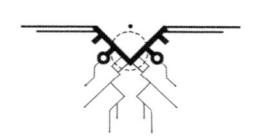

When her family had Ascended, she hadn't really considered it. So many people were Ascending that it was just what happened. No big deal – at least when they could afford Spot access.

"I know you'll all look after grandma, but can you promise me?" Tears swelled on her lashes as Fade took her hand.

"Don't be silly, of course we will. I promise!"

"I've never wanted to think about the day that she would leave me. I never supposed it would be me leaving her. That's not the natural way around is it?"

"At least you'll never get wrinkles." Fade attempted to lighten the mood.

"Can we do it now?"

"Now?" Fade asked, leaning back. "You mean, right this second?"

Lex nodded. "Yes. I don't want the idea of her to talk me out of it."

"… I don't know Lex."

"This is bigger than us! Let me be brave." Lex snatched both of the hacker's hands. "Too much is resting on this."

"You are brave. You're the bravest person I know." Fade stood up. "I guess, I can plug things in. Let me go tell Meshi. You should… do whatever you need to do. And make sure you're not wearing anything metal."

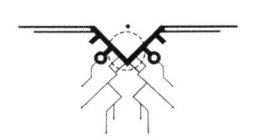

How strange it sounded, something so sweet followed by something so logical. She realized then, that this was going to be hard for all of them. Even Fade was flustered. Then, why shouldn't she be? Without government permission Ascension wasn't a blessing, it was murder. Fade had done a lot of illegal things in her life, many of which she had bragged about, Lex was sure she had never killed anyone though. They weren't murderers. Although, if the bombing were anything to go by, they may as well have been. Some said they were. The lines were beyond blurry. It was hard to even see them.

Lex took out her phone. Should she call Damian? What would she say if she did? It wasn't as though she could just say "Hi! Loved our dinners together, always wanted them to go on a bit more, but funny thing! I'm about to kill my body!" That was just a stupid though. Not only that, he'd try to talk her out of it too – and it just might work. It was too important. If it meant she had to betray them, she would, in this small way so that she didn't have to risk a bigger pain later. It was just like a vaccine, one sharp scratch so that things weren't awful in the long run. It was still going to be painful though, for everyone involved.

She looked at her phone and turned on record.

"Hi Grandma, I know things have been a little weird, but you always said I was as rebellious as you – and that's something that I'm really proud of. I just wanted to tell you from this body, though I'm sure you'll hardly know the difference. The technology is amazing now." She rubbed the back of her head. "I suppose that I just wanted to send you a message and apologise for what I'm doing, but I want you to know more than anything that I love you, and everyone, me included, will look out for you; not that a badass lady like you needs it. I couldn't have you here to see this, so while Akoni was on his way I decided to take a step. I love you. All of you actually. I won't name names because – well – you know." She realized she was rambling, blew a kiss at the screen and said one last time, with all the warmth in the world, "I love you."

"Lex," Fade's voice called. "It's time."

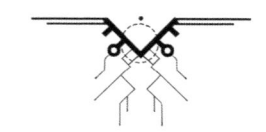

Chapter Twenty-Nine

Akoni knocked on the door to the old lady's house, with a smile on his face. He had only been there once, but there was something about being in her home which felt like he was very welcome. That was partially because of the nature of Chinese citizens becoming one big, blended family, driving to support each other as much as they could, especially in the poorer districts, like where he was from. Whatever the case was, he had taken a particular soft spot for Alice. In many ways he saw her as his own grandmother, taking her under his very overprotective Wing. It was for that reason; he was not going to let her miss Lex's Ascension. Damn the consequences.

Akoni knew that it wasn't his place but staying in his place was something he had never done very well. He wasn't about to let the kindly old dear have any regrets. If that meant annoying the others by telling her exactly what was going on and bringing her in to watch it, albeit probably kicking and screaming, that was what he was going to do. Not to mention, her putting up an argument might allow him some semblance of his former reputation, which was starting to get soft – something that had been pointed out to him several times over the last few weeks by Fade; all in jest but still highly irritating.

He rapped his knuckles on the door three times, about as loudly as a debt collector, not that it was a profession that existed anymore. There were only gangs and mercenaries, and as far as he was concerned police fell into the latter category.

"Akoni! This is a pleasant surprise. Is your stomach feeling empty again?" Alice chuckled, as her phone message tone went off somewhere in the house.

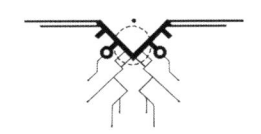

He shook his head, giving the woman a smile.

"No, but if you've got anything going I won't say no, not to your cooking."

"What a charming young man! If I were 30 years younger," she teased.

"Let's not let that get around the streets." He gave her a wink as she moved back to let him walk into the door. "Besides, I'd have only said 20 years younger."

"That's a charm. In the days before all of this chaos began, I would have scolded you for your career choices when you can behave so politely, but I suppose those are lost times, aren't they? And people like me who used to work forever Dawn are part of the problem." She closed the door behind him.

"I don't think you should say that. You were just doing what you had to, to protect your family. Any good person would do the same in your position, which brings me onto the reason I'm here."

"Oh? You're not here to argue with me to let Lex Ascend, are you? I really have heard quite enough about it, and I would not have it ruin your company."

He gave a noise like a grunt. Conversation wasn't exactly his way of getting things done. He didn't mind insulting or threatening, but when it came to Alice, he had the question whether he had a soft enough tongue to deliver the messages he wanted to. After everything they had been through, it seemed that this was the thing his stomach was too weak for.

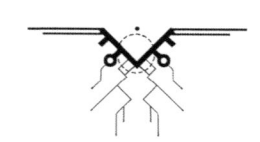

"Got any tea on the brew? I wouldn't mind some more of your Ritz-Carlton blend or whatever it was."

"Ha! Now there's a name I haven't heard in years. I'll put a cup on now, but I'll tell you this, no granddaughter of mine is going to become a pile of binary in a system that could just one day erase her."

There was a steady trickle of water as the kettle was filled up, and the two of them sat in silence as it boiled. He could tell by the look in the woman's eyes that she knew what he had come for was bad. She just did not know the extent of it.

By the time the kettle reached its boil and the whistle began, he couldn't keep it to himself anymore.

"Alice," he started as she picked it up. "I feel like I have to tell you, because of the way things were left. The Ascension, it's going ahead today."

"When?" Alice's eyes grew as wide as the moon and she gripped the kettle so hard that white appeared on her fingers.

"Right now. I didn't want you to miss it. You deserve that much."

He started to wonder if he had said the complete wrong thing, since he got no reply.

"Alice? Alice?"

The kettle clanged on the floor. Steaming water pooled around her feet and yet she didn't seem to notice. He called her name again, rushing over to her, catching her just as she fell against the counter.

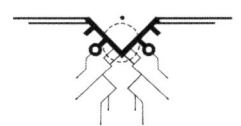

"Pull it fucking together!" he shouted at her, holding her up as best he could. Her hand was shaking over her chest, and she was gasping for air. Having pulled over so many people on the Metro, Akoni knew exactly what a panic attack looked like – and had been expecting her to have one. This was not a panic attack.

The woman managed to spit out two words, "Chest pain."

He knew exactly what she meant then. The news of what Lex was doing, had given Alice a heart attack. If he could get her to hospital quick enough, she would make it through – but god damn it! She would never get those final moments with her granddaughter's body. There would be no final hug, only an ice-cold corpse.

He knew that it was all for the greater good, but it didn't seem like a price worth paying. Carrying Alice as best he could, he lifted her out of a front door, and ran as fast as he could with a struggling woman in his arms. They had to get to a hospital. As he left there was a beep, a reminder of a message that she hadn't opened.

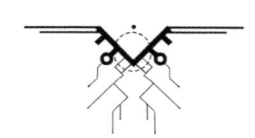

Chapter Thirty

So, this was what it had come to. Lex couldn't quite believe it. There was no changing her fate now though, not when they have come so far. It didn't mean it didn't hurt though, knowing what she was about to do, and how permanent it was going to be.

Hot tears pricked her eyes, settling on her lashes before spilling down her face. Throughout this entire thing she had been so strong. She was the one that had said no to the unreasonable charges at the Spot. It had been her that drew the moustache on the poster of the president and drawn everyone together for that initial meeting. Of course, she had thought about where it could go, but it had never seemed like a reality. Not really. Then again, what was reality? Giving what she was about to do it seems like a perfectly understandable question. It just seemed to her like an unfortunate situation to be having to ask it right then. That was the thing about philosophy, wasn't it? A person never really could make a judgement call until they were living it. What was reality?

People liked to act like they could take a single moment and stretch it out into forever. The end was always around the corner, but never something that you really had to face. And yet here she was, standing on the precipice at the end of everything. Here she was looking the final moments of her reality in the eyes.

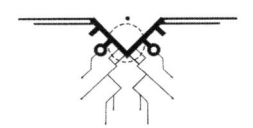

The only thing she could do to satisfy her mind was think about that, and what it really meant. Holding onto the moment seems like the only way to keep control of herself. Her lips pressed together, as if that would somehow slow the barrage of tears that was waiting for her. Her eyes were burning. Her throat was tight. It was as though the weight of her entire journey was bearing down on her now, trying to press her into this moment. Lex wouldn't be able to let her mind drift. She wouldn't be able to pretend that everything she had ever come to know was about to end.

Slowly she reached out, hovering over the button. It felt cold when she pressed her fingertip down. The world seemed too still around her. Lex could hear the sound of her own racing heartbeat. It crashed down like a drum, like thunder, like the tides against the shore. It beat along with the machine tracking it, almost drowning it out entirely.

The button felt so cold. It was then that a feeling struck her and she snatched her hand away, grabbing hold of her wrist just in case it had a mind of its own. The coldness of that plastic around the button, that was going to be the temperature of her body soon. The warmth of her flesh was going to leave her. The body that she had known for all of her life was going to be no more than a cold corpse.

Just like the plastics that had poisoned the world, she was about to become disposable – and she was going to do it willingly. It sent a chill down her spine, thinking about it like that.

But that was the truth.

The world would die from this poison, and so would she.

"This is it," she said out loud to herself, savouring the sound of her own voice. That gave her a half chuckle. Even from the time that she was just a little girl she had always hated hearing herself speak or sing on recordings. Now she cherished her voice, just as she was about to lose it. There are so many things that people take for granted, and so many that can be taken away.

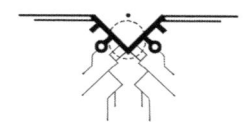

Rebellion's Martyr

There was a saying along those lines, she thought. You never know what you have until it's gone. It seemed that the same thing applied even when you were losing it on purpose. Even when you were making the choice to give it up.

She could sing. Right there. The urge struck her. Lex could sing and hear her voice one last time. She could rage and curse. She could profess love of the profoundest sort. It wouldn't matter. Dying words would become a dying breath… and then there would be nothing but silence.

It was starting to dawn on her then; EverDawn, maybe it was called that because it would forever be a morning without her seeing the sun rise. Maybe there would be a peace there, found just outside of the reach of someone still living?

Lex once again extended her hand, touching the button so lightly that it did not press and trying to pull together her thoughts. This would be her final moments. She didn't want to leave them without gaining at least some amount of clarity. There would be no chance to come back here, after all. There would be no chance to tie up any loose ends.

There was just going to be now – and nothing.

If her body was going to die and become nothing more than a corpse or a cadaver, was that death? Did that mean that her act of uploading herself was some sort of martyrdom? Maybe even suicide?

Lex always had trouble understanding religious guidelines on this sort of thing. It wasn't like any bit of any holy scriptures had digital uploads written into them. Regardless of that fact, it had always felt a little wrong, a little blasphemous. At one time in her life, she would have said that was just the influence of Grandma Alice. In fact,

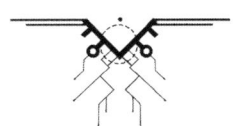

Lex had considered uploading herself before. The difference was that it had only been considered up until that point. It was a passing thought, something that came up in a fit of rage or sorrow or childish grief, back before Lex even fully understood the process.

There had been no real desire to reach this other plane. There had been no aching curiosity. It was just what people were supposed to say, what they were supposed to think – I wish I was dead, I wish I was uploaded. And then the calendar date had flipped over, day became night became day again, and Lex was able to move on from her, at the time, irrational thought.

Now, in this very moment, sitting in an uncomfortable chair without her loved ones around her, it was a very tangible and palpable decision – one that had already been made for her. There was no choice, so why was she pretending like there was? It had to be done. All she was doing was delaying the inevitable.

More tears spilled from her eyes and she whimpered. Her breath hitched, catching in her throat and then spilling out as a twisted, rattling thing. The back of her throat itched.

"You sound pathetic Lex," she attempted to give herself a talking to, but even by the last word of the short phrase her voice was cracking. "You need to pull yourself together. This is the end. You don't – you don't want to leave this place crying, right?"

Right.

She wanted to be brave. She wanted to upload with some semblance of dignity left about her. And that meant not crying.

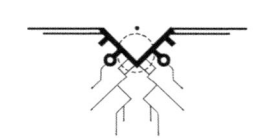

Except... once the tears had started, it didn't seem as though there was any way to make them stop. They ran openly down her face. It was so hard to pull in an even breath of air that her shoulders were shaking.

She closed her eyes, squeezing them tightly together.

Pull it together, she thought. Just hold onto things a little bit longer. You started all of this with a brave face. You can end it that way, too!

Her body and her brain didn't want to work on the same level, though. No matter how much Lex tried to will the tears to stop, they just kept coming. Her lower lip trembled. She bit it in an attempt to stop the next whine from becoming audible. It only worked a little.

Lex looked around the room, closing her eyes and feeling for one last time what it was like to have the senses of the human body. There was a slightly chemical smell, disinfectant no doubt. The seat beneath her buttocks was well-worn, a far cry from the blanket she had at Granny Alice's house. And then Lex tried to listen. For the most part there was silence, but the heart monitor at her side bleeped monotonously. Beep. Beep. Beep. Beep. How cruel it was, the last sounds you would ever hear would be the things she was going to snuff out.

"Fuck. And fuck President Mason." The words rolled right off her lips. For a second she considered that it might be her last and wondered if she should say something more monumental. After all, they were so close to accomplishing everything, right on the brink of success, but it all depended on Lex's ability to press in one singular button. She really didn't want her last word to be "fuck", but her mouth was drying up with fear.

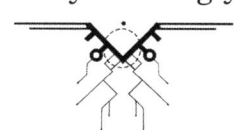

What else was she supposed to say, anyway? How could you pick what was worthy of being your last word? And what did it matter when there was no one around to hear her say it?

Maybe fuck wasn't the most eloquent thing to go out after, but it sure seemed to sum the situation up well enough.

Lex had to wonder if the books and movies she had read and seen throughout her life had lied to her on purpose? Was it a kindness that they gave heroes such a glorious death? In all of the great stories, the champion went out with a bang – something brave and unrelentingly beautiful, a mark of what the human spirit could really put on itself and achieve in order to save everyone else. Lex didn't feel like one of those heroes. She just felt like they were all liars, putting on a brave face because inside they were shit scared. Lex was petrified.

She didn't know how to hide it, either. Her brave face had been used up. It was gone. Empty. Lost somewhere outside of this room, outside of this moment. The only thing that still existed was her terror, that button, and the sound of her heart monitor. There was no place here for false confidence and untrue realities.

Lex wouldn't lie to herself at the end. She couldn't.

There was no more to it. It had to be done. She just kept telling herself that, but no matter how many times her mind related it, her heart disagreed.

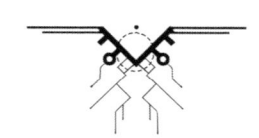

Her finger pressed down on the button a little more and it gave a slight click. The sound made her wince and she pulled away quickly, wiping her hand roughly across her eyes. She was furious at herself. This was too important to mess up. There are too many people relying on her. At that moment she didn't care as much about the rest of the world. That was another movie lie. All she gave a damn about were the people closest to her. Damian. Alice. Meshi. God damn it, she even thought about Akoni.

Thinking about them helped a little bit, but only for a second. Shortly after images of them all and what they had been through popped into her mind, and she felt a stab in her chest. If she couldn't protect those people, life wasn't worth living. It wasn't worth fighting for anything else.

Lex let out a long and heart-breaking wail, letting her head fall back and her cries ruminate throughout the room – heard by no-one. The very last moments of her physical life would be spent alone with nothing but bleeping machinery to bear witness to her pain and suffering.

Her hand dropped to the button. This time it had been pressed. Lex sobbed outright, then. She cried as if she were a child again, searching for someone's arms to fall into. Her breath heaved out of her, the force of her tears enough to make her choke and hack. There was no beauty in this. There was no sense of accomplishment. There was just fear.

True terror. The knowledge that the absolute choice had been made. There was no undoing this. There was no going back. There were just the long, steady seconds passing by. The trill of the heartbeat monitor. The despair and resignation that was choking Lex. It was just Lex, left there with her own soured grief.

Lex had no idea what it would feel like to Ascend. How could a common layperson know what it was like to be uploaded into a computer? It wasn't right. It wasn't normal. It was going to happen. She was going to be Uploaded. No more pauses. No more breaks. No more hesitations.

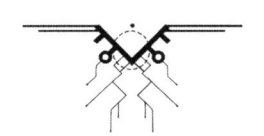

269

It shouldn't be possible, but it was. Lex was going to do the impossible. She was going to do the unthinkable. She was stopping this reality and entering into another. It was done, and there was no way to undo it. There would be no going back. There was nothing to go back to.

Lex's eyes turned glassy, remaining open, and her lips parted ever so slightly. Every muscle in her body seemed to relax as if it knew things were finally over, but her fingertip clung on. Some part of her knew that this wasn't the end. Or at least, it shouldn't have been. With the light finally leaving her eyes, and the acrid stench of her own urination, Lex was gone. Only then did her hand slip away from the button. It fell limply by her side.

Lex's breathing could no longer be heard in the room. There was only one sound – the lone, uninterrupted tone of the heart monitor.

There was no doctor to call the time of death, only a machine giving out the one singular note. Lex was gone.

On the other side of the wall, Fade waited. Her breath was hitched in her chest, not daring to come out.

"What's going on?" demanded Meshi. He may not have been a technological genius like she was, but he was old enough and wise enough to know the sound of a heart monitor packing in when someone left this world. More so, he knew that paralysed look on Fade's face.

Nothing was happening. Nothing.

Was Lex's blood on her hands?

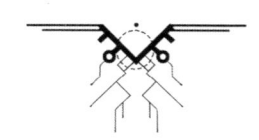

"What is it?" demanded Meshi. "Why isn't the screen doing anything?" he forced out the question in the faint hopes that he might get a different answer to the one he suspected. He desperately wanted Fade to say that there had been a problem with the internet connection, or that this was routine maintenance and always fine. Fade said nothing.

The air in the room hung as heavily as the grave, and then as if an angel was making their presence known, the screen lit up.

Fade gasped, and her hand darted to her chest. Meshi could have shaken her. Thankfully she spoke, finally capturing some oxygen.

"She's in."

They looked at each other, full of mixed emotions. They'd achieved the impossible, but this was just the beginning. Lex had been uploaded.

But the story didn't end there. This was just the beginning.

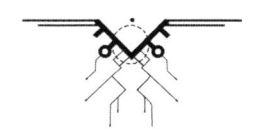

Printed in Great Britain
by Amazon